Sam Casanova

Sam Casanova

Max Catto

HEINEMANN : LONDON

William Heinemann Ltd
15 Queen Street, Mayfair, London W1X 8BE

LONDON MELBOURNE TORONTO
JOHANNESBURG AUCKLAND

First published 1973
© Max Catto 1973
434 11060 4

Printed in Great Britain by
Willmer Brothers Limited, Birkenhead

I

'ANIMAL. You are abusing me. What large bones you have. So you will kill this Joey for me?'

'Oh, God.'

'Is it so much to ask? A small favour. All right, then, if you are so squeamish. Just break a leg.'

'Lie still.'

'Sam, you are not listening. A gentleman would *want* to protect me. Perhaps a few bones in the wrist. Anything. Break something!'

'*Oh, God.*'

'*Chéri*, are you putting on weight? I feed you too well. My nerves are all on edge. That Joey! I have been insulted beyond endurance. Did you say something?'

'No.'

'Ease yourself on me, Sam. Ah, that is better. I am entitled to your sympathy. All I am asking for is a chivalrous gesture from your strong right arm. Say, knock out a tooth . . .'

'Sybilla, will you *shut up*? This isn't the time for talk.'

'Would you want me to suppress my feelings?'

'Yes.'

'How callous you are. You do not know what I have suffered. Infamy! This Joey . . .'

'Screw this Joey.'

'Sam, it is unworthy of you to address me like that. I am a woman of the most delicate sensibility. You are not finished?'

'Never even took off.'

'Then throw me my bra. It will be better later. You will come round for dinner. I shall make you a nice steak *à la Bourgogne*. You must keep up your strength.'

'What for?'

'Now you are being amusing. Say, at nine?'

'Don't wait for me. I may be busy.'

'Fetch a bottle of Beaujolais. Now about this unspeakable . . .'

'Who in hell *is* Joey?'

'If you would only let me tell you . . .'

'No, I don't want to know.'

'A monster in human form . . .'

'The world's full of them. See you later. Maybe.'

'*A bientôt*, Sam. A kiss?'

'Sex'll get you nowhere.'

'At nine, then. Be happy. And remember. Steak *à la Bourgogne*.'

He came into the gaudy glitter of Pigalle, thick bodied, heavy shouldered, still shivering with natural frustration. The wind was bleak. He turned up his collar; a few greasy snowflakes licked his face. The violet neon on the dark skyline advertising France's favourite smoke sizzled like fat in a hot pan. The G and the L had flickered out like blown candles. It was a bad time all round. You couldn't even trust Gauloises these days. Every *brasserie* he passed exuded the drool of accordion music that excites Frenchmen and sets the teeth of *l'étranger* on edge like a dentist's drill. He shrugged distastefully and pushed on. Watch him as he goes plunging absently across the mad bustle of Clichy, spattered by the slush of skidding taxis, the deep V of worry creased between his eyes. He is a great worrier, this man. He worries about the human condition, moral pollution and the ingratitude of society that stings like the biblical serpent's tooth. It is a cruel, cruel world. Be glad you are alive.

There he goes, borne across Place Blanche by the pre-Christmas shopping mob, turning into the dark thread of Rue des Six Anges. No angels live here; you will certainly not count six. Every tenth door is a *boîte*, a night-club, a clip-joint. They are open all hours and the kerbs are permanently parked with cars so that the refuse carts never get to clean them. It is a refinement Rue des Six Anges has learned to do without. Lift your head and you see wooden shutters that have not felt a lick of paint since Napoleon left Elba; the bricks of the aged tenements glued together by the awful corrosion of time. A woman leans out of a lighted window, her bosom propped on the sill, her fair hair glistening like virgin gold in the shine of the lamp. There is nothing virginal in her expectant posture, nor in the rowdy conversation she is conducting with the iceman who is delivering a late load to one of the clubs. The Americans must have ice? Let them pay for it. He nods familiarly to Sam Casanova (yes, the name is authentic) and says politely, 'M'sieu,' as he goes by. Out of the continuous strip-show comes the sexually incitive hammer of music; the cracked photographs that line the door are all bare breasts and athletic poses and as much pubic hair as the Parisian censor will allow. Which is plenty. The tout in the ill-fitting tuxedo fastens on

Sam and follows him a few yards down the dark street, whispering fervently in his ear until he recognizes him and lets him go with a useless shrug. He knows that Sam is in a similar business himself, if less profitable. Even dying.

Le Kasbah Marrakesh. Belly-dancing no less. There is no market these days for semi-respectability and pseudo North-African charm.

Stay with our friends. The Kasbah is at the darkest, frowsiest end of the street, a few doors from a small warm bar into which Sam now turns. Follow him. The bar is run by a burly Corsican with the impossible name of Garfunkel. It is one of the improbabilities of the Parisian scene. Accept it. He leans on the zinc, listening dreamily to the radio playing a Bach gavotte. That in itself is an absurdity. Accept it, too. It is a little early for trade and there is nobody there but a crone from the nearby market dunking a croissant into a bowl of coffee. She is so small and insignificant, so intent on the sodden croissant, that the bar still seems empty. Garfunkel likes company.

He looked up brightly as his guest came in. He began pleasantly, 'M'sieu Sam,' taking in his sad dourness with one shrewd sympathetic glance. He knew what was wrong. It made him shudder. Bankruptcy was a terrible thing! His bar was separated from the Kasbah by only a few walls; if he cocked a sharp ear he could hear the faint wail of Moroccan music, the hollow thump of drums, and he knew how many — or rather how few — customers went in, what little business it drew. Not that the Kasbah was a bad club. Very tasteful, very atmospheric; if you liked swarthy voluptuous dancers exercising their navels in your face. Garfunkel could think of more interesting vices. He reached for the right bottle. Armagnac. As he poured out a heavy slug for his guest he wondered pensively if he had the money to pay for it. He thought he had.

He went on, 'It looks as if it is going to be a white Christmas.'

'That's good news. I'm booked for St Moritz. Join me there, Garfunkel,' Sam said.

'I have my business to look after, my friend.'

'I'll swap you mine. There isn't much to look after.'

Garfunkel said softly, 'Bad, is it?' As if he didn't know.

'Not bad. Not good. Just non-existent.'

That *was* bad. 'It's the monetary situation,' Garfunkel sighed. 'The franc is over-valued. The financial wizards have fouled it all up . . .'

'Fetch them along to the Kasbah. We'll find them something to take their minds off it,' Sam said. He gave Garfunkel a humorous look. 'You're wondering if I'm going to pay for the drink.'

'It did cross my mind for a moment.'

'I can. I don't want to, but I will. You'll trust me for the next?'

'This one on the house.' I will be as poor as him if I go on like this, Garfunkel shrugged. 'How are your partners?'

'Guess.'

Garfunkel didn't need to. Stricken. The three partners, Papa Miche, Willie Tobias and Stefan, the Hungarian with the unpronounceable name, came occasionally into his bar for their drinks. He used to wonder why they didn't drink off their own bar, until it occurred to him with astonishment that they were ludicrously honest; that a man couldn't measure the exact cost of his personal liquor and charge it up to an impoverished club; it was fairer to buy it outside. Garfunkel had a poignant word for them. *Schlemiels*. Meaning pathetics. That was honesty gone mad.

'Sam,' he said with slight exasperation, 'a word of advice. If I may.'

'So long as it doesn't cost.'

'Do not give up. You are young and enthusiastic. The human spirit is indestructible. You must not yield to despair.' He found himself getting genuinely worked up. 'Look at that creature over there.' He nodded across at the shrunken crone from the second-hand clothes market. She had finished the croissant and was supping the dregs of the coffee out of the bowl. She did it with unnecessary loudness. Garfunkel was aware that she had no front teeth. 'What has she to live for? Yet her spirit is indestructible. She lusts for life.' It was something of an exaggeration. She moaned petulantly every time she came in. 'So you are temporarily ruined. Something will turn up. On the other side of every cloud,' Garfunkel said, 'is a lining of gold,' and Sam Casanova looked at him wonderingly as if he had uttered the crashing cliché of the century: as he had. 'Listen. I will give you a tip.'

'Using your money?'

Garfunkel ignored the suggestion. 'This Kasbah business is *fou*. Finished. After the Algerian trouble nobody wants to know. Put your belly-dancers into the museum. That is where they belong. They do *real* business down the street. You know? Get a new band. Le jazz hot! Modern. Engage a few bright girls . . .'

'No whores,' Sam said.

'Not exactly whores. Just a little permissive,' Garfunkel said. 'How stuffy you Anglo-Saxons are. Nobody is talking about private rooms upstairs. So they take the occasional gentleman home . . .'

Sam said adamantly, 'No whores.'

'You will die in the gutter, my friend.'

4

'It's where you find the best company,' Sam said. 'See you in St Moritz.'

'Funny!'

'Isn't it. How many drinks do I pay you for?'

'Just the one.'

'For the hell of it I'll pay for both.' He put the money on the zinc. Garfunkel watched him wryly as he went out. The radio had finished the Bach gavotte and was playing one of the trendy, tone-mad compositions of the modernists that went through him like the screech of pencil on slate. He switched it off. The old lady had shuffled out absently during his last words with Sam and had taken the opportunity of forgetting to pay. It is I who will end up in the gutter, Garfunkel sighed. The coffee-machine hissed. Over the hiss, like the thump of Moors capering to battle on camels, he could hear the beat of drums and the ululating wail of pipes from the Kasbah. That was one war the Moors weren't going to win. Business was too important to be left to incompetents. The Kasbah was done.

I knew Le Kasbah Marrakesh when it was all the rage. It was owned by a smart Algerian operator named Durocq, who was cashing in on erotic North-African mysticism, all things Islamic, the cult of the yashmak, a hint of the lascivious seraglio with its fearsome black eunuchs. He had managed to combine the strip-routine with the belly-dance, so that his dusky stomach-quivering damsels suggested Salome divesting herself of her seven veils. It gave the Kasbah a kind of amusing chic. He had the walls draped with Meknes carpets, keeping the lighting as dim as a mosque. It wasn't wholly for effect; it was to conceal the cracked plaster and the fact that the middle-aged houris weren't as enticing as they looked. It paid off for a while. But already Durocq had seen the storm-signals. The jazzy strip-shows down the street, verging on roaring obscenity, were beginning to scoop the pool. It was time to move on. There were other reasons for alacrity. Interpol was taking an unhealthy interest in him; he had once run a club in Casablanca that was a transit-depot for the despatch of nubile Spanish maidens to the vice-spots of the Levant. With a little deft cooking of the books he interested a down-at-heel impresario named Papa Miche, with two equally gullible associates, in the club. They had only a little capital between them. Durocq wondered how they had managed to induce a benefactor named Sam Casanova to put up most of the cash.

The Durocqs of this world never question the limitless credulity of the mug. He departed swiftly for warmer climes, making particu-

5

larly for Marseilles where heroin distillation was now the profitable thing.

To watch the Kasbah fail was like watching the aged tenements of Rue des Six Anges crumble away. The process was distressing. The truth, they say, will set you free. All it told Sam Casanova and his associates was that they were financially trapped. Accounts, like the wooden lips of a ventriloquist's dummy, can be made to say anything. And what Durocq's accounts had told them was a palpable lie. During the couple of weeks of negotiation he had had the bar packed with patrons attracted by the lure of free drinks. There is an organization in Paris that supplies enthusiastic non-paying audiences for a reasonable fee. Durocq thought the fee reasonable. It got him off the hook. It impaled the new proprietors on it instead. The hook hurt more and more as the months went by. Takings slumped. Bar profits – the very pillar of the club – began to slip. Rent had to be paid. There is no charity in a landlord's heart. The performers grew querulous when salaries were a week or two behind. Then a month behind. The Moorish band grumbled incoherent threats. Bad, bad, bad. The bank was suddenly adamant. Then brutal.

The hook was particularly agonizing that evening when Sam Casanova walked with an air of bitterest finality into the club.

I was there at the time. God alone knows why. It certainly wasn't to drink the execrable champagne. I saw Sam come into the doorway, squinting past the dazzle of the floods. He told me he always entered with an expectant sniff. What did he expect? The healthy fug of fine cigars? All he ever got was the choking haze from the smattering of locals smoking cheap Gitanes. The Kasbah echoed like an abandoned church. Where had all the American tourists gone? To the clip-joints up the street where *les girls* mimed the sexual act. Culture is dead, Sam thought, watching the plump dancer oscillating her bloated navel in the blinding flush of the lamps. It disgusted him, he said. She wasn't even *good*. The Egyptians wouldn't work for him any more; and the drabs from the back streets of Tangier didn't have the art. The Moorish band, tambourines jangling, pipes squealing like anguished cats, sounded as if they were playing from the hollow-ness of a drum. The tables laid for dinner weren't a quarter filled. It was hardly worth keeping on the chef; if that was what you called the Turk in the kitchen who maltreated the food. That Durocq, Sam growled; one day I'll run him down . . . but nobody ever runs the Durocqs down. They are faster than hares. Sam stood by the *vestiaire* for a moment, getting over that heart-stopping wave of sheer madness and futility. I am broke. We are all broke, he sighed.

6

He glanced along the shadowy bar, the stools empty. They were inhabited by ghosts. No, there was a solitary human figure hunched on the end stool, the shock of wiry white hair aglow like silver spray in the shifting beams of the lamps, head bent. Like Job sunk in sorrow. Sam knew – he couldn't hear it – that Papa Miche was whispering to himself with despair. Somebody stirred in the gloom. Willie Tobias, the bartender. One of the partners. He murmured to Sam, 'Let him be.'

'No good, Willie. We have to talk.'

'Talk tomorrow.'

'Tomorrow the bank stops talking. It'll foreclose.'

'Terrible. Too terrible,' Willie gasped. He blinked violently. It was a discomforting nervous affliction. He brought down a bottle. 'Sam, have a brandy. Before the bank gets at it.'

'How long's he been like that?'

'Papa? All day.'

'Give me the brandy. And come across. You have to listen, too.'

'Yes.' Willie's eyes continued to twitch as if ants were running up and down his face. It was a very special affliction he had. The neck of the bottle rapped spasmodically on the glass. Sam steadied his hand with another sigh and took the glass from him. Then shifted across to Papa Miche at the end of the bar.

So how was he to start? Come on, Papa. Face it. We're broke. Busted. It all belongs to the bank. And it's getting no bargain. Certainly not in the podgy Salome who'd shed two of her tawdry veils and was shimmering her abdomen to pleasure a patron absently gnawing a chop. It excited him no more than if the local butcher were displaying a side of beef. Half down with the spangled bra. All terribly arch. One breast revealed. A big one. Sam turned away with a grimace. Big deal. He told me that he felt a pang of suffocating shame. He'd struck low levels in his time; who hadn't? This one had him wallowing in the gutter. 'Papa,' he said painfully, 'you have company. Look round.'

No sound.

'You think the trouble'll run away if you play deaf? It won't. We're stuck with it. Like the plague. Papa, *look round*.'

'So all right. I'm looking.' Papa Miche twisted to show his stubborn old face. 'You want to see me cry?' and Sam caught his breath with dismay at the glint of tears in the outraged eyes. He rasped his face. Sybilla should have told him he needed a shave. He didn't know what to say. I could have told him. The old freedom fighter was weeping because he was inadequate. A born loser. Some men have only to touch dross and it automatically turns into gold. I have met quite a few. And there are men who cannot back a horse, but it unfailingly goes lame and comes in last. If at all. Papa Miche was that kind of man. Providence is very cruel. It has to have its butts, its figures of fun. I never thought there was anything funny about Papa Miche. He deserved better of life. His history was a mess of ruined ideals. He'd fought with the International Brigade in Spain as a lad and all he'd got for his passion for freedom was an embarrassing bullet in one buttock. And a lost cause. Ludicrous. Providence was already beginning to laugh. The theatre was his great love. At least, he *looked* like an impresario. And every venture he backed died on the boards. Operas failed. A vista of financial wreckage. One of his productions cost me a little money. Once bitten, twice shy. Sam stared at the rocky obdurate face, the glazed angry eyes, the shock of silver hair that reminded one of the late Albert Einstein; though the lamented professor, notoriously absent-minded, could scarcely have handled his affairs worse.

'Stop it,' Sam said irritably. 'It'll be all right.' But it wouldn't. Papa Miche had ended up with Le Kasbah Marrakesh, which promised to be the biggest failure of them all.

Sam thought: I'm another. How did I let him talk me into it? Sybilla had warned him crudely, 'You are *fou*. Crazy like a horse. You will lose your shirt.' He still had his shirt, but very little else. If he didn't guard it with care the bank might take it, too.

Willie Tobias, the second partner, said in his sweet voice, 'We must all keep our heads.'

At least, the bank won't get *those*, Sam thought. 'Yes, Willie,' he said.

'We've been through worse.' A lot worse. Willie's twitch had now become uncontrolled. Another *schlemiel*. But there was no derision in Sam Casanova as he stared at him; his heart moved perceptibly with compassion and again he put out his hand to steady him down. It was, as I said, a very special affliction. Willie had spent his formative years in a camp not ideally designed for children. Dachau, to be precise. He still bore his enrolment number tattooed on his wrist, and it wouldn't wash off nor grow out with the years. A lost waif. How had he survived? Ask God. At twelve he'd been detailed to the job of sanitary commando: which meant that he stripped the processed bodies of such useful by-products as wedding rings and gold teeth. If the war hadn't ended just about then he wouldn't have survived, of course. He was left with the tattoo and the twitch. He wore long cuffs to hide the first, but nothing could control the second when he became agitated. It didn't take much anxiety to set him off. An unfortunate asset in a bartender, for it made superstitious patrons think he had given their drinks the evil eye.

I thought him the gentlest, most unmilitant soul I have ever met. Like the Indian guru he would always walk considerately around a spider. Sam Casanova looked from Willie's jumpy cheeks to Papa Miche's brimming eyes. Two of my prime partners. God help me. So where was the third?

He said brusquely, 'Get Stefan. He has to be here,' but already he was approaching rapidly from behind the band. The first thing you noticed about Stefan's expression was its curious contradiction. His luminous happy eyes simply didn't match his long lugubrious face. It was just a trick of the muscles. There was nothing lugubrious about him. He was a joyous, if rather clumsy man. I never knew what he had to be joyous about. Thin as a stick, with the look of excessive hunger – a not infrequent condition – he was always in a hurry, especially when excited, which tended to make him walk into things. He was probably slightly myopic. He should have been an outstanding concert pianist. He had been trained at the Budapest *Conservatoiré*. His over-confident friends got him out during the Hungarian uprising; they planned it like an adventure epic. Western movie fashion, and like so many Western movies it all went wrong. The truck he shouldn't have been riding in skidded across the frontier, crushing the knuckles of both his hands. You would see him absently flexing the distorted fingers as if they might loosen up in time. They wouldn't. They would never be any use for playing the piano.

Something stunning like that happened to Beethoven. He went on to write the 'Eroica'. (Or was that before he grew deaf?) Stefan was less ambitious; he was content to be musical director of Le Kasbah Marrakesh. There was a strict apportionment of duties between the partners. Papa Miche ran the front office and the commissariat. Willie Tobias saw to the bar and the Turk in the kitchen. Sam, having put up most of the capital, kept a generally morbid eye on things, which enabled him to watch Le Kasbah slide to its inevitable doom.

He waited for Stefan to come hurrying up; he had brushed the table of the patron gnawing the chop. No damage done. But Willie Tobias said to him kindly, 'Stefan, *please*. Don't run.'

Stefan said breathlessly, 'I just saw Sam walk in.'

And Papa Miche rebuked him indulgently, 'How many times do I have to tell you to watch where you are going? You hit things!'

Me, hardest of all. Sam winced. I ache from them in every bone. He made a frustrated sound. Listen to them. Already they were accustoming themselves to the disaster; getting their heads down, preparing to bend with the wind, and wait for the next blow. It would come. For Papa Miche, Willie Tobias and Stefan (why *did* fate so have it in for them?) life was a series of disasters. Each worse than the last. Sam watched them with pity, but without hope. They were the incompetents. The pathetic ones. Humanity's evolutionary flops. And there was nothing, simply nothing, they could do to retrieve themselves. It was the kind of men they were; the kind of luck they had. They reminded Sam of the broken debris the ocean tossed up on the beach with the ebb and flow of the tide. He glanced back with a long sigh. Salome from Tangier was weaving between the tables, heavy breasts swinging with enough impetus to fell an ox. A man had to be hare-brained to put money into a sleazy venture like this. And for the hundredth time he asked himself the poignant question: how did I let myself get involved?

A waste of breath. He knew. He owed Papa Miche a debt. There was a dark area of horror in Sam Casanova's life he couldn't bear to recall. An alcoholic wife, given to raging nymphomania in her cups; the old man had helped him over the hump before she died. So now I'm insolvent. I've paid the debt. He'd have to start borrowing eating money. Living on Sybilla's indulgence for a while. Terribly hurtful to a man's pride; assuming he had much of that useless commodity left.

Papa Miche was staring keenly into his face. 'Sam,' he said fervently, in the most assured voice, 'I swear to you, everything is going to be all right.'

Not for me. Certainly not for you. Unless God takes a sudden fancy to you: and I see no reason why He should.

'Sam, try to believe me,' Papa Miche went on passionately, 'things are going to change.'

Only for the worse. Oh, grow up. How they depress me. Sam shrugged. He was in one of his dark moods.

Willie Tobias asked uneasily, 'So when do we close?'

'Get ready to be out in ten days.'

'So soon?'

'Best deal I could get.'

Willie said with an unsteady laugh, 'At least, we have a little time to breathe!'

'If you call it breathing.'

And Papa Miche peered nostalgically about the club. Sam knew what he was thinking. All that wonderful North African atmosphere lost! The mystique of the harem. The houris of Paradise.

He said defeatedly, 'And we go out with nothing? Just our two legs?'

'We could be lucky. If there was a hospital market for legs we mightn't even keep those.'

Stefan patted Sam's hand. 'It can't be so bad, can it? See, you can still joke!'

With my guts bleeding. 'Papa,' Sam said wearily, 'let's stop playing funny. It's finished. Drink up what's left in the bar. Then face it. *Kaput.*'

'And you hate us for it?'

'No, no.'

'We love you for it. You will never know how grateful we are. You have been very kind to us. Kinder than we deserve. A son,' Papa Miche said, 'couldn't have shown us more regard,' and Sam rasped uneasily the cheek Sybilla should have told him needed a shave. Now they were going to get emotional. Papa Miche watched him with a dry smile. 'Not to worry, my friend. At least, it will get you a little credit in heaven.'

Long-term prospect. I'd rather have a little short-term credit down here.

'Sam,' Papa Miche said forcefully, 'don't discount yourself. You are a better man than you think.' Sam found his hand enclosed in the old man's moist warm grip. 'Do you hear? We are going to repay you.' In heaven? 'It is the truth. This time it is going to be more than words . . .' his voice tailing off to a curious emptiness as if his attention had suddenly strayed. Willie Tobias and Stefan had stopped concentrating on Sam. They were staring narrowly over his shoulder. There was even a marked change in the atmosphere of the club; the rattle of plates stilled as if somebody important had just walked in. Nobody had. Nobody ever would. But a scurrying waiter slowed down perceptibly, head slanted interestedly towards the floor. Sam half twisted on his stool. He had never heard the ruffianly gang of Moroccans they called the band play with such bawdy zest; they were stretched forward to catch a full frontal view of the Salome who'd appeared in the blinding glitter of the floods. Sam had to adjust his eyes to the glare. All he caught for the moment were smooth young shoulders; milk-white. No coffee-tinted Tangier sunburn here. The Kasbah had half a dozen performers, ranging in plumpness from the massive to the disgustingly fat. He'd never set eyes on this slender sprig. He murmured wonderingly to Papa Miche, 'Who the hell is . . .' but she'd swirled about in a gust of filmy veils, flat stomach tensed. Navel gently oscillating. Not much revealed in the frontal view: as yet. Just one veil gone. Now the second discarded with a disarming impropriety he thought queerly disconcerting in one so young. It had the drummer guffawing. His beard split. The pipes, each as strident as a bitch in heat, wailed about the half notes; the fiddles whined.

The monotonous sensuality of North African music appeals to some people; it sets other's teeth on edge. I prefer the nightly chorus of cats. Sam looked sharply at Papa Miche. The old man had averted his head. Sam pressed his arm; it felt unnaturally stiff.

Another veil gone. A little more sleek flesh to be seen. It throbbed enticingly. Sam watched her critically. By the standards of practised Arabian belly-dancers she was a naive amateur; she invested the ritual with a lascivious delicacy, if such a combination of words made sense. That body couldn't be more than twenty. When the full flood of the lights caught her face it looked twenty-five.

He said to Papa Miche with cool annoyance, 'When did this arrive?'

Papa Miche said nothing. Still averted his head.

Sullen? What for? Sam said softly, 'Fire her.'

Papa Miche looked round. His face was a dusky red; his mouth stubbornly set. 'Let her stay,' he said.

'She'll want paying.'

'No.' Papa Miche shook his head.

Sam ignored this foolish response. 'What'll you use for money? Cowrie shells?' he asked sarcastically. 'Or draw on your vast credit with the Banque Lyonnaise?'

Papa Miche glared. Willie's twitch had begun to crawl. Stefan darted a fleeting glance of alarm at Sam. What was the matter with them? 'She isn't interested in money,' Papa Miche said.

'What then? Love?' Sam looked impatiently from Willie and Stefan to Papa Miche. Absurd! Even in this penny-pinching audience there were better pickings to be found. The patron with the chop had lost interest in it. Another, and more subtle, appetite had taken its place. Sam had never seen a man so nakedly and loosely agog.

He couldn't understand his partners' agitation. He wondered if they wanted him to get them off the hook. He said with more kindness, 'You want me to fire her for you?'

'No.'

'Somebody has to.'

Stefan muttered faintly, 'She will bring us luck.'

12

'We're all out of luck. All out of money. Ten days from now we're going to be all out of time,' Sam said.

Papa Miche said with a belligerent grumble, 'She is going to stay.' And that was that. The Moroccans began a tremulous nasal chant. Hoodlums. How many veils gone? Five. Firm pink buttocks emerged. Firm hard breasts a-quiver. Belly voluptuously alive. It was a smoothly synthetic simulation of the act of love. She let loose the last of the veils; as stark as Eve before the fig-leaf was introduced. Sam – for no reason he could understand – felt the hairs rise on the back of his neck. He studied her. Golden girl. Very calm. Very naked. Very fair. He thought the patron with the chop would die.

He made a gesture of defeat. The hell with it. It would be the best day of his life when he walked for the last time out of Le Kasbah Marrakesh. It would figure in his worst nightmares for months to come. One last begrudging glance at the girl. Six months ago, he shrugged dubiously, she might have brought in a little business . . . but nothing could save the Kasbah at the frowsy end of Rue des Six Anges. The miracle would need more than six angels. He doubted if this tender sprig was in that heavenly class. She had finished her act; the Moroccans rumbled a hoarse sexuality. The patron with the chop was gone; presumably to the loo to relieve his leaking loins. Ten days from now she could sing for her money; and she'd need to sing at least as well as she could strip. She had her arms crossed demurely over her breasts, pink, shapely, unadorned, pubic hair golden. Golden girl. She slipped off with a gleam of flesh, the patrons returned to their drinks and sanity was restored.

Not quite. What *was* the matter with his partners? There was still that palpable unease. Papa Miche wouldn't meet Sam's eyes. Willie began convulsively to wipe the bar to hide his face. Stefan absently kneading the mashed fingers that no amount of exercise would loosen up. All of them so very evasive. Why? *Why?*

'At least,' Papa Miche growled defensively, 'you won't have to worry about us for a while. Willie and I have found ourselves jobs.'

Ah. Now we're coming to it. 'You have?' Sam pretended gratification. 'Where?'

'We're not proud. Just for the week,' Papa Miche said with a dismissive shrug. 'It'll keep body and soul together for a few days.'

A week wasn't much. And he wasn't being very forthcoming. He still hadn't said where it was. Sam repeated the question. 'Where?'

'You will not believe me.'

I probably won't. I'll try to. 'So where?' Sam asked again.

'At the Alcazar.'

Sam found his head swivelling stiffly in the old man's direction. '*The* Alcazar? In Avenue Foch?'

'Is there another?'

'*You?*'

Papa Miche pouted huffily, 'Why should you be so surprised? Because God lives there?'

'Papa, it's a little select.'

'So what?' He was growing truculent again. 'The rich need looking after. People work there. They earn their daily bread.'

A week's work wouldn't produce too many loaves. Sam waited patiently. There was something more to it than that. To say that the Alcazar was a little select was rather like saying that the blood of a prime monarch was slightly blue. There was nothing quite like it in Paris. It was breathless luxury, packaged for God's elect. The great tycoons who moved world power had their *pieds-à-terre* in it; a scattering of diplomats, one of the wealthier Latin American ambassadors, the ultra-smart socialites who figured seasonally in the glossy magazines. It had an oil sheikh. A royal exile or two. It was, in effect, a socially reserved apartment block with all the appurtenances of a private hotel. God, of course, didn't live there. If He applied for one of the apartments He might have to wait for a vacancy the best part of a year. There were only twelve of them, each secluded from the common ruck of humanity. Nobody knew what they cost. The people who occupied them didn't particularly care.

'It's three days to Christmas. You know how it is with the festive season,' Papa Miche said carelessly. 'They're desperate for staff.'

Not that desperate, Sam thought. Go on. I'm still waiting. There's bound to be some more. 'The manager's off for his vacation to Bermuda. The head porter's getting his holiday ski-ing in at St Moritz. The serfs know how to live,' Papa Miche grinned sardonically. 'They learn from the best teachers at the Alcazar.'

'Finished?' Sam asked.

'What else is there to tell?'

'What's the job?'

'Night porter. The midnight shift. Midnight to breakfast. I never sleep well. It won't worry me much.'

'I'll tell you what worries *me*,' Sam said brutally. 'I'd have expected them to be pretty choosey.'

'They are. I came with the best references from the managers of the Bayerischer Hof in Munich and the Hotel Beau-Rivage Palace in Lausanne.'

Sam grew very still. 'You *what?*'

And Papa Miche gave him a flat sullen stare. 'A little quick print-ing. A couple of letterheads. Nobody could give me a better refer-ence than I gave myself.'

'Forgery, Papa.'

'So it's forgery. So what?' Papa Miche's voice rose. 'What did I forge? Hundred-dollar bills? All I forged was a licence to eat a little before we close down.'

No, it isn't that simple. Sam was sure of it. It seemed a lot of trouble to go to for so little. A week's work.

Papa Miche began suddenly to shout. 'Life owes us something.' His eyes were inflamed. 'For this!' He grabbed hold of Stefan's mal-treated hands. Stefan recoiled with a horrified gasp. 'And that!' Papa Miche stabbed a finger at the tattooed number on Willie Tobias's bony wrist. Willie covered it up hastily as if something obscene had been exposed. 'I fought for human freedom. And what did I get for it? A bullet in the arse.' In his great rage Papa Miche was actually trying to drag down his pants as if to display the buttock that still bore the scar. Sam had to control him with a hiss. Where did he think he was posturing? Doing a senile strip?

Mother of God. What did I do to deserve them? They were drain-ing him of his strength. What *were* they up to? No, he didn't want to know.

'They'll check up on you,' he said.

'They already have. Do you think they're mad? I'm not mad, either. I didn't give them my real name. I've knocked about both hotels. I knew the right name to use.'

A shock-haired professor was giving him a lecture in chicanery. Sam pressed the flats of his hands hard on the bar. He shook his head.

He could hear Stefan's unsteady breath. Willie was very pale. Sam stared at him. 'And Willie?' he asked.

'I have a little authority,' Papa Miche muttered. 'I have had him taken on as a lift-attendant and kitchen relief.'

'At night?'

'The upper crust don't live by the clock. And they don't operate lifts on their own. That is what menials are for. If they ring down for *pâté de foie gras* and champagne at three in the morning they have to have it. That is what kitchen reliefs are for.'

Behind that insufferable twitch Willie had suddenly become two men. Lift-attendant and kitchen relief. Sam drew a tired breath. He'd had enough. Somebody had to get them off his back. And then he sighed. He wasn't a bad man; though I wouldn't call him particularly good. Walk around Pigalle and you might find six better men inside the hour. He had unruly appetites. He could afford them; he was physically strong. He was subject to violent spasms of exasperation; he found it hard to suffer fools gladly. The world was bad enough without the idiot fringe making it worse. Another long sigh. He stared at the three of them with distress. Even the idiot fringe had to live.

He followed Stefan's eyes. Golden girl had appeared from the shadows, wearing a thin wrapper. She now sat quietly behind the band.

'She is very good, isn't she?' Stefan said softly. 'She is going to bring us luck. That Joey.'

'I don't know about luck.' I don't even know about being good, Sam thought. And then something clicked like a gramophone needle on the turntable of his mind. 'What did you call her?'

'Joey. For Josephine.'

Queer. I must find out about that. 'Where does she come from?'

'Who asks?'

I'll ask, Sam thought. He glanced at her again. Calm, unobtrusive, whispering demurely to the drummer. He had the notion that she was watching him from the twist of her head.

He got up, patting Papa Miche's hand. 'Don't go forging any cheques,' he said frostily and went out.

He walked towards Place Blanche. Getting colder. Might be a white Christmas, after all. A drizzly curtain of snow coated the cars lining Rue des Six Anges. Be very goose-pimpling for the strip-specialists on the unheated stage of the clubs. What they had to suffer for their art. He went into the nearest *bureau de tabac* to use the phone. He rang Sybilla.

'Sam?' Her voice instantly alive. 'You are coming round?'

'No, no. I'm busy. Listen, Sybilla. About this Joey . . .'

She crowed exultantly, 'So you are going to break something after all?'

'Will you listen? What did he do to you?'

An astonished pause. 'He? Who is talking about a he? She is a she.'

Ah. We're getting close. 'She's rather small?' Sam said inquiringly. 'Very fair? Quite pretty?'

'You must have seen her in the dark!'

'She dances . . .'

Sybilla said scathingly, 'She struts! She does a dirty act at that terrible club The Dying Duck.'

Not any more. She does something stupefyingly sexual at Le Kasbah Marrakesh. He said interestedly, 'What *did* she do to you, Sybilla?'

'She's a plunderer. A pirate. She moves in on one's men.' She grew suddenly cautious. 'Sam, we are people of the world. You understand? One still has some cherished old friends,' meaning that though he was her favourite he could scarcely expect to be the only man in her life. 'But that Joey. Insatiable! Sam, break her . . .'

'I'll be ringing you.'

'My steak *à la Bourgogne* . . . ?'

Give it to the deserving poor. Or share it with the cherished old friends. 'We'll eat it for Christmas,' he said, and rang off.

He had dinner at a *brasserie* in Clichy. They were serving turkey *américain* for the tourists. The bird antedated the *Mayflower*. He had never chewed anything so tough. He spent a long time over his brandy, dreamily smoking a cigar. He was pleasuring himself; he didn't expect to be able to afford one for many months to come. Presently, when the waiter began to yawn significantly, hand itchy for his tip, he let himself drift with the late shopping crowds, stocking up for the festive season. A store blared out a *chant de Noël*. He had nobody to sing a carol with. An Ishmael. He would end up lonely, songless, toothless, unable even to chew turkey *américain*.

Out of sheer habit he found himself drawn back to Rue des Six Anges. Here the herald angels might sing. They bleated from the radio in Garfunkel's bar. Although there was almost no pre-Christmas business, he wasn't alone. Golden girl, still in the thin silk wrapper she wore between acts, as if waiting for somebody from the Kasbah to call her when she was due, sat demurely at a table over a glass. Garfunkel brightened perceptibly as Sam came in. He said generously, 'Christmas is for giving. This drink is on the house.'

'Garfunkel that's no way to make money.'

'Who wants to make money? Money means taxes. Taxes mean headaches.' Garfunkel didn't suffer from them; he ignored the tax-inspector clinically as if he had the plague. 'What'll it be?'

'Make it Scotch.'

Garfunkel said reproachfully, 'One should support one's home industries.'

'A *good* Scotch. Let the home industries start supporting me.' Sam thought he heard golden girl chuckle.

Garfunkel whispered to him over the bottle, 'This is some filly, eh? I hear she's rather special.'

'She is.'

'I must get a look at her act.'

'Do.' She'll show you all she has. Sam raised his voice for her benefit. 'Shouldn't you extend your hospitality to the lady at the table?'
She had been watching him all the time.

Garfunkel called across, 'If m'selle will join us?'

'A pleasure.' She rose. Soft husky voice. A young voice. Nothing could be younger than the slim, virginally wrapped body. She came over to the bar, tightening the wrapper as if Garfunkel might get a glimpse of her vital formation without paying to see the act. 'Another orange, m'sieu.' Abstemious, too. Sam stared into her face. She lifted it to him without affectation. Good clear skin, scattered with soft freckles, warm brown eyes seemingly ready to bubble. She'd looked twenty-five in the floods; she hadn't aged. She examined him as frankly as he was examining her. Pleased with him? She nodded. 'I am Joey.'

'So I've heard.'

She said with surprise, 'Do we have a mutual friend?'

'I wouldn't call her your friend. She says you're a plunderer. You move in on her men.'

Garfunkel made a shocked noise. Golden girl chuckled again. Joey was a better name for her; juvenile, impish. Let's stick to Joey, Sam thought. She said, with a disarming shrug, 'You know how it is with women. All they have for each other is claws.'

'It's just a comment. No business of mine. She said you did a dirty act at The Dying Duck.'

She looked at him guilelessly. 'You know what they say?'

'No. Tell me.'

'*Honni soit qui mal y pense.*' Educated, too. 'If one has a dirty mind everything one sees is dirty.' She settled herself pleasantly at the bar. Garfunkel couldn't take his distended eyes off her. 'Mind you, it *was* a little near the knuckle,' she confessed. 'Very realistic.' Meaning very sexy. Very filthy. 'It meant nothing to me. Art makes its own demands,' she shrugged. Listen to Sarah Bernhardt talking. 'It was strictly for the tourists. Did *you* see it?' she asked.

'No.'

'I am glad,' she said seriously. 'It *wasn't* very nice. I would like you to keep a good opinion of me.'

'Joey what?'

'St Claire.'

Josephine St Claire. Straight out of the top drawer; one of the fine old Versailles families. Accent not from the best finishing school, though.

'My stage name,' she said. 'I never knew my own. Only the one the orphanage gave me.'

The orphanage, of course. He stared at her. Everything worked in for effect. A studied delicacy. Innocence undefiled. (Oh, come off it!) Eyes as bland as a child's. Freckles to match. Nobody who'd discarded Salome's seven veils the way she had, nipples, quivering belly and pubic hair setting the senses agog so that the patron with the chop had to hasten to the loo, could be that innocent. She glanced at him sidelong as if defying him to laugh. He grinned.

It seemed to cement a friendship. 'Are you going to pay me?' she asked.

'No.'

'It is hard to work for nothing.'

'Nobody asked you to.'

'It's all right. I don't mind. There are going to be opportunities for us both.' Now what did *that* mean? His stare sharpened.

She said, quite calmly, 'You are flat broke.'

'You've been talking to my accountants.'

'No. Just to Papa. He trusts me.' He does, does he? I don't, Sam thought. 'You mustn't worry. These things pass. You are a strong and virile man. You will be better off and flat broke another ten times before you get old. And it will be a long time,' she said, studying him without embarrassment, 'before that happens.' Somebody from the Kasbah banged at the door. It was her cue. She finished the orange juice and rose. 'You are very kind, m'sieu,' she said to Garfunkel. 'Come in and see my act. You will find it both refined and oriental.'

Oriental perhaps. Refined never. She stopped at the door to stare back at Sam. 'Did Papa tell you?'

'Tell me what?'

'I just wondered.' And she was gone.

She left a lot of unanswered questions. Garfunkel said in a disgruntled voice, as if blaming Sam for the fall of Eve, 'What is a gentle girl like that doing in your kind of business?'

'What kind of business?'

'Exposing herself to men. Ten times a day.'

'Six. She was doing it before she reached puberty,' Sam said.

Did Papa tell you? Queer. It put him on his guard. Garfunkel said holily, 'Thank God, I earn my money the nice way.'

Like watering the Scotch. It was just brown enough to be recognizable as whisky, but not alcoholic enough to go to his head. Sam peered out. The damp wind was blowing the snowflakes almost horizontal. It fluttered the garbage in the gutter. Tomorrow it would be white. 'Compliments of the season to you, Garfunkel.' He turned up his coat collar and went.

Almost without conscious direction he headed for the Métro. It was a nagging curiosity. He took a train to Etoile. He came out into the slushy cold of Champs-Elysées. It was a fairy highway; the shops blazed. The headlamps of the packed cars poked militantly into the snowy sky, horns blaring; there wasn't much fraternal spirit abroad tonight. He idled absently along Avenue Foch until he came to the status symbol. That hallowed edifice, the Alcazar. And there he stopped. No glittering neons here; its bronze arcade shed a soft religious glow like the halo of the saints. A wide *porte cochère* that would admit a Rolls. Heavy swing-doors that would open at the lightest touch, as would the portals of heaven to the souls of the pious. Sam drew close. Without going inside he could sense the comfort of the central heating; without setting foot on the deep carpeting he knew that it would muffle his tread; that the sound-insulation shut out the raucous crudity of life. The Alcazar was a protective chrysalis. It was gone midnight. He wondered if Papa Miche and Willie Tobias had started work.

He looked through the glass. They had. He hesitated to intrude upon them. The peacefulness was ineffable. Papa Miche was ensconced behind the deep desk, fronting a battery of phones. He sat reading *Le Monde*, silver-rimmed spectacles low on his nose, like Einstein contemplating the Theory of Relativity. A little way off, as if aware that he was of a lower social order, Willie sat by the foot of the marble stairs. He waited for somebody to call for the lift or ring down for *pâté de foie gras* and champagne. Nobody did. The apartments were probably all empty. The lords of finance, the smart set and the diplomats, were no doubt on safari, ski-ing on the best slopes or sunning themselves in the Caribbean. Who wants to be in Paris off-season? That's the way to live, Sam thought admiringly. His shoes were beginning to let in slush. He drew his coat tighter about him and trudged home.

II

HE spent an unprofitable morning wrestling with the Kasbah's accounts. Whichever way he added up the figures the result was the same. Dismal. Papa Miche's custody of the books had been catastrophic. He had no sense of order; paid and unpaid bills crossed each other like tangled threads, Willie's bar chits were indecipherable, cheques had been drawn haphazardly on the bank. They were transparently honest. It went without saying. But slipshod. They had to be kept away from the complexity of double-entry book-keeping, the way children were kept away from matches.

The Moroccan band hadn't been paid for two weeks. They would grow murderous. The bank would certainly grow coldly legal. Perhaps even vicious; the police might be called in.

A wise old professor had once said to Sam, 'This isn't a world for the unwary. It's filled with narks, shysters and sharks. Every human foetus should be confronted with a sign before it emerges. Beware!'

The sum total of the professor's advice was, 'Never take a step without sound professional advice.'

And that's what I'll do, Sam thought. Take professional advice. The soundest. He knew the supervisory auditor at one of the American charitable agencies. He went to see him with the books.

'For God's sake, Sam.' The auditor riffled through them with disgust. 'What do you expect me to say? They'd give any public accountant a thrombosis. These people aren't rational. In a well-ordered society they'd be inside a cage. What in hell induced you to get involved with nuts like these?'

Affection, humanity . . . financial inducements like that. It was too long a story to tell. Sam sighed. 'What do you advise me to do?'

'Pay off the bank.'

'With what?'

'Then pray for divine guidance. Flop on your knees. Join the church.'

'Is that the best you can do?'

The auditor stared at him with sympathy. 'Sam, I wouldn't worry too much. There's bound to be some kind of collateral. Somebody must have given the bank a bond. Which of the idiots signed it?'

'I did.'

'*You* guaranteed them?'

'Somebody had to. They needed help.'

'Sam, it's you who needs help. You're going to have a *juge d'instruction* on your back. He'll claw you right down to the spine. You're not even French,' the auditor said with exasperation. 'He'll love you for that. This Papa Miche. What's he?'

'A citizen of the world. He doesn't believe in national frontiers.'

'Tell him to get the citizens of the world to rally round. And this Willie Tobias?'

'Stateless. One of the privileged from Dachau.'

'It gets worse and worse. This Stefan's Hungarian, is he?'

'That's right. What do you think they should do?'

'Sam, I love you like a brother. Straight talk? No punches pulled?'

'That's what I want.'

'Emigrate fast. Run for cover. Throw themselves into the Seine. Let's cheer you up. The time of carol-singing and sweet charity's here. I'll buy you a drink.'

'I'm a proud man,' Sam said. 'I'll buy my own.'

Two thousand francs might tide him over for a while. It was the season of giving. He looked in at Sybilla's for lunch. She was out. There were dents in both pillows on the unmade bed; she'd been in a giving mood too. If he didn't know women for what they were, if he'd had any particular attachment to her, he might feel betrayed. He rang up a few drinking acquaintances. From three of them, in the festive blaze of generosity, he got the dubious promise of a couple of hundred francs. Christmas was a fraud. He felt a growing sense of anxiety. He didn't look forward to a prolonged interrogation by an examining magistrate. They could keep him making depositions until his hair was white.

One last small chance. He'd done a minor Washington diplomat some special favours. There might be a fistful of dollars in response. He was usually to be found before dusk in Angus's American Bar in Rue St Honoré; a step or two from the embassy. The place was a fug of fine cigars when he pushed in. He had his back slapped. He would rather have had his hand crossed with silver. He shouted across the sea of heads to a familiar face, raising his voice above the din, 'Larry somewhere about?'

'Sure is.'

'Can you call him for me?'

'If I had that kind of yell.' It produced a hiccup of laughter. They were celebrating Noël rather early. 'Larry's back home in New York.'

Sam winced. Fate is spitting hilariously into my face.

From now on a sandwich for lunch. We are going to be very economical. *Vin ordinaire* by the half carafe instead of a lovingly selected bottle of Beaujolais.

He ordered a double Cognac. One last improvident splash. Let's finish this misbegotten year in style.

Sitting pensively at the bar he had the sensation in his back that somebody was trying to draw his eyes. He turned to search the crowd. Well, well! The junior Salome. Golden girl herself. And not alone, either. A thick-set man, very craggy of face, sat impassively and protectively at her side. Champagne on the table; the kind that made pre-Christmas rejoicing bearable. Sam could recognize the label of a noble Veuve Clicquot at a glance. She wore a small white fur cap that might have been mink, but almost certainly wasn't. On it bounced a jaunty pompon. *Très jolie.* A short white jacket of the same dubious fur, a muff likewise. A dazzlingly crimson scarf pleated at the throat by a presumably near-gold ring. Wonderfully *jeune fille.* She could wear that sort of thing. She was beckoning to him. Her teeth flashed. He wasn't much in the mood for bar-chatter; but curious to see who her current 'protector' was. Plunderer. Some bitterly deprived woman was no doubt biting her nails.

He picked up his glass and went across. He said ironically, bowing over her hand, 'M'selle St Claire.'

She chuckled. 'Don't laugh.'

He glanced significantly at his watch. 'Not at the club?' She should be doing her afternoon stint.

'Papa gave me two hours off for shopping.'

Since nobody was paying her, nothing was being lost. He wondered who was paying for her shopping. His eyes wandered to the man at her side. Powerfully built, his face a deep Mediterranean brown; an Italian face; that fleshy prow of a nose came from somewhere south of Palermo. A small tight wordless mouth. Why should Sam feel faintly chilled? He thought it was the eyes; cold, unfeeling, unblinking. A lizard's eyes. They had a hard boot-button polish. He bore a deep scar under his Adam's apple; so deep that the accident must very nearly have cut his throat. Sam thought: this is the kind of man who will get it cut in the end. But not until he cuts a few himself. His suit was American cut. Sleek mohair. That classic tie would have bought Sam lunch for a week. He licked, rather than smoked, his cigar. Nobody will move in on our Joey while this man is about.

And she wouldn't make any move to filch some other woman's man; she might well get a scar to match the one he had.

Did she know what he was thinking? She said demurely to Sam, 'Do sit down.'

'Do you mind? I'm a bit pushed for time.'

'This is Vic.'

Vic. The man nodded slightly, his tongue fondling the butt of the cigar. He had finished examining Sam. He spoke. It was as appalling as the scar; a thick cavernous mumble. That cut in the throat must have damaged the voice-box. Well, he was alive with it, if not too articulate. 'Don't sit down,' he said to Sam.

Very direct. Some people would be offended. Sam merely shrugged.

'I'm leaving,' he said.

'Vic, you're being aggressive.' Joey laughed. She wasn't in the least afraid of him. Sam scrutinized her again. His casual guess about the fur that garnished her face and body was wrong: it *was* mink. And the ring that held the scarf wasn't brass. She has a natural taste for the very nicest things, Sam thought. That gay young radiance. How old was she really? God knew. A lot of men in the bar were watching her furtively. They could see more of her, in fact everything that was physically available, any night they cared to look in at the Kasbah. I missed a good chance; I should have brought some printed handouts along, Sam thought. She completed the introduction calmly, touching her companion's arm. 'This is M'sieu Casanova. He will not object to you calling him Sam. Sam' – using his first name so easily that he was taken aback, as if a precocious child were taking liberties – 'this is Victor Diamond. He is from Seattle.'

And Palermo previous to that. Sam glanced slantwise at the heavy craggy face. Vittorio Dimanti was probably nearer the name given to him at some Sicilian font. Indeed, he was nearer the truth than he knew. Vittorio Adamanti was the name attached to the man with the cracked voice-box when the priest marked his forehead wetly with the cross. Holy water was never so wasted. Joey said, 'Vic, don't make me ashamed of you.'

He smiled faintly. 'O.K. Have your fun.'

'This is a civilized country.'

'I'm not a civilized man.' He relented. 'If your friend wants, he can sit down.'

24

'He is my employer.'

'This is the guy who owns the Kasbah?'

He looked with sharper eyes at Sam.

'Much of it,' Joey said.

'Gamey kind of name. Casanova. Stage-name or something?'

'Vic!'

Sam said to her, with a rueful shake of his head, 'You must really scour Paris to pick them out. This one's something special.'

'Sam,' she said softly, 'he will hit you.'

'No, he won't.'

'Shoot you, even.'

'Not even that. Not with witnesses. He's a cut-throat. He's got the trade-mark.'

The man Vic said pleasantly, 'Friend, go away.'

'My joy. Your loss. See you later, Joey St Claire.'

'Now you're vexed with me. That will make me unhappy.' But she was still laughing. Minx.

Cry your eyes out, Sam thought. He felt hot with annoyance. The day didn't get any sweeter as it went along. He left them, aware of the cavernous chuckle of the man with the damaged voice-box. He sweated out his humiliation. Still snowing. It swirled virginally out of the dark sky. He lifted his hand to hail a cab; but it was a habit best forgotten. He would walk.

A solitary dinner at a small restaurant close to the Crillon; not necessarily in the same class. Sybilla was still out. He had nowhere particular to go. When he left the snow had stopped. The pure white drift was turning into slush. There was an intoxicated circus whirl of cars around Concorde; the Egyptian obelisk in the middle, that in two thousand years had seen humanity's every silliness, jutted like a huge phallus into the night. It probably signified the only sane human activity likely to persist. He had left it rather late. He had no inclination to go home. Something magnetic was drawing him. He found himself idling towards Avenue Foch and he knew what it was. An uneasy instinct; something humming like a suffocated alarm in his over-tired brain. It had had him faintly on edge all day. He halted in the street, facing the Alcazar. Midnight past. He let himself go across, up to the swing-doors and again looked through the glass.

And there they were: the caretakers. Papa Miche seated behind the ornate desk, encompassed by phones like a busy industrialist who had a dozen countries to ring. Still reading *Le Monde*, though a different edition, the silver-rimmed spectacles still low on his nose. Willie stationed tranquilly by the lift doors, luxuriating in the hot-house warmth; he'd risen startlingly in the world, that late tenant of Dachau. How quiet it was. No other soul about. Sam pushed open the doors slowly and went in.

Papa Miche lifted his head. He stared fixedly at Sam, then smiled. Serenely. Willie rose with a hiss of welcome. Strange. It sounded like relief. Almost as if they'd expected him; and here he was at last.

Better late than never. 'Sam,' Papa Miche beckoned to him gently, 'come on in.'

'They keeping you busy?'

'You can see how busy. I read *Le Monde* until two in the morning. Willie makes coffee at three. I read *Figaro* until five. We discuss the world situation. The various wars. Then more coffee. Time passes as if on greased wheels. Willie snores now and then.' Willie twitched unoffendedly. 'He tires easily. He does not have my strength.'

'Doesn't anything ever happen?'

'What can? There is almost nobody here to make anything happen.'

They'd fallen on lush days; pity they weren't going to last very long. 'It's nice,' Sam said, glancing about.

'Nice.' Willie looked at him with surprise. I have been through the Alcazar. It is overpowering. Even I would have looked at him with surprise. 'Sam, it is fabulous,' Papa Miche reproached him in a hushed voice. 'This is only the skin of the orange. The real rich fruit is inside.'

I'll never get to suck it, Sam thought. He'd walked too far. He wished he'd gone straight home. 'Touch this desk,' Papa Miche said.

'What would I feel?'

'Nigerian mahogany. Hand polished. Satin doesn't feel like this. Walk on the carpet and you could be treading on springs.' Like a proud guide displaying the treasures of a museum to a tourist. 'See all the marble?'

'I've seen marble before.'

'From Carrara. Where Michelangelo went for his David. They say from the very same cliff! Willie,' Papa Miche said imperiously, 'give Sam a drink.'

Sam said with a faint smile, 'I'm nobody's guest in this place.'

'*We* have made you our guest. Willie, just coffee for me.'

Willie poured Armagnac into a glass. Crystal? For the menials? Damn my eyes, Sam thought, it really is. It did nothing special to the taste.

26

'Well, Sam?' Papa Miche sipped the hot coffee.

'I wondered about you.'

'You saw from our faces. We were wondering about you.'

Yes. What is it about them that troubles me so? I haven't been at ease since I came through that door.

'Sam,' Papa Miche said breezily, 'don't be embarrassed. Nobody is going to disturb us. I just told you. The tenants are almost all away. Who can blame them? Paris, come Christmas, is a mess. The sun shines upon the ski-slopes. Very nice. Bermuda is very nice, too. Especially if you have a yacht. One of our people' – he was beginning to talk about them possessively – 'is shooting leopards in Kenya. Isn't that a marvellous way to spend a vacation?' He seemed to be indulging remotely in the pleasure himself. 'You just have to have the inclination. And one other small necessity. You have to be very, very rich.'

'Papa, I have to be off.'

'What's the hurry?'

'It's late.'

'It's beastly outside. Stay a while in the warmth. Sam,' Papa Miche inquired pleasantly, 'would you like to look around upstairs?'

'No.'

'You're not curious to see how the other two per cent lives?'

'No.'

'I have to check the doors every two hours. I don't know why.' He chuckled hoarsely. 'I think it's to make sure we stay awake. It's time for the grand tour.' He took a jangling bunch of keys out of the desk. 'Come with me, Sam.'

'Good night, Papa.'

'You don't need to be shy. There's only one resident home. Eighty-two years of age and sleeping sound.' Sam stared at Willie. How pale he'd grown; all in an instant. Any moment now the twitch would leap spasmodically to life. 'Take over the desk, Willie. Come, Sam,' Papa Miche said firmly, leading him to the lift.

Why the hell do I let myself be led? Sam couldn't resolve the question even when he was inside the lift. 'Smell,' Papa Miche said, lifting his nose. 'Jasmine.' The cabin was impregnated with the scent. 'They come twice a week to renew it. One of the many fine services of the Alcazar.' They'd already whispered past the second floor. 'That one's Swiss.' Sam caught a sliding glimpse of a massive door through the grille. 'Banker.' Papa Miche said secretively, 'Better not to mention his name. Keeps two dollies for company when he's home.' He'd learned quite a lot in a very short time. 'The other side of the corridor's Gabrielle Tone.'

'Should I know her?'

'You surprise me.' A soft chuckle. 'But of course. Dresses two ex-queens and Jill St John. I never cared for her collections. Too fussy.' So he wouldn't let her dress him. They'd left a floor unidentified. Who lived there? The sporting type shooting leopards in Kenya? The one yachting in Bermuda? On and up. Papa Miche pointed. The recital of the Alcazar's population went on. 'The Duchess di Ravenna. She's the only one at home. Old, old, old. Older than Mrs Methuselah. Keeps a basket of jewels locked away in her bank. They should be adorning some beautiful woman. Life's one vast waste.' And the lift suddenly halted as if heaven had been reached. Perhaps St Peter was waiting for them outside the grille.

'We'll start at the top,' Papa Miche said. Heaven couldn't be as hushed as this. Two doors faced the corridor. He inserted two curious looking keys in one of them. 'A Maharajah lives here.' He swung open the door. 'You think they went out with history? They're still about. A very pleasant gentleman, they say.' Papa Miche wouldn't be here long enough to meet him. 'Sam,' he murmured, 'you don't have to stand in the doorway. They're just walls. Uninhabited. No ghosts, I promise you. *Come* in.'

Sam entered. A furry odour compounded of strange essences, overheated air and damask drapes. The lights clicked on. He blinked. A vast lounge; the windows overlooking Avenue Foch seemed fifty steps distant. A half-open door revealed a vast bed. All the appurtenances of ceiling-high closets and mirrors; rather womanish. Beyond it was a bathroom that was somewhat larger than Sam's apartment. Could a man get claustrophobic in the bath? A wide honey-brown bureau caught his eye, all glistening marquetry and intricate brass. Gold perhaps? Louis Quatorze, he thought vaguely; something like it. He wouldn't know. Chairs as spindly as an aged ballet-dancer's legs. Pictures; one of them faintly reminiscent. Papa Miche watched him all the time.

'You think that bureau's a nice bit of classical reproduction? The Maharajah would rather die than own a reproduction. He can afford the original. This is genuine Louis Quatorze. You recognize the Utrillo? It's on lots of Christmas calendars. This is the picture they took it from. As authentic as the Gospel of St John. The Maharajah doesn't know much about Impressionists, but he knows a good investment when he sees one. If ever he runs short, which is about as likely as the Chase Manhattan running out of cash, it'll go on sale at two hundred thousand dollars. Pin money for a week. Sam, *do* sit down,' he said tetchily. 'The Maharajah won't mind.'

'He might.'

Papa Miche said carelessly, 'He's in India. Chasing tigers. Whatever it is Maharajahs do.' He opened the door of an antique commode. It revealed a drinks cupboard. He poured out a little brandy. He was making himself very free with the Alcazar's services. He raised the decanter invitingly to Sam, who shook his head. He said with a wry shrug, 'I feel the need of a restorative. I must be getting old. I sometimes lie in bed and my feet grow cold.' He settled himself cosily on a couch. 'We're going to have visitors here on Christmas Eve. Just for a few days. The Maharajah's loaned the apartment to a friend. The friend's invited some of *his* friends.' His eyes were much brighter now. Was it the brandy? Or was he coming to the point? 'They're really rather special friends.'

Sam looked at his watch with a yawn. I must be getting old, too; I should be in bed by one. Papa Miche said, 'The Maharajah's friend is Parnassus,' and Sam gave him a sharp brief glance. It woke him up. 'You've heard of him?'

'Theo Parnassus?' Who hadn't. 'Ships?'

'Ships.' Papa Miche nodded. He'd made an impression. He seemed content. 'About half of everything that floats.' Something of an exaggeration; it was still a lot of the world's shipping. 'Macedonian Airlines. A few chains of de luxe hotels. Some holiday resort developments. Everybody has to diversify,' Papa Miche said seriously, as if he were faced with the same problem himself. Sam thought: you're gabbling. *Get* to the point. 'I rate him number one,' Papa Miche said.

'Number one in what?'

Papa Miche looked at him with surprise, as if he were being rather obtuse. 'The ranks of the super-colossi. The mass-billionaires. There's an American oil independent who once had the edge on him, but too much of his money's in the Middle East and they're shifting sands.' Sam thought sardonically: so I'll keep my money out of the Middle East. He looked at his watch again. This time blatantly. Papa Miche ignored the hint. 'Guess who's number two.'

'God?'

'Be serious, Sam.'

'Why?' Sam shrugged. 'Does it matter?' I've a long walk home. My shoes are letting in damp. Who cares?

'Caesar Vinci. The automobile industry in Milan. He'll be here, too.' Sam stopped looking at his watch. Something was making him uneasy; his belly a little cold. Now he sat. 'Caesar Vinci's big, big, big. He's made the motor car into the new Latin god. Almost as powerful as the Vatican, which can't run you down to the coast with the *bambinos* once a week.' Papa Miche said teasingly, 'So now you're going to ask me: who's number three?'

I'm not; but you're going to tell me, Sam thought. Would *he* be here, too?

'Yes,' Papa Miche said, as if reading his thoughts. 'He'll be here, too. Gregor Kassem. Number three in the club.'

Him I never heard of, Sam thought; I could actually pass him in the street, be pushed over by his limousine, and I wouldn't even know.

'Grigori Sayed el Quassem. An Iraqui. He's Westernized his name. Everything in oil,' Papa Miche said. All the statistics at his fingertips, like an executive accountant. Probably even the returns the tax-man never saw. 'Gasoline. Lubricants. Petrochemicals. You can't run a car, spray an aerosol, but a little of it goes to Gregor Kassem. You've heard of the legendary Mister Five Per Cent?' Sam nodded. His sleepiness was gone; and his stomach wasn't any less tense. 'Well, Gregor Kassem's Mister Half Per Cent. Don't be too sorry for him. Half per cent of most of the crude that flows out of the Gulf is still a very great deal.'

Sam rasped his cheek. This is going to be my problem. I'm always going to need a shave. He peered at Papa Miche. What in the Holy name was he getting at? If I go to the door it may make him . . .

But already he was opening up. Papa Miche said in a brittle voice, 'There used to be a fourth.' Used to be? '*De mortuis nil nisi bonum.* Speak no evil of the dead.' So even God's elect couldn't duck death's cold hand. They all had to go; and they'd still found no way of taking it with them. Maybe that would come in time. 'Never mind his name. South African diamonds. Rather small time. Not really in their class.' Just a very ordinary billionaire; not a super-star. 'It's a funny quirk of fate; it was one of Caesar Vinci's mass-produced cars that killed him on an Italian road. Probably running on Gregor Kassem's gasoline. For all I know, coming from one of Theo Parnassus's de luxe hotels.'

Sam sighed. Not to worry. He'd probably paid his bill. And the mortgage on his car couldn't have run out. His eyes were growing heavy again. 'Papa,' he said tiredly, 'you're talking yourself dry.' You're making me dry, too. And more than a little nervous. Where's all this leading? 'Do you know what time it is? I have to get some sleep.'

'Sam, I won't keep you long.' Presumably he had to be kept.

What made it so important? 'I'm going to tell you something about these super-colossi,' Papa Miche said. Sam wished he wouldn't use that emotive term; he made an impatient sound. 'There aren't too many of them left. They're a little like the dinosaurs. You know? Out of date. Nobody likes them much. They're never out of the full glare of publicity. It's an uncomfortable sensation. They have to watch their images. Day and night. They're the prisoners of their press-relations men. What good's that wealth and power, what's the use of bestriding the world like Croesus, if you have to live like a spinster afraid of the dark? They have to relieve their feelings. Lift the safety valve once in a while.' Now we're coming to it, Sam thought starkly. Here it is.

'They meet every Christmas Eve,' Papa Miche said. 'They've been doing it for years. Every year a different place. Geneva once, Turin another, St Moritz the next. Nobody knows about it; not their closest aides, not even their wives. It's the best kept secret since D-Day . . .'

Sam interrupted him with a wolfish growl, 'If it's so damn secret how do you know about it?'

'I know,' Papa Miche said stubbornly. He needed the brandy; he'd begun to look as worn as an old coin. 'I know for sure. Shall I tell you what they do?' No, don't, Sam thought. This is where I should go. I don't want to hear any more. He was moving to the door as Papa Miche said, 'They play poker,' and he stopped. That was *all*? 'A very select kind of poker. Poker as it's never been played before. A million dollars stake each, four million dollars in – what do you call it? – the pot. Not in banker's drafts, either. Even for the giants there's no thrill like laying your hands on somebody else's cash. They play two, three, even four days non-stop. There was a marathon game in Turin that lasted six days.' Sam licked dry lips. He seemed to know a lot.

He's mad. No, he isn't; the bleared old eyes looked sane. 'This is where they'll be playing this year,' Papa Miche said. 'Here in this very room.' Sam peered about. He needed to touch something solid to reassure himself that it wasn't a dream. The Utrillo looked real. His stomach suddenly contracted. He blew up.

I said before that he wasn't a bad man; just easily inflamed. It could make him unpleasantly violent. Pity. He had so many excellent faults. He said savagely, 'Shut up. I don't want to hear another word.'

But Papa Miche was too wound up. 'That's what they do, these descendents of the medieval barons,' he said in a thick disgruntled voice. 'They play poker. With four million dollars in the pot. On Christmas Eve, too,' and Sam glared at him. He'd never heard Papa Miche declare any particular affiliation to God. 'It's an affront to society!' Again the old man muttered hypnotically, 'Four million dollars in the pot . . .'

And that's what's convulsing him, Sam thought cruelly. With a little effort he could almost let it bedazzle him, too. Four million dollars in the pot! 'Papa, stop it. Do you hear? You've gone gaga.' He wasn't speaking very coherently. Dark unspeakable fears were crossing his mind. 'Don't even talk about it.'

'There's worse to come . . .'

Not for me. 'I don't want to know.' They were yelling at each other. Just as well the Alcazar was near empty; someone might hear. Christ's name, how do I get him to shut up?

'Sam, listen to me . . .'

'No.' He held up his hands. Look. They're sweating. 'Just shut up.'

'Somebody's stepped into the dead man's shoes. Number four in the club. Ask me who.'

'I won't.'

'Lew Cask. You never heard of him?' Sam hadn't. 'Go to the Pacific Coast. Up as far as Seattle.' It stiffened Sam. Now where did I hear that place mentioned? Dear Joey, of course. The gentleman friend from Seattle. It's too involved for a tired brain to work out at this time of night. 'Ask about him there,' Papa Miche said. His eyes went red; an old man's futile rage. 'He is Mafia. *Cosa Nostra* on the West Coast. He is very eager to polish up his social image. Eh? Isn't that something? To actually rub shoulders with Parnassus and Caesar Vinci and Gregor Kassem.' Papa Miche shouted, 'It's enough to make you vomit.' Sam stared at him. It was a physical possibility the way he was working himself up. 'The man's a monster. A moral outrage. He put a little squeeze on Gregor Kassem, who owed him a favour or two. So he's in! Never have they regretted anything more. It's too late to get rid of him. Nobody throws the Mafia out. Not if you're sensitive to bullets in the back of the neck.'

'Finished?'

'I am hoarse. Yes, I've finished.'

'Then that's the lot. I've heard enough. One more crazy word and I'll dump you . . .'

Papa Miche said sullenly, 'It is spitting in humanity's face.'

And here's where I spit in yours. Sam said harshly, 'Don't come back to the club. I want you out of your room.' Papa Miche slept in a small cubicle over the Kasbah. 'That's all.' He went to the door, sick with guilt and compunction, and looked back. The old man had slumped loosely into the couch; his face yellow. He stared hauntedly at Sam. They'll be the end of me, the three of them; God help me. I've had enough.

He went down in the lift. He passed Willie Tobias seated behind the desk. Still enraged he said to him brutally, 'You, too?' and Willie made a piteous sound of despair. He put out his hands fluttering-ly, revealing the terrible tattooed mementoes on the bony wrists. I hate them, Sam thought morosely; they'll drive me insane. He went out into Avenue Foch where there were no worse problems than leaky shoes, barely enough francs for a taxi, and the near certainty that if he went to Sybilla's for consolation he'd find his pillow occupied. Which could only lead to violence. It was, after all, the season of good will to all men. The Métro gates were barred. The good will didn't extend to the public transport system. He turned up his collar with fortitude and trudged home.

It had been a bad day; the night, already a third advanced, promised to be even worse. He lived up on the heights of Montmartre, alongside the *Sacré-Coeur*. His apartment – the word dignified the accommodation – consisted of a room and a half, flanked by a bath-room whose antique plumbing deserved a place in a museum. It was reached by a perilous flight of greasy stone steps. In summer you could see the artists displaying their pictures under the trees in Place du Tertre; in winter you had restricted glimpses of the sleaziest roofs in Paris shrouded by mist. He had taken over the place from an Algerian painter in exchange for a bad debt. I had a drink with him there once; I thought he would have been better advised to write off the debt. It lay over a garage that opened with a shriek of iron shutters at seven; since he rarely got home from the Kasbah before midnight it cut severely into his hours of sleep. I sometimes thought it was why he was so unpredictably edgy.

He was overtired, overwrought. He decided to soak away his anxiety in a hot bath, but the rusted water ran chill. He was no Eskimo. He made himself a cup of coffee and lighted a Gauloise. He looked out. A dark lowering sky. The roofs already rimmed with

33

white. Soon Father Christmas would come skimming over the tiles with his reindeers, dropping bags of goodies on the way. One for me, please; it's time my luck turned. *Bonhomme Noël!*

He couldn't rest. Couldn't get Papa Miche's haggard reproachful face out of his mind. He couldn't even pin-point his foreboding; come to think of it, nothing definite had been said. Mostly the bitter outpouring of an old man's disillusioned heart. What were they up to? Were all three of them in it? He'd never known them act apart. He was overdoing it; everything was at its blackest in these dismal hours before dawn. Yawn, yawn, yawn. If I could only sleep. He took off his shoes, stretched out on the bed and lighted a last cigarette. He woke to the screech of the garage shutters; the cigarette had fallen out of his mouth and burned a hole in his shirt. Not a promising start to a new day.

And yet . . . hope began to burn timidly in his breast. He toured a few bars during the morning and raked in another four hundred francs. He still had friends! He rang Sybilla before lunch. He might eat with her. But she sounded cool. She said remotely, 'Why have I seen nothing of you?'

As if she needed to ask. 'I looked in. You'd had company.'

Pause. 'My sister, of course.'

Of course. '*Chéri*,' she rebuked him, 'you are surely not getting dirty thoughts? I hope I am a nice woman.'

He hoped so too; without much cause. 'Sam, what are you doing?'

'Rounding up a little money.'

'I have a few francs in the bank . . .'

'I don't take money from women.' Though the situation could change. 'Will you come round to dinner, *chéri?*' she asked.

'I may at that. Don't make anything special. Just a plain *entrecôte*. Garden peas will do. Some *crêpes*. A few wild strawberries. No need to put yourself out.'

He heard her giggle. I forgive her for the pillow, he thought.

He went round to the Kasbah at dusk. He was in a calmer frame of mind. He'd forget that curious bursting of the old man's heart at the Alcazar. Despair was the privilege of the aged. He even felt a little guilty; as if he'd failed to sustain Papa Miche in his hour of distress. There was the strong smell of dinner, but few customers eating. Another poorish night. The moorish band in rough and careless form. It would be a pleasure to fire them. The dazzling floods trailed the belly-dancer as she writhed about the tables; she looked duskily pregnant. Perhaps she was. By any one or all of the band. Willie Tobias was behind the bar. There was nobody to keep him busy; he was whispering with Stefan, who sat on a stool, both breaking off sharply as Sam approached. Both looked gaunt. Or was it a trick of the lights?

Stefan said nervously, '*Bonsoir*, Sam.'

Sam patted his back. How stiff he was. 'Willie, I think I'll treat myself to a brandy. Put it on my slate.'

'No more slates, Sam. Everything you want on the house.'

Nice to be a guest in one's own club. 'I don't see Papa about.'

'He's upstairs.'

'Sleeping?'

'Packing.'

For God's sake! Sam winced. 'Willie, tell him to stop. Get him for me, will you?'

'You think I should?'

'Any reason why you shouldn't?'

'You've upset him. He's a very theatrical man.'

Sam grunted. I'm apt to be a little theatrical myself. 'Willie, fetch him down. Leave me the brandy. Stefan,' gripping his arm firmly as he felt him shift, 'don't go away.'

Stefan muttered rebelliously, 'I have some music to arrange . . .'

'Sit still.' Sam pushed him back. He said unkindly, 'We'll book you the Carnegie Hall.' Not very nice. But the little suppressed buzzer in his brain was signalling to him again; triggered off by Willie's jumpy face, by the glazed look in Stefan's eyes. He sighed. I'll never be able to look at them without a sick guilt I don't deserve and a generally bilious stomach. I'm the one who's going to be the war wounded; they'll invalid me of life. He watched Stefan slant-wise. How pale he was. He tried to make it up to him by softening his voice. 'You look peaked. Aren't you eating?'

'Enough.' Barely enough. He could do with a little more blood in his cheeks. 'One gets worried,' Stefan said. As he was; he was busy kneading the crushed knuckles again. 'We shall be closing down in a few days.'

'Nobody's going to let you starve.'

Stefan said in a high voice, 'And that's the best I can ever expect? That nobody will let me starve?' Sam's head swivelled. Listen to the fire-eater. 'If it's to be like that,' Stefan said passionately, 'I *would* rather starve. It is not a way to live. I am entitled to something better than charity. Even yours.' Sam looked round the club. For once he was grateful for the Moroccan band's coarse jangle. He framed the words with his lips: this isn't a football field. Be quiet. He tried not to look at Stefan's eyes. They had grown suddenly wet.

35

'Sam, don't press us. We are all terribly upset. We don't want to talk.'

We? So they were all in it; whatever it was. Mother of God. All the dark insane premonitions had come flooding back. Willie was leading Papa Miche across. The old man looked drained. He couldn't have slept much. There were heavy black pouches under his eyes. He hadn't even combed his hair; the thick white mane flopped about his ears. He came up with great dignity. 'You wished to see me, Sam?'

'Yes. I just wanted to . . .'

'Let me apologize first. I was rude to you at the Alcazar last night. You are the best man I know. The only friend we have in the world. I would rather cut off my tongue than abuse you again.'

Mamma mia. He's taking the wind out of my sails. He won't even give me the chance of shaking him by the throat. 'Papa, you don't have to leave . . .'

'Better that I should.'

'Why?'

Papa Miche looked him steadily in the eye and said, 'Because I do not wish you to get involved.'

And this is where I should drink up my brandy; collect myself calmly and remove myself from the scene. With that shattering pathos of theirs, that enormous helplessness, they're going to suck me into the maw. Sam, don't open your mouth; not another word. He heard himself say imprudently, 'Involved in what?'

Papa Miche continued to stare at him woodenly.

Willie Tobias said in an agonized voice, 'May I talk to him, Papa?'

'What would you say? Sam is not stupid. He knows what we are going to do.'

'Just to tell him about our personal anxiety, our frustration. At least, let me explain . . .'

'There is nothing to explain. What we are doing is morally justifiable, but wrong in law.'

And if ever there was a classic understatement I just heard one, Sam thought. He felt a little prick of sweat. He had never set eyes on Parnassus, barely knew of Caesar Vinci's and Gregor Kassem's existence; he still cursed them furiously in his heart. That damned four million dollar pot! 'Papa, for God's sake. You're out of your mind.'

'Maybe a little. Not much. It has to be done.'

'They'll eat you alive.'

'Maybe that, too. We shall try not to be too appetizing. We know what we are going to do.'

Don't tell me. Mother of mercy; they can send *me* out of my mind. He found himself controlling his breath. 'Papa, listen. Willie, Stefan . . .'

'Hush, Sam. Not so loud. We are not entirely alone.'

'What do you think you're going to do? Just walk in on them and say: this is anti-social. All that money on the table. It must give you nothing but trouble. We've come to relieve you of the headache. Hand it over to us.'

Hard to believe that his hearing wasn't impaired. Papa Miche said in a tone of sweet simplicity, 'Yes, Sam. Exactly like that.'

'You *are* mad.'

'We have reason to be.' And everything that was sweet and deceptively simple in Papa Miche's voice dissolved in a sudden spasm of mindless rage. 'You do not know what it is like to live in our shoes. We have suffered enough.' Somebody at a not-too-distant table put his finger to his lips and hissed, 'This is a place of entertainment, not a debating society.' Sam could have debated the point with him; he'd never found much entertainment in his own club. He wondered what was so intriguing the man. Joey? Joey, of course. She was already near nude; indeed as he squinted into the glare of the floods she discarded the last veil. He studied the firm sleek loins, the pink-nippled breasts . . . she would have intrigued a Trappist monk. But Papa Miche had seized his arm and was whispering throatily into his ear. 'Sam, you have to listen. We are naked bodies, too!' It startled Sam. Queer thing to say. Papa Miche's voice rose, 'We are human derelicts. The debris of society. Do you hear?' Who could help but hear? Papa Miche's voice was choked with rage.

'The world would like to sweep us under the carpet where we would cease to be a reproach. We are an embarrassment to life! We have lost out in the race. We cannot keep up. How can we?' Sam tried to free his arm, but Papa Miche held on to it as if clutching a lifebelt in a tormented sea. 'Who wants a theatrical old clown like me?' Sam stared defeatedly into the wild bloodshot eyes, at the professorial silver mane flopping loosely about his ears. 'Eh? What good is Willie with a face like that?' It was cruel; Willie averted his head with hurt dignity. Nobody wanted to see his tic. 'Or a musician with smashed hands?' Stefan shoved them shamedly into his pockets as if he knew that they would be the next object of reproach.

Stop it, Sam thought. You're shaming us all. Apart from disturbing the patrons who'd paid good money to see the show. Nothing short of a gag could stop Papa Miche. 'We are people! Not derelicts. It is time for the worms to fight back. We are going to take what we deserve from those who will never miss it.' And that made it right? Even legal? 'What is a million or so to them?' Ask Parnassus that. 'Right or wrong, we are going to do it,' Papa Miche said.

'You won't . . .'

'Oh, yes, Sam, we will. And no Machiavellian schemes, either. Everything blindingly simple. Just a quick show of force. In and out with this.'

It rattled as Papa Miche laid it on the bar. Sam found himself staring with incredulity at a heavy old-fashioned pistol; it had a scarred sheen as if someone had cherished it as a museum piece. It still looked hideously forbidding. He heard Willie's breath tremble. Stefan looked quickly away. He whispered, 'Jesus God. Put it away.'

'It is perfectly safe.'

'Is the thing loaded?'

Papa Miche said with a touch of asperity, 'There is no firing pin. It doesn't work. I hope I am a civilized man.' He returned it to his breast pocket where it bulged. 'It came back with me from Spain. It never did me much good. Perhaps it will be luckier for us here.'

Sam squeezed his kneecaps hard; punishing his flesh for something he was sure he hadn't done. Unless compassion was a sin. He was beginning to think it was. 'They'll kill you.'

Papa Miche shrugged indifferently. 'No, they won't. The superrich abhor violence. When you accumulate great wealth you get to be very attached to your health. Separate a billionaire from his life and what does he become? Just like any other man. A corpse.'

'They'll look for you.'

'Let them try. They'll have to look a long way.'

'They'll never give up. The police . . .'

'Nobody will call the police,' Papa Miche said. 'The police ask questions. There are some questions they wouldn't care to be asked. Such as what was happening in the Alcazar on Christmas Eve. With a man like Lew Cask.'

They make me sweat. Sam got up. He looked from Willie to Stefan. They drew away from him, closer to Papa Miche. They were committed. There was a tag Sam remembered from his schooldays, 'Whom the gods wish to destroy they first make mad . . .' They were stark staring mad. He said roughly to Papa Miche, 'You're as good as dead. You know it?' and the old man said, 'We have been dead for years. The three of us. Now we refuse to lie down.'

How they make me sweat! Sam stared across the floor. He could

38

see Joey in the reflected glare sitting behind the band in her robe. Something still needled his mind. He had to know. 'The whole thing's supposed to be so damned secret. Who put you up to it?'

Papa Miche hesitated. His gaze wandered across to the band.

'Joey? Who told *her*?'

Papa Miche hesitated again. 'You see the man sitting next to her?' Sam could just make out the silhouette of a thick body at her side. 'His name is Vic Diamond.' Ah, the gentleman from Seattle. 'He is besotted with her. He tells her everything. A man like Lew Cask goes nowhere without a gun to guard his body. This Vic Diamond is his gun.'

Sam's tongue felt too thick for his mouth. 'You're on your own. You're sticking your neck into a noose. Good luck to you. Choke.' He was out in the street before he remembered his coat. He went back for it to the *vestiaire*. Papa Miche had hired a young negro from Ghana to run it for dramatic effect. A hint of the harem. The eunuch touch! It had misfired like all Papa Miche's ventures. The lad was as insatiable as an oversexed goat.

Nobody should be surprised by the quality of Garfunkel's trade. He had only Rue des Six Anges to call on; few tourists ever reach the dark end of the street. The titillated specialists in *le strip* don't bother to go on after seeing the stupefying photographs outside the nearer clubs. Perhaps Garfunkel runs his bar as a hobby. He doesn't need the money; his bulky wife, the widow of a cat-food manufacturer, is very comfortably fixed. Nevertheless, the onrush of Christmas had brought on a minor boom. He had to turn down his radio because of the din. Cheek by jowl along his zinc were a pair of *commissaires* from the *stripperies*, one wearing a tuxedo with an Egyptian fez, the other the dressy uniform of an officer in the army of a developing African state. A thin silent girl from the *bordel* at the corner of Rue Sidon. Two strapping laundresses from the *blanchis-serie* that catered for the clubs and also served as a *clandestin*; a place of assignation that was somewhat less professional than the *bordel*. They were hardworking girls with rough red hands who would one day return to their villages with a useful *dot*.

Garfunkel enjoyed the company. He presided amiably over the mixed rabble. He had also been made curiously agog. Five minutes ago Sam Casanova had walked in with a stony face and gripped his arm. 'Where's madame?' he asked.

'My wife? Why should you want . . .'

39

'Send her into the Kasbah. Tell her to fetch the girl Joey in here. She's resting between shows. You know who I mean?'

Garfunkel knew who he meant. There had been times when he would have liked to know her even better; in the biblical sense, that is. But not with Madame Garfunkel about. 'Is something wrong?'

Sam said impatiently, 'Nothing I can't cure. Hurry her up. You don't want to lose my custom, do you?'

Garfunkel shrugged non-committally. 'I don't want to lose what you owe.' He had sent his wife into the club. Presently she returned with an affirmative nod. A few minutes later the girl Joey walked in. Draped over her shoulders was a cheap fur coat. M'sieu Casanova, Garfunkel saw, was waiting for her at a corner table with the same granite-like expression on his face. He beckoned. She approached and sat. Garfunkel would have given a great deal to hear what was about to be said. Madame Garfunkel was watching him narrowly. He sent her across to the table instead.

'Scotch,' Sam said. He glanced begrudgingly at Joey. Garfunkel's wife thought with astonishment: he would rather hit her than buy her a drink. The girl smiled. She said simply, 'I will have a cherry, if I may.' It was a less innocuous drink than it sounded; a crystallized cherry embalmed in neat brandy. Madame Garfunkel looked at her with surprise. Two of them could turn a strong man's head.

Not a word wasted. Sam said grimly the instant Madame left, 'You know why you're here?'

'I think so.' She put a cigarette between her lips. She waited for him to light it. She could have waited for the New Year to arrive. She flicked open her own lighter. It wasn't quite gold; but still not cheap. She saw him glance at it. 'From a dear friend,' she said.

'You have a lot of them?'

'Not to sleep with. If that is what you mean. Friends are a substitute for the family I never had,' she said.

'I've just been talking to Papa Miche. I saw you watching me.'

She patted his fingers. 'I watch you all the time,' she said.

'Whatever you're up to . . .'

'Hush, Sam. Control your temper. The drinks are coming. Try to be discreet.'

Madame Garfunkel arrived. She served them with a sidelong glance at Joey. She had seen her Salome act. It still troubled her. She thought: she is either a very sweet girl who has wandered into the wrong place, or M'sieu Casanova should get out of here before she has his head on a plate. If Garfunkel looks at her twice I will break his wrist.

40

Sam was thinking: if I have to break some part of her let it be her neck. He saw her eyes dance. It might be a privilege to black those, too. He said softly, 'What have you been feeding Papa Miche?'

'Surely he told you?'

'You fence words with me and I'll kick you under the table. You'll crawl out of here on your knees.'

And she threw back her head and laughed. Silly; coming the heavy gangster. He bit his lip. The two touts from the clubs turned to stare at her with a kind of absent-minded lust. Sam knew that if she were alone the one with the Egyptian fez would be across to proposition her. And he wasn't even sure how she would respond.

'Come, *chéri.*' She stopped laughing. How intimate we've become. 'You are a very assertive man but you do not kick girls under the table.' She put the cherry between her teeth and crunched it. It oozed brandy. She watched him meditatively. 'I think you *could* be violent. I don't mind men who erupt. You must have a lot of women. Have you?'

They throng my staircase, he thought morosely; I have gendarmes holding them back. She was at his fingers again. Her skin felt silky. He withdrew his hand. 'All right,' she said briskly. 'So you want to ask me questions? Ask.'

'I'm not sure they're worth asking. I think you're a liar.'

'But of course,' she said with staggering candour. 'It's a terrible world we live in. How could a girl survive if she spoke nothing but the truth?' She looked at him reproachfully as if he were being rather naive. 'The truth can be very painful. Not many people can bear it.' He still thought he could bear it. She went on calmly, 'I came out of the worst gutter in Paris. I do not intend ever to go back.' As good a reason as any for lying in her teeth. Now she grew serious. 'There are some things I would not lie about, and some men I would not lie to.' Her warm brown eyes met his. 'I would not lie to you.'

And there was as rich a whopper as he'd ever heard. He drank off his Scotch. Talking to her was like running up an endless hill. 'Your gentleman friend from Seattle . . .'

'He has a name. Name him.'

'This Vic Diamond. He's Mafia.' She nodded casually as if she'd just been told: he's a grocer. 'It's a pretty dangerous profession. He seems to have stuck his neck out telling you so much . . .'

'There are moments in time when a man will tell a woman everything,' she said. Such as when they were in bed? She didn't even shrug. 'You don't even have to coax them. They give out the way a cow gives milk.' It made him wince. The milk was getting to be sour. 'Every word he told me was the truth.'

'And you thought it safe to tell Papa Miche?'

'Why not?'

Why not? God damn it. 'I'll tell you why.' He was trying not to erupt. 'Because . . .'

'Because it amused me? Yes, it did. A little.'

I'll hit her. He rubbed his eyes. How he wished he'd slept better last night . . . 'Sam, calm yourself,' she whispered. 'Your face gives away too much. Do you think I would do anything to harm Papa Miche? Or Stefan and poor Willie Tobias who has forgotten how to smile? I pity them from the bottom of my heart. I have grown very fond of them. Even fonder of them than you.' If you could believe her. And he didn't. 'Life has been cruel to them. It has beaten them into the ground. I am young. I have certain natural gifts.' He had only to look at them. She'd been using them on him since she sat down. 'I can fight back. They cannot. They are frail and battered and have no weapons. All right. I have put one into their hands,' she said.

'I want you to let them be . . .'

'No, chéri.'

'It'll blow up in their faces.'

'What have they to lose?' she demanded. 'Is their existence so sweet?' Almost thou persuadest me, he thought. But not quite. 'They are human derelicts,' she said. Something twanged recollectively in Sam's mind. Papa Miche had used that expression; he wondered if the old man had been speaking with her mouth. 'Think of it, petit.' Getting fonder by the minute. She was touching his fingers again. 'There will be four million dollars up in the Alcazar. On Christmas Eve, too. Christmas is the time of giving. Let a little be given to them.'

Like being washed with warm soothing oil. Glib as Delilah. Samson was about to lose his hair. 'It isn't a little,' he said.

She shrugged carelessly. 'What is a million or so to these super-stars of wealth?' Queer. 'Superstars' had been another of Papa's expressions; it was like listening to a familiar record being played back. 'Sam, don't worry. They will get away with it,' she said.

'They won't.'

'Let them try. Where is your spirit of adventure? Sam, cher ami,' she rebuked him almost with despair, 'you are getting to be what

42

les Anglais call a stuffed shirt. Doesn't it excite you? Not even a little? It does me. Fate's a callous bitch; she has been laughing at them for years.' She didn't seem to have much respect for her sex. 'I want to see our poor maltreated friends laugh back.' Her face shone. She reached forward to seize his arms; the jerk twitched the coat off her shoulder, dragging with it the thin robe underneath, revealing a bare arm and the upper swell of a breast. She drew it back with an indifferent shrug. 'They will do it. They will! I am all for them . . .'

'And who's for you?'

'Sam, you are being vicious.'

'What do you expect to get out of it?'

She stared at him gravely. She stroked the worn skin of her cheap coat. 'Perhaps a little mink. Nothing much. I am not greedy.' She saw the tout with the Egyptian fez watching her with a benevolent leer. He'd seen the coat slip; perhaps he expected to see the rest of the breast. She muttered with disdain, '*Il est méchant*. If I had time I would spit in his teeth.'

She got up hastily. 'It's time for my act. I must go. Sam,' she murmured, 'encourage your friends. It is the only hope they have. They are like candles fluttering in the wind; do not let them blow out,' and she was gone with a whisk of cheap fur. It was remarkable how many heads turned to watch her pass through the door.

Madame Garfunkel came to the table. She said with rough compassion, 'M'sieu Sam, you are upset.'

He sighed. 'I'd like to stop the world for a second. I want to get off.'

'We are stuck with it. We shall not have a better one until we pass St Peter who guards the Golden Gates.' She looked at him sadly as if she didn't think he would get through. He didn't think so, either. 'Twelve francs, m'sieu.'

'Put it on the slate.'

'Garfunkel has changed his accountancy methods. There is no slate.'

He paid her. He went by the bar, bumping hard at the thin shoulder of the tout with the Egyptian fez. The man reeled. Sam said sternly, 'Watch yourself, Pharaoh. You could find yourself back in your pyramid before you swallowed another drink,' hearing Garfunkel utter a nervous gasp. Pity to distress him. He left.

No snow? The night sky was heavy with unshed gloom. The psalmist had said, 'Heaviness may endure for a night, but joy cometh in the morning.' It was a long time coming. The chariot that was fetching it seemed to have stalled somewhere along the road. Sam, he told himself, like the Kasbah you've run out of luck, now you're rapidly running out of joy. Let's bury the whole damned sleazy world in sleep. He ached for his bed. He went home.

But he couldn't sleep. His room was peopled by ghosts. He lay flat on the bed, smoking a cigarette. Presently he switched out the light. He must have fallen into a doze; for that was when it began. Papa Miche whispering from the darkest corner of the room. 'Sam, we are going to do it.'

'No, Papa, you mustn't!'

'We must. What have we to lose?' He was speaking with Joey's voice again.

And then Willie Tobias's ghastly mutter, 'Sam, it will be all right. All we have to do is show the gun. They will cringe.'

'They'll stiffen. They'll even let you walk off with the money.'

'That is all we want . . .'

'But it won't be all. These people are very proud. They never forgive a slight. They'll find you if it takes six years. They have antennae all over the world. Shipping lines, airports, hotels. This man, Lew Cask, has Mafia cells between Sicily and Hong Kong. He'll hunt you down and kill you in the nastiest possible way.'

Next Stefan's shocked gasp. 'Sam, you are making us very frightened . . .'

'I *want* you to be frightened!'

And finally Joey's husky chuckle. Laughing Girl herself! 'You are talking yourselves into a panic. All you have to fear is fear . . .'

And that was when Sam jerked out of the doze. He sat up. He was damp with sweat. He got out of bed and took a heavy swig of brandy in the hope that it would help him sleep. All it did was put him more frantically on edge. He began to walk up and down the room. Fifteen steps from wall to wall. The floorboards creaked. He should have brought Sybilla to stay with him; a brisk bout of sex might have exorcized the ghosts. Fifteen steps back. Creak, creak, creak. Something was needling into his mind; not quite a plan, something practical, some kind of project. He couldn't see it very clearly; only as a vague shape without details . . . in his agitation he dropped an ashtray and the man in the next apartment began to bang on the wall.

I'm too tired to think, Sam sighed. In the morning it would all be gone . . . and he dropped exhaustedly back on to the bed, not bothering to strip off his robe. When he woke at first light every detail of the plan was starkly clear in his mind; it was as if a busy computer had been working while he slept, programming every move for him, putting each step precisely into place. He had never been so shaken. He had a viable ghost of his own.

III

YOU have probably never been in a nightclub before noon. It is the ruination of one's illusions. All glamour gone; the chairs are piled on the tables, surly waiters sweep up, a scrubwoman squats mopping the foulest corners of the floor. If there are cracks in the ceiling you see them. There is the smell of raw lysol, of food that an Inspector of Health would unhesitatingly condemn. I once visited the Kasbah in this frowsy state; it was like waking up in a whore's bedroom and seeing her with disgust in the cold light of dawn. This was in the days when the crook Durocq ran it; Durocq who is now in Marseilles making a fortune out of heroin. I never believed that the wages of sin is death.

Normally Sam Casanova never entered the Kasbah before dusk. He came in before breakfast to find Papa Miche sorting out the bar chits with Willie Tobias, while Stefan tapped absently on the piano. The scrub-woman's bucket was perched on the lid. Artur Rubinstein would never have stood for it. Papa Miche gave Sam a startled glance. Willie Tobias twitched; poor Willie whose facial nerves were disrupted for life. Stefan stopped in the middle of a chord of Mozart . . . all three moved defensively together at the bar. Sam said mildly, 'I've had no breakfast.'

It broke the tension like glass. 'Willie,' Papa said, 'go into Garfunkel's for croissants and coffee for Sam.'

'Yes.' Willie hesitated. 'Sam, you are not . . . ?'

'Not what?'

'It is so early. You don't normally . . .'

'There's nothing normal about me. Tell Garfunkel I want hot fresh coffee, not yesterday's parboiled tar.'

'Don't talk till I come back!'

'I'm dumb.'

Sam sat on a stool. He lit a cigarette. He glanced through the bar chits. Papa watched him intensely. Sam had never seen him look so sleepless, so gaunt. 'What were you playing, Stefan?'

'*Eine Kleine Nachtmusik* . . .'

I had a little *Nachtmusik* myself, Sam thought. Willie came in with the coffee and croissants. The coffee was hot, but not fresh. Garfunkel worked his percolator until the grounds ran pale. Sam dunked a croissant pensively. He looked at his partners while he munched. 'Where does our good friend Joey live?'

Silence. Papa said uncertainly, 'Why would you want her . . .'

'Where?'

'Rue Pierre Morceau,' Stefan said.

'Fetch her.'

'But you will not find her there,' Stefan said.

Sam waited. Stefan said in an embarrassed voice, 'She is residing temporarily at the Hotel Antoine.' Near the Palais-Royal. She was coming up in the world. 'With her gentleman from Seattle no doubt?' Stefan looked down. 'Fetch them both,' Sam said.

Stefan blanched. 'Sam, he is not a very amiable man. There is a certain natural brutality . . .'

'Tell Joey I want them both. Inside the hour. They'll be here.'

He finished his breakfast. He glanced about. Not much longer; I'll have this incubus off my back. He had begun to detest the Kasbah fiercely as one grows to detest a slatternly wife. He stared into Papa's tragic face. 'You're still set on it?'

'Yes.'

'God help you.'

'He will. My life is running out. I am not much; but I don't know how Willie and Stefan will survive without me. I cannot be nurse-maid to them for ever. Sam, why are you mixing yourself up in it? Go away.'

'I'm not sure God quite knows what to do with you. He may need a little help.'

Stefan returned. He looked ravaged. He could barely speak; he had to make three efforts to get it out. 'It was terrible. He upbraided me. He would have hit me if Joey were not there.'

'But they're coming?'

'She is. Not him. She says, give her ten minutes to dress.'

Having emerged, warm and sleek, from the exertions of the bed. Sam dispelled the vision with a sour shrug. She arrived almost at once, wrapped in the skinny fur that he was sure would be quickly changed to mink. Her breasts heaved with her haste; probably con-trived to draw his eyes. He felt them drawn. She said with a smiling gasp, 'See? Not even ten minutes. I have hardly had time to put on my face.'

She couldn't improve on the one she had. Her colour heightened the honeyed freckles that dusted her cheeks. He wondered if her body, which he'd seen only in the deceptive glitter of the floods, was as honeyed as her . . . and was astonished to feel a tiny stir in his loins that wasn't hideously removed from sex. Ah, he thought with a grimace, we're all vulnerable; we're all flesh. 'How did you come?'

She looked at him blankly. 'By taxi, of course. You wanted me quickly.'

'And your friend from Seattle?'

'He takes orders only from Lew Cask.'

M'sieu Frightful. Borgia himself. 'He's waiting in the taxi,' Sam said, and saw her chuckle without embarrassment. 'Stefan, go out and fetch him in.'

Stefan shrank. 'I am not afraid of him,' Papa Miche said staunchly, and went into the street.

Joey glanced demurely at Sam. '*Chéri*,' she said apologetically, 'it's a habit I am trying to break. I am such a terrible liar. I had to learn it in the . . .'

'Worst gutter in Paris. So you said.' He didn't think she'd be any different if she'd had the aristocratic upbringing of Marie Antoinette. They had to wait for Papa Miche quite a while. He seemed to be having trouble in the street. When he came back he looked as if he'd been savaged by a bear. Indeed, the animal followed him in. Vic Diamond sat beside Joey, clapping his thick hand possessively on hers, glancing at her warily as if to say: watch your tongue. Sam had first set eyes on him in the mellow shadows of Angus's American Bar. Here, in the raw light of the Kasbah, he was a more ominous beast. The dark face seemed to have been scraped out of coarse terra-cotta, the hooded glazed eyes very still as if some flicker of emotion might betray weakness. He lighted one of his poker-like cigars. To do it he had to loosen the thin lipless mouth. The other signs of his ferocity hadn't changed. The cracked voice-box, the eye-catching scar across the throat. He waved about the Kasbah, grinning disparagingly, and said with his raven's croak, 'Such a crummy joint.'

Willie Tobias had never heard him speak. He backed away from him with fear.

Sam said dryly, 'You don't exactly enhance it.' But he licked his lips. The description wasn't inapt. The scrubwoman seemed to have found some trinket under a table. The surly waiters gathered about her greedily. She got to her knees with a defensive splutter as if she would hit back. It was unfortunate that one of the Moroccan bandsmen should arrive at that moment to add a note of North African bluster to the scene. Disorder and insolvency wherever you looked. Somewhere in the last ten years, Sam thought, I began to mess up my life. Couldn't God have warned me? He looked at the plate he was using as an ash-tray; he'd stubbed out six half-smoked cigarettes in the last half hour. I'm growing into a nicotine neurotic. A major financial support of the Gauloises concern. It was very hard to laugh.

The man Vic Diamond was waiting for him to speak. He went on with a muffled sigh, 'You sent your creep to me with a message.' Stefan flushed sensitively. Nobody in his life had ever called him a 'creep'. 'You said, come quick. Quick, quick, quick. You have something to say?'

'Yes.'

'So say it.' The thick brown hand fondled Joey's with unabashed sexuality. She hardly noticed it. She was watching Sam with a lurking glint of amusement in her eyes. 'You took us out of bed.'

She chastened him with a faint smile, removing her hand. Sam turned away. He hadn't realized how very tired he was. He'd had that flash of inspiration in the night; he'd come in the most civilized way to show them how it could be done. It might even work. All he wanted was to get them forever off his aching back! He couldn't bear to look at Papa Miche. The old man's bloodshot eyes burned with a bitter urgent plea. Stefan, in his great passion, had taken to sucking his knuckles. Willie Tobias's fluid face leapt. Why, in Christ's sweet name, should I always feel guilt? Sam heard himself mutter: 'I don't want to be involved.' I'm sick with misguided pity, I'm stupid, it must be solid cement in my brain. It's nothing to do with me!

Then he was aware that Vic Diamond was watching him chillingly, taking his features apart, one by one, as if trying to get through the bony structure to see what lay in his skull. He felt a little tremor of disgust, not unmixed with fear.

Let me digress. The movies have conditioned us to the stylized gunman. He either prances maniacally like James Cagney or he has the Bogart slanted sardonic mouth. These are actor's gunmen. The practical varieties do not look like that. They never have. *Cosa Nostra* selects its recruits with meticulous care. They need to have only one negative quality; to be born without those feelings of compassion that make ordinary people soft. They rise in a hazardous profession, watched, not without affection, by their mentors. It is an industrial training school. They live well. They are apt, admittedly, not to live too long. The life expectancy of a professional is perhaps thirty years. If they survive that long they are rich enough to retire.

And few men get so elaborate a funeral, or their widows a better pension, if they don't.

Let me finish. I am almost done. *Cosa Nostra* has many branches; it covers a variety of economic areas, such as gambling, business protection, call girls and narcotics. The competition is intense. Now and again fraternity gets lost in the squeeze; then the gunmen turn on each other. These bouts of internecine warfare rarely last long; they are too wasteful. They attract press headlines and *Cosa Nostra* likes to live a quiet unnoticed life. When all the shootings and the garrotings are over there is room in the thinned ranks for the veterans to rise. This was how Vic Diamond had risen. He had matured in the aura of Lew Cask's benevolence. He was now thirty-eight years of age, which was approaching senility in his profession. Lew Cask had perhaps six trusted aides. Vic Diamond was one of those aides.

Joey said gently, 'Sam, you are getting angry.'

'No, I'm calm.'

'I can see by your face. Don't say anything indiscreet.'

Never mind my face, Sam thought; watch his. There was a kind of lustre about Vic Diamond's eyes he didn't like. It produced the sensation in his stomach one gets when a plane climbs too fast. He heard himself say, 'He's an overdressed thug,' and knew he'd said something indiscreet. Joey sighed. 'He's a paid gun. A knife in the dark. Whatever he uses to earn his disgusting keep.' So far nothing happened to Vic Diamond's face. He didn't seem annoyed; in fact he nodded perceptibly as if he couldn't have chosen better terms. '*A condottiero*,' Sam said, and that pleased Vic Diamond more; for it was a word he clearly understood. But it was all deception. A faint flush stained his dusky cheeks and Sam stiffened with ugly anticipation, as if a cobra had reared its head in the club.

Joey said, 'Vic, he's baiting you. Behave yourself.'

The man said angrily, 'I should wash his mouth out for him.'

With raw lysol, Sam thought; arsenic perhaps. He had begun a little shiver. He didn't know if the man carried a gun; but he was as big as he was, even bigger, and he was sure he could inflict a quick hernia before he reached it. And then he thought with self-disgust: say what you have to say and get out. You deserve a more dignified life than this.

'Now everybody calm down,' he said, and Joey laughed out loud. 'Just tell your *compañero* that this is Paris. We're in a civilized town.' A few hundred thousand Parisians could have argued with him strenuously on that score. 'And tell him not to wait for me round any dark corner. We have *flics* who know how to deal with tricks like that.' As indeed they do. Have you ever seen an angry *flic* use his rolled-up cape as a club? It is heavily weighted with lead pellets. It is as lethal as a gun.

The dissension over by the scrubwoman had ceased. They'd reached some kind of equitable division; Sam wondered vaguely what she had found. Chairs clattered; tables scraped; the Moroccan began to practise softly on his oboe. Normality of life returned. Sam stopped shaking. He had put Papa Miche into terrible shape. Stefan's pallor was ghastly. And these were the headstrong adventurers who proposed to go plunging into the Alcazar on Christmas Eve. Goose pimples rose on his skin. He said to Vic Diamond as mildly as he could, 'I think you've been a little foolish. Do you mind?'

'Think what you like.' He crushed out half an expensive cigar to show his utter disdain.

'You're in a precarious business. A man never knows when the scimitar's going to fall. You have to be careful. And you're too vulnerable to sex.' He didn't glance at Joey. 'It wouldn't please your chieftain.' If that was what one called Lew Cask. Or was it *padrone*? 'You talk too freely in bed.'

And it seemed to take a little while for the words to reach Vic Diamond's brain. When it did the effect was spasmodic; his head swivelled dully in Joey's direction. He looked at her with total incredulity; not with rage, he was too besotted with her. She patted his hand gently to reassure him. Nothing would. He looked like a man who had been tied to a stake for execution.

Sam went on, 'She's been priming our friends with what's going to happen you know where and when.' And again the man stared hard at Joey. He was unutterably shaken. A glisten of sweat appeared on his upper lip. Sam added, 'She told you, of course?'

She hadn't. She looked at Sam with wide-eyed reproach as if he'd jumped the gun. He probably had. He just wasn't sure at whom the gun was pointed.

Vic Diamond reverted to the Sicilian. Sam heard him mutter huskily, '*Morto mio*.' He thought it meant: I am dead.

He stared at the man with a curious pang. He probably wasn't very clever. His line of work didn't call for high intelligence; indeed it could be something of a disadvantage. The history of gangland was filled with epics of ambitious gunmen who had taken over the boss's empire. The supreme virtues for the job were unbreakable loyalty, that touch of animal brutality; and strict obedience to the principle of silence. Never open your mouth; never in any circumstances betray your chief. And Vic Diamond had indiscreetly done something like that. He might well say: '*Morto mio.*' I am dead. Bed was a trap for an oversexed man.

Sam glanced at Joey. Now she has him over a barrel. Let's see which way she's going to roll him. He thought he could guess.

He beckoned with his elbow to Papa Miche and Willie Tobias and Stefan. He said to Vic Diamond, 'They know all about the Alcazar. The big game. You understand?'

Vic Diamond said nothing. He lighted another cigar; it shook like a loose spar. He had understood.

'What would you think they're going to do?'

'*What?*' Vic Diamond started violently.

'You might have tried it when you were young.'

'These crummy wrecks?' Papa Miche stiffened sullenly. Willie and Stefan flushed. Vic Diamond said wildly, 'Jesus God in Paradise. They're out of their crazy minds.'

'They'll still try.'

'They won't live to walk out.'

'Oh, they will. For a while. Ask Joey. She has a high understanding of the instinctive reactions of very rich men. They never argue with the gun. They only look for it afterwards. And then . . .'

'Joey. You told them that?'

'Vic, he is confusing you.'

'But you *told* them.'

'I told them, yes.'

'Why? Why? Why?'

'You will listen?'

'Christ, I am stricken. You have put me in my coffin. These twittering dummies, you have put them in their coffins, too.' He gasped with horror, looking down. There was a flood of water about his feet. The scrubwoman mumbled, '*A la garde,*' dragging the bucket along his legs. She had heard nothing; understood nothing; nothing convulsed her but the sordid battle with the vulturous waiters. It gave them a breathing space, a minute or two to recover composure while she swabbed around them. When she had removed her bucket Joey said earnestly, 'Vic, *now* will you listen?'

'You betrayed my confidence. I trusted you. You should never have breathed it to anybody, much less these crazy bums. What have you done to them? What have you done to me?' He wiped a drop from his nose. Sam had never seen a man sweat so much. 'There is nothing you can do to help.'

'I can help you.'

'Then stop these idiots. The *padrone* will have me shot.'

She said fatalistically, 'But you already know that you are going to
be shot. In your line of business how long can you go on? Another
year? Perhaps two? You once told me that your luck cannot go on for
ever. Maybe the coffin that will contain you is already made.' He
tried to speak. He couldn't. 'They will find you in some gutter
with a knife in your kidney or a bullet in your head.' He could only
look at her frozenly. 'Do you think it will lose Lew Cask a minute's
sleep?'

'He is my *padrone* . . .'

'He has to be your executioner. You know it. There always has to
be somebody to step into your shoes. For you? *Fini*. There will be a
nice wreath at your funeral but you will get no pleasure out of it. You
will get no pleasure out of anything, not anywhere, for you will have
run out of life.' Sam watched her with wry admiration; whoever had
written the play for her it was a remarkable performance. He
thought he could see how it was going to end. She pointed from
Papa Miche to Willie Tobias and Stefan. She had a captive audience in them, too. 'So why not help them?'

'Are you mad?' Vic Diamond shrank. 'It would be an act of
betrayal . . .'

'An act of self-defence. You are entitled to survive. You have served
your turn.' She was stroking the palm of his hand; the sexuality was
blatant. Sam could see the craggy lines of the man's face blur the
way rough iron softens under heat. We're not far off the curtain now,
he thought. 'Think of it, Vic,' she said. 'There will be four million
dollars on the table. Only four of you to share. A million for each.
One can live very well on a million dollars. One can simply vanish,
change one's name, grow a beard,' she shrugged. 'I know a man
in Clichy who can supply an excellent false passport for a thousand
francs.' Vic Diamond stretched his knuckles. He fumbled for a silk
handkerchief. He didn't know what to do with all the sweat. She
said softly, 'Have you ever been to Buenos Aires? I often dream of
it. It is very gay. The sun always shines . . .'

'I dare not! They would find me . . .'

She touched his arm. 'Then listen to our friend Sam. I think he
has something in his mind. Perhaps your *padrone* will never even
know that you are involved.'

Vic Diamond's head dragged round to Sam. 'Is it possible?'

'It's just possible.'

'Only *just*?'

53

Sam said dryly, 'For four million dollars you have to risk a few "justs".'

'I am listening.'

'You'll have to do more than that. You'll have to go on with it. You don't really have any option, do you? You've already stuck your neck out. You've put it into a silken noose.' Joey laughed softly. Some noose! Sam watched her under his lashes; she should be careful. There was still a lot of emotional gunpowder about and she was prancing in the vicinity with a lighted taper in her hand. He went on cruelly to Vic Diamond, 'You'll never be able to deny it. Lew Cask would never trust you again. He'd take no chances.' Sam motioned carelessly to Joey and said, 'He'd take her and twist it out of her if he had to break her legs.' It sobered her for an instant; her dazzling little play had its dangers, too. 'Well?'

'Jesus Christ. Let me think.'

It's all been thought out for you, Sam mused. 'You've got yourself committed.'

'Betrayal is a fearful thing. We have a word for such men. *Traditore*. It deserves death . . .'

'Too bad for you. I don't give a damn. I do give a damn about my friends,' Sam said. He touched Papa Miche's hand. The old man shivered. 'They're my people. I don't want any kind of *morte* to happen to them. You can still walk out.'

'Joey?'

'Do it, Vic. Better long life with much much money where the sun shines for ever. Better than one of Lew Cask's wreaths.'

'God help me.' He would need all the help God could give him 'All right. If it can be done I will do it. Tell me how.'

Sam told him. He'd seen the plan vaguely in his mind as a stark leafless tree. But his voice seemed to give it life. It began to suck up sap, take on foliage, throw out branches. And suddenly it was a great tree of a plan that would stand any gale. He was curiously pleased with it. It could work. In fact, it *would* work, God willing. It was the only dubious factor. Just how willing was God?

Papa Miche's mouth worked like a gasping fish. He stared at Sam his bloodshot eyes ashine with unshed tears. Willie Tobias bent his head. Sam thought he was both moved and afraid. Stefan broke into an excited mutter of unintelligible Hungarian. Joey began to laugh. Louder and louder, pealing out, so that the scrubwoman ten paces off peered up as if wondering what there was to laugh at in a life of bruised knees and buckets of suds. Vic Diamond took ten

frozen seconds to absorb it. He said begrudgingly, 'It's too clever.'
But Sam could see that he was greatly impressed.

Joey said, 'That's what every good plan should be. A little too
clever. If something should go wrong there's still enough cleverness
left to carry it along.'

'I like things to be simple.'

'Like death,' Joey said. 'And that's the wonderful thing about it.
Nobody is going to die. Nobody is even going to be seen.'

He was like an uneasy dog worrying a gritty bone. He glanced
sidelong at Sam. 'There's something he forgot to mention.'

'And what is that?'

'Where does he fit in?'

'He doesn't,' Sam said.

And every anxiety in Vic Diamond was suddenly acute. 'You
thought it up . . .'

Sam said impatiently, 'But I'm not involved.' What was making
him so angry? He found his eyes straying to Joey. Am I getting to
be jealous? Sam, you're out of your infantile mind. He went on
irritably, getting it out of his system, 'Do I have to paint it on a wall
for you? I'm not involved! There's nothing in it for me. Not a
dollar, not even my *Métro* fare. I want no part of it. I'm giving it
to you free of patent rights. Copyright it, do what you like with it,
but I walk out of this club in ten minutes and I never want to see
any of you again.'

Joey put out her hand to subdue him. 'Sam, *chéri* . . .'

'Don't *chéri* me. *Chéri* your bedmate.' He twitched her off.

Vic Diamond said with stilted dignity, 'You have no manners.'

Sam stared at him. He had to laugh. 'That's right. I disgraced my
finishing school. They threw me out.' He had been thrown out of
la société des notaires, the law society, but that was another story. A
painful one.

'So what's in it for you?'

Sam said tiredly, 'Oh, – off.' He disgraced himself again. It
wasn't the language of his finishing school; it was the argot of the
lowest Parisian gutter, and there is nothing much lower than that.

Papa Miche said in a faint voice, 'Can we not behave like civilized
human beings?'

'You can, Papa. I can't. Good bye, my friends,' glancing at Willie
and Stefan. 'Make yourselves rich.' But not at my expense.

'You are not going just like that?'

'Watch me. I'll be through that door in thirty seconds.'

'Sam, I beg of you. One last blessing . . .'

'No more talk. No more blessings. I know what you want. Talk to Auguste yourself.'

Vic Diamond asked roughly, 'Who in hell is Auguste?'

'My uncle,' Stefan said. His distress was naked. 'He is consultant registrar at the Hospital of St Germain-des-Prés.'

'The doctor? God damn it, you can always fix some doctor . . .'

'They need Auguste,' Sam said. He looked at them, one by one, with a kind of bitter valediction. His gaze lingered on Joey. He went through the door.

He found the young negro from Ghana by the *vestiaire*. Why so early? His duties didn't begin until dusk. The lad whispered, 'M'sieu Sam, am I going to be paid?'

'You need the money?'

'I have large appetites.'

So have I. But I'm not going to subsidize yours, Sam thought. 'Women will only corrupt you,' he said. 'Be chaste. Try to manage on your tips,' and went into the street.

Up with the collar. It was beginning to snow again. The thin drizzly variety that grows grey as it passes through the upper atmosphere and befouls Paris when it lands. It never solidifies; all it can form is slush. He went up the street, passing Garfunkel standing in his doorway. He gave him a brief nod. Then rage caught up with him; he had to relieve his feelings or bust. He went back to Garfunkel and said scathingly, 'Don't you have anything better to do than stand here watching the tarts?'

'Do you know of a better pastime?'

'It's character destroying.'

'Mine was ruined a long time ago,' Garfunkel said. He was surprised by the tremble in Sam's voice. 'Sam, my friend, why are you in such a frenzy? You will tear your nerves to tatters if you don't learn to relax.'

'I might if I had a rich wife.' Sam glanced into the bar where Madame Garfunkel was slicing bread.

Garfunkel admitted unoffendedly, 'It helps.' He was curious. What had happened in the club? 'I enjoy your conversation. Come in and share a bottle of *pinard* with me.' He might find out.

Sam hesitated. A taxi rolled up to the Kasbah. Two figures emerged. They stood talking on the sidewalk. Vic Diamond gesticulating vehemently. Joey shaking her head. Presently Vic Diamond got into the taxi and drove off. He gave Sam a militant glare through the window as he passed. Joey slowly approached. She said sweetly to

Garfunkel, 'I am starving. It has been such a rush this morning. I have had no time to eat.'

Garfunkel beckoned hospitably into the bar. 'My place is warm. The bread is fresh.' The coffee almost drinkable. 'Please enter. I am sure your employer, M'sieur Sam, will keep you company while you wait.'

'That would be very nice,' she said, tugging at Sam's sleeve and drawing him in. They sat well away from the bar. Garfunkel whispered to his wife, 'Something is going on there. I wonder what it is. I sense terrible passions.'

Madame Garfunkel glanced at him sharply. She was interested only in the passion that drew his inquisitive eyes to Joey. 'Attend to your own business,' she said.

'I am a bartender. Their business is mine. The day I cease to interest myself in my customers I lose interest in life.' He prepared the coffee. Poured half a bottle of *pinard* into a carafe. He might pick up a few words as he approached.

Joey was murmuring reproachfully to Sam, 'Was it necessary to embarrass me so?'

He glanced at her with mock surprise. '*Can* you be embarrassed?'

'Talking of me as his bedmate. It was not very nice. It was also unjust. I am quite alone. There is nobody to guard my interests but myself.' She couldn't wish for a better guardian. Sam gave her another dry look. 'A girl is sometimes forced to do things for which she can feel only revulsion.'

'Such as sleeping with . . . ?'

'There is no need to spell it out. I do not like him very much.'

Poor Vic. They stopped talking instantly as Garfunkel brought over the wine, the coffee and the bread. He had left the butter behind. He might still hear something when he returned.

'Sam,' she said, meditatively dunking a crust into the coffee, 'why did you think it necessary to fetch Vic Diamond into the business?' Was she already preparing to ditch him? He couldn't believe his ears. 'You are tempting him with a vast amount of money.' She shrugged diffidently. 'It seems a very great waste.'

'He's Lew Cask's gun. He's employed to guard his body day and night. He'll be somewhere in the vicinity on Christmas Eve. Papa Miche and the boys' – silly way to talk of Willie and Stefan, but in their wretched simplicity he would always think of them as 'the boys' – 'are in greater danger than they think. Vic Diamond has to be neutralized.'

She smiled shyly as if she could have neutralized him herself with

57

c

less expense. She probably could. 'Sam, do you think you'll ever be able to walk away from your friends?'

'You saw me do it.'

'I saw you take a little step. The Chinese say that if you stretch out your hand to help somebody you assume responsibility for him for life.' She chuckled as he stared at her. 'It was something I read in a book.'

'You don't have to believe everything you read.'

But she shook her head seriously. 'You're never going to get them off your back.' And then Garfunkel appeared with the butter. They grew silent again.

Garfunkel did something he would be ashamed of. Later, perhaps. On the other side of the wall was the store-room. Above their heads was a small ventilator. He went next door and pricked up his ears. He could hear their faint murmur. And what he heard astounded him.

'Sam, *chéri*,' he caught her husky voice, 'I have a great feeling for you. Do not look on me as an enemy. We have an affinity for each other.'

Then Sam's cynical mutter, 'Don't make it an excuse for me to slide into your bed.'

She laughed. Minx. 'It doesn't have to be quite like that. I was thinking more of sliding into yours.'

I would never have thought it of her. So guileless; the essence of sweet femininity. One can no longer trust one's instincts, Garfunkel thought. When he came back to the bar they had already paid and gone. He said nothing about it to Madame Garfunkel; she had a puritanical view of life he found restrictive. And a tongue to match. I must slip into the Kasbah and take another look at this girl *à la nature*, he mused. There are facets to her I have evidently not seen.

It was time to get away from Paris. Sam was tired of the chilling slime, the sleaziness of Rue des Six Anges, the mental burden of Papa Miche and the boys. There was an Italian movie director he had once represented; he was shooting location scenes in Nice. He was a generous man. What Sam most needed at that moment of time was human generosity, expressed in terms of francs. The garage that lay beneath his apartment would hire him a car to drive to Nice. He packed a bag and went below. As he threaded his way through the battered autos in the dark oily cavern he heard one of the mechanics shouting his name. He had no phone of his own; people sometimes reached him through the garage office.

He went inside. It was stacked with tyres and reeked of cheap *essence*. The counter-hand offered him the phone. 'There is a call for you, m'sieu.'

'I just left.'

'It is from your club. One of the ladies. You know the one?' Sam could guess. 'She is quite insistent.'

Sam hesitated; he sighed. He took the phone. He heard Joey's cool voice. 'Sam?'

'Who else?'

'I have been trying to get you all afternoon. Sam, you sound very far away?'

In another few minutes I would have been. Driving along the A6 to Nice. But God won't let me off the hook.

'This Hungarian doctor has been to see Papa Miche,' she said. 'There was a terrible scene. He refuses to even listen to them. They do not know what to do with him.'

Pity. 'Neither do I.'

'So they are in a very great state. You will come here, then?'

'No.'

'Sam, they need your help. I know it is an imposition. But it will be for the last time.'

'There'll never be a last time. I have to ditch them now.'

Sam could see from the rigidity of the counter-hand's neck that he was trying to fathom the conversation. Listening to only one party made it hard.

'You cannot be so inhuman.' She waited for him to speak. He didn't. She went on with sorrowful emphasis, 'You remember the Chinese?' He remembered. 'You assumed responsibility for them. You must continue the responsibility a little longer. Do not walk away from them.'

The phone slipped within Sam's sweaty hand. He had been carrying his bag all the time; he put it down. 'Is Stefan there?'

'Yes.'

'Put him on the line.' Presently he heard Stefan's fluttering voice. 'Sam, it was so distressing . . .'

'Never mind. I want you to go to the hospital and talk to your uncle. Tell him I want him in the Kasbah inside two hours. If he won't come tell him I'll send him a postcard from Chateau d'If. It's outside Marseilles.'

'I never heard of it.'

'He has. If that doesn't fetch him give him fraternal greetings from Inspector Massime.'

'Sam, you mystify me . . .'

'Yes.' I mystify myself. I'm stupidity incarnate; thick bone from the neck up. Sybilla had once told him with angry scorn, "You are the softest touch in Paris. You are like the blind, you should not be let loose without a guard dog." 'Stefan, don't waste time.'

'We take such advantage of you, Sam . . .'

'Hurry.' He put down the phone. He said to the counter-hand with a shrug, 'I shall not be needing the car until tomorrow.'

The man watched him strangely. 'Very good, m'sieu.' From now on they'll regard me as a cool customer. The *Rififi* type. They'll never trust me with a franc, but they'll treat me with respect.

He unpacked his bag and prolonged the two hours with a leisurely lunch. Let them wait. He walked into the Kasbah mid-afternoon to find them assembled at the bar. Always at the bar; the tribal gathering place. Vic Diamond was there. Probably Joey had fetched him along. Sensitive girl; she had guessed that Sam would prefer it. He wanted the man to be involved deeper and deeper in every move.

The club was unnaturally quiet. It was that desolate hour between the racket of the cleaners and the first blast of the band that would start off the early show. There was a face at a nearby table Sam hadn't seen for some years. The man gave him a quick anxious glance; then turned away. A pale beaky face with small darting eyes partially masked by absurdly old-fashioned pince-nez. He looked like a village school-teacher one wouldn't trust with the children's welfare fund. But teachers do not wear clothes like that. Sam and I first met him on the Riviera where we were running a little chain of unprofitable boutiques. I lost a little money over it. Nothing to make me weep. The money had been put up by a consortium, a big slice of it by a Hungarian named Augustus Beniszki. He lived in a style to which few doctors, unless they are abortionists, can aspire. He had an opulent flat in Cannes. He was supposed to run a pharmaceutical laboratory in Chateau d'If which lies by Marseilles. He suddenly sold out his share in the consortium to some Parisian *marquereau* with a bad record. It got the police interested in us, which is always bad for business. It was Dr Augustus Beniszki they were chiefly interested in. It seemed that his laboratory specialized in dubious pharmaceuticals like heroin; there was an efficient chain that fed the stuff into the pusher's rackets in the United States.

Perhaps there was some row? Who knows? There was a rumour that he turned the names of his associates over to the police and fled. And here he was, covered with respectability, Dr Auguste Benes, consultant registrar at the Hospital of St Germain-des-Prés. Not one of the smarter clinics; a working man's hospital. He still looked well off. Probably abortions on the side. The world makes cynics of us all! Sam stared ruefully at the sleek mohair suit, the silk shirt and the fine English shoes that seemed to have been sculpted to fit the bony feet.

'Well, Augustus? You never once dropped me a postcard all this while.'

The doctor gave him another furtive glance as if he would disclaim recognition; but it would have been a waste of breath. He said huffily, 'It is Auguste Benes. Kindly remember. I am now . . .'

'I know what you are. Forgive me. I forgot about your name. Have they offered you a drink?'

'I have no time for social frippery . . .'

'Don't go.' The doctor sat down again. It was Vic Diamond he was queerly aware of; a scamp, particularly if he is a doctor, which is rare, knows a dangerous animal on sight. He probably saw them by the dozen in his surgery at the Hospital of St Germain-des-Prés. 'You were here for a little chat with Papa Miche this morning,' Sam said.

'Yes.'

'So go on. Take it from there.'

The doctor grumbled irritably, 'Some ludicrous rubbish about . . .'

'It isn't, though.'

'What?'

'Not rubbish. Not ludicrous at all. No more ludicrous, say, than the very practical laboratory you used to run in Chateau d'If. By the way, do you still hear from your friends?'

The doctor took off his pince-nez and wiped them. It gave him time to think. He pursed his mouth disdainfully. Of course, he hadn't heard from his friends. First they would have to find him; next to get out of prison on parole. In Marseilles it takes many years. It wasn't easy to puff out his skinny body like a frog. He almost achieved it. Sam said in a kind voice, 'Inspector Massime of the narcotics squad would dearly like to know how well you are,' and the doctor's hollow chest fell in.

He said to his nephew, Stefan, who was watching him with horrid fascination, 'What is in that bottle?'

'Cognac.'

'A drop or two.' Stefan half filled a glass. The doctor drank it with a wry twitch of his nostrils; he was used to better. He muttered to Sam, 'This orgiastic game.' He evidently knew nothing about poker. 'These unbelievably rich men . . .'

'Did Papa tell you who they were?'

'No.'

'But he told you what he wanted of you?'

'Yes.'

'And you were only too eager to help?'

'Do you think I am mad?' Again the pince-nez flashed. The good doctor, I remember, always used them with theatrical effect in the South of France. 'My medical integrity is at stake. As registrar at the hospital . . .'

'Auguste, don't work yourself into a state. The brandy isn't that bad. I know about your medical integrity. Our friends here would like the benefit of it.'

'Impossible!'

'Napoleon said nothing is impossible if one wills it. I trust him,' Sam said. 'Auguste, listen.' He pressed the bony clinical hands. 'You are a greedy man. Yes?'

'No.'

'Auguste!'

'All right. So I am. What of it?'

'Would a quarter of a million dollars assuage that pathological greed of yours?'

'*What?*'

'In cash.'

Sam heard Joey's soft chuckle. There was really nothing to laugh at. The doctor glared angrily about. 'If I did not know that you are not a fool . . .'

'I can be. On occasion. I was a fool when I trusted you in Cannes. This time I am perfectly sane. Now listen again. Auguste, you are not feeling sick?'

'This idiocy about a quarter of a million dollars . . .'

'I know. Money on that scale can make healthy people feel ill. In 1968 you got your brother, who is Stefan's father, out of Hungary. I like to feel that it was an act of charity.'

'For my own brother? It was!'

'At five thousand francs. Stefan always tells the truth. You took him out by train in a coffin. You gave him a capsule that induced a deep coma near enough to the appearance of death to fool the frontier guards. It is this capsule Papa wants.'

'This game . . .'

'At the Alcazar. On Christmas Eve. Some kind of ritual. Four million dollars, as the professionals say, in the pot.'

'Gibberish!'

62

'Not with men like that. They are the *crème de la crème*.'

'You did not tell me who they are.'

'Forgive me. Theo Parnassus for one.'

Auguste Benes rose with a convulsive jerk. 'I do not believe it . . .'

'Caesar Vinci. The Italian.'

'The industrialist?' The doctor shouted, 'You are making it up.'

'Gregor Kassem you never heard of. The big oil barons have heard of him. You have *certainly* never heard of the fourth. Lew Cask. I think he is the most powerful and ominous of them all. He is Mafia.'

Nothing was said. The pince-nez glittered. There was sweat on them. Again they were wiped. Dr Auguste Benes uttered a tired sigh.

Sam said, touching Vic Diamond's arm, 'This is his man. His guard. His *condottiero*. How would you wish him to confirm it? By showing you his gun?'

'I want no part of it,' the doctor said, making for the door. A heavy hairy hand brushed him back. Vic Diamond said, 'You let us tell you too much. You have a part in it, like it or not.' He grinned without humour. 'You would really like to see the gun?'

'No.'

'Then sit down. And comply. We are *camerati*,' which Dr Benes took to mean comrades. It filled him with distaste.

Sam said, 'This capsule . . .'

'It has to be used with care.'

'You are a careful man. You used it on your brother who was sixty-eight years of age and he walked about Vienna two hours after he woke up.'

'On whom is it to be used?'

'Parnassus.'

Auguste Benes flinched. He said huskily, 'He is a well man?'

'He is immortal. Have you seen him play tennis? He skis, he swims, he high dives. He came second in the European bob-sleigh race at Cortina last month.'

The doctor nodded. Another sigh. 'What else would you want of me?'

'One of your ambulances, of course.'

The doctor started. 'I cannot be sure . . .'

'There'll be almost no traffic on Christmas Eve. You will have a whole fleet of them available. There'll be a quarter of a million dollars on tap for you. Surely you have some co-operative driver who is amenable to a large gift?'

The doctor gave it passionate thought. 'Yes,' he nodded. 'I have.'

There was a different glaze to his eyes; a considerable glow. He muttered, 'The money . . .'

'It's guaranteed for you by Papa Miche.'

'I would rather you guaranteed it.'

'No.' Sam shook his head.

'Why not?' It was piling shock upon shock for Dr Benes.

'I'm not in it,' Sam said. 'Auguste, you know me from Cannes. I'll be a poor man all my life. I have no talent for roguery. I'd just be useless baggage to the rest.'

If one could only believe it. Auguste Benes sighed. 'Very well,' he said. A patch of sweat defaced his silk shirt. 'I will ring Stefan in the morning to tell him what is to be done.' There was just one other thing. It had been troubling him all the time. He stared at Joey. 'What is the girl doing in it?'

'Every plan has to have a hook,' Sam said. 'This girl is the hook.' He didn't explain how. Auguste Benes no longer wanted to know. He already knew enough. He muttered to Stefan, 'In the morning. Early,' and he went, feet dragging a little, bowed by a banker's anxiety: the plague of money in bulk that only an auditor could count.

Vic Diamond said to Sam, 'Can he be trusted?'

'Can you?'

Vic Diamond flushed offendedly. He glared.

'He can be trusted,' Sam said. 'Auguste Benes is the greediest man between Calais and Cannes. He's had a glimpse of the Promised Land. He won't sleep, he won't rest, he'll sweat away his life until he wades ankle deep in thousand-dollar bills.'

'Joey.' Vic Diamond touched her arm.

'Yes?' She came out of a dream.

'Let's get out of this joint. Let's go some place they pour something that's fit to drink.'

'*Chéri*, you go.' Her eyes drooped. 'I am so tired. I seem to have been bustling about all day. I have my first show in two hours. I think I would like to lie down.'

'Okay, honey. Rest.' He pressed her hand affectionately. Sam wouldn't have thought him capable of such tenderness. 'I'll look in tonight.' He got up, giving Sam an acid look; his eyes ranged despisingly from Stefan's knuckles to Willie Tobias, who reddened because he couldn't control the twitch. He went into the street. They heard him whistle. A taxi rattled up. It drove off and he was gone.

'Sam, you are a blessing to us,' Papa Miche said in a choked voice. 'We do not know how to thank you . . .'

'Don't try. Just forget me.' The boy scout's done his good deed for the day; it's going to be the very last. He went out without looking at them. As he moved along the street he heard the quick patter of heels behind him and Joey caught up. 'I thought you were going to rest,' he said.

She laughed. 'I feel suddenly revived. Where are you going?'

'I don't know why I should have to tell you.'

'May I walk with you?'

'It's a free country. It's a free street.' Repellent as it was. He gave her a slanted look. 'What in hell *are* you after?'

'You, Sam.'

'I'm not God's gift to women.'

'You are to me. Do you have to walk so fast? It's impolite to a lady.'

Lady. He grinned dryly; how this *gamine*'s cracking herself up. 'I need a drink,' he said, 'and I can't afford to pay for two.'

'I have enough for four.' She drew him into one of the gaudier bars in Place Blanche. Because of the bleak snowy weather it sheltered more whores than usual. They ranged the tables like characters from a Toulouse-Lautrec print. The place smelled of stale scent and dubious drinks. They sat. He faced her. 'What will you have? Another cherry?'

'Oh, that was just for fun. No, I'll have a *limonade gazeuse*.'

'That I can afford.' He beckoned to a waiter and ordered a Scotch for himself. 'I'm leaving for Nice tomorrow.'

She frowned. 'Must you?'

'I need eating cash.' She stirred and he said, 'Don't offer me your purse. I'd hate to think where the money came from.'

'Sam, there's no need to be so unkind.'

He stared keenly into her face. Her cheeks were flushed. Her eyes elated. He said to her softly, 'Joey, don't try playing Delilah to my Samson. My hair isn't long enough. If I had to I'd pick up the jawbone of the nearest ass and smack you down.'

'You are not that kind of man. We have an affinity for each other, *petit*.'

'What we have for each other is trouble. And I've had enough to fill two men's lives.' He finished his Scotch. He felt suddenly restless. The way she was looking at him. His loins were stiffening up. He said irritably, 'Drink up that damned gassy lemonade. I want to get away.'

'Where are you going?'

'Home.' Silly word for it; a bed, four walls and the companionable bedlam of a garage beneath.

'I wondered where you lived. Sam, don't run. I've been making inquiries about you.'

'I could have saved you the trouble. My credit rating's nil.'

'I know. It's terrible.' She was quite put out. Her puzzlement was real. 'You don't have any money. You never will have. What you said to that Hungarian doctor is true: you'll be a poor man all your life.'

He looked round. A fracas had begun between the *patron* and one of the 'floating ladies' who had occupied a table too long. She was painted up like a Follies girl; a hawkish fifty-five. Maybe Joey would look like that one day.

'Sam, are you listening?'

'No.'

'That's another terrible habit you have. You never listen to what you don't want to hear. This wonderful plan you thought up. It's clever; it's going to succeed, I feel it in my bones. And all for your worn-out battered friends.' What had happened to the womanly compassion she'd felt for them? 'Such a colossal amount of money.' Ah, that was different. Money killed compassion. 'They'll never be able to enjoy it,' she said. Her dark eyes shone with bewilderment. 'I keep asking myself: why, why, why?'

The screeching that was going on behind. The *patron* had a hammer-lock on the 'floating lady's' arm and was wheeling her like a bouncer to the door. The French had a no-nonsense approach to women. It was probably the right way.

'Vic can't understand it,' she said. She couldn't, either. She squeezed Sam's hands as if trying to infuse some sense into him. 'What's in it for *you*?'

'Does there have to be something?'

'Well, of course.'

'Joey, when you're old and toothless' – she grimaced at the mere thought – 'you still won't be able to understand.' He said with mock sternness, 'Don't you know what the Good Book says? The meek have to inherit the earth.'

'Never!' She shook her head.

No hope for the meek?

'They never have, and never will,' she cried. 'I am not meek!' He knew that. 'You know where I began.' Ah, we're going to have the gutter-saga again. 'If I were meek do you know what I would be

66

doing now? Picking up old gentlemen at the corner of Place Blanche.'

And she'd lifted herself heroically out of that unfortunate class. Doing a nude belly-dance at the Kasbah.

'Oh, come on,' he said breezily. 'I have to go.'

'Just one thing.' She drew him back secretively. She didn't have to lower her voice; the howl of the tart trying to get back into the bar was horrific. She murmured, 'Sam, don't be antagonistic to Vic Diamond. He isn't a bad man.'

'You mean he doesn't kick animals? He writes home to his old mama twice a week?'

'He is very rough, but he will play fair with you. He can be trusted.'

'And you?'

'I would be shocked if you didn't trust me.'

'But I don't have to trust anybody, do I? I'm finished with the thing. Goodbye, Joey,' and he pushed past the *poule* in the doorway who was still abusing the boss. What Women's Lib have done to the sweet sex, he thought; bad language, loose breasts and the abrasive charm of a dockside hustler. He went briskly across Place Blanche, feeling the lightest touch on his arm.

He wasn't going to shake her off. 'I would like to see where you live,' Joey said.

He hazarded a guess. 'You've already looked it over.'

'Just once. Sam, it is not very genteel. You should be living better than that.'

The garage man's eyes narrowed as they approached. Now this is some chicken, he thought enviously, studying Joey with anatomical thoroughness; some men have too much luck. He watched them go upstairs with a little surge of vicarious sex.

'I am sure it is nicer inside,' Joey said. They entered the apartment. She looked about with a sigh. But there was a bed; it's all that interests her, Sam thought.

She watched him amusedly. 'You are a grown-up boy. You are not going to be embarrassed, are you?'

She undressed so swiftly that he hardly had time to take off his coat. 'Let me help you,' she said, kneeling with a kind of Oriental obeisance to take off his shoes. She stripped him as clean as a wand, dealing efficiently with every button and zip. Suddenly she fell on him. He'd never known such ferocity; he'd expected to direct the operation, but she was using him, manipulating him, sweeping him urgently into the maelstrom. She hardly gave him a moment's chance

67

to regain masculine control. He didn't wholly enjoy it. It was an experience he wouldn't forget. When it was all over she lay back, recovering her breath. Her eyes twinkled. 'You gave me much pleasure, Sam,' she said.

IV

THE four exalted players were now converging on Paris. Three of them, Theo Parnassus, Gregor Kassem and Caesar Vinci, would arrive tomorrow: on Christmas Eve that is. They would be coming from different parts of the globe, using their highly individual forms of transport like the Caliphs of the Arabian Nights who were wafted from city to city on magic carpets. A three-engine executive jet, reserved for one man, *is* a kind of magic carpet. They had to snatch their leisure hours when they could. They were very complex and over-extended people; in fact they had long ceased to be people, for they had become too vast to be wholly human. Their lives were more and more programmed for them by busy armies of secretariats, never an hour wasted; a daily calendar of engagements could actually be disjointed if they lingered in the toilet too long. It is not a way to live. Did Theo Parnassus sometimes look back nostalgically on the exuberance of the Turkish bazaar in which he was born? Did Gregor Kassem occasionally sigh for the freedom of the Bedouin tent of his boyhood? And Caesar Vinci, the great auto industrialist, now and again yearn for the lusty comradeship of his racing car days?

No wonder they had to burst out of the suffocation of their huge commitments; the Christmas Eve poker-rampage was the mental safety-valve blowing off. Billionaires can go mad, too.

There is one in Las Vegas who lets nobody near who is not sterilized, who sees human beings only over closed-circuit television. Ordinary people like us should be content with what we have. A hundred thousand a year is enough for anybody. Dollars I mean.

The fourth player, Lew Cask, was already over Paris, circling Orly International Airport in the PanAm arrival from New York. Vic Diamond was waiting edgily in the arrival lounge for the touchdown; he had a lush Renault limousine ready for his *padrone*. Coarse though he was and barely literate – he had to have the Wall Street Journal read out to him – Lew Cask liked and expected the good things of life. He could afford the best. His *régime*, meaning his particular clan of the West Coast *Cosa Nostra*, was a copious source of wealth. Almost all of it untaxed. How does one tax a narcotics ring? Is there a federal office that can assess the proceeds of business protection rackets, the revenues of organized call-girls? Mafia money puts its lofty chieftains in the Theo Parnassus class. (Not socially, of course.) Lew Cask was accompanied by the *consigliori* who was his counsellor and financial adviser, with an aide in the seat behind. He went nowhere without carefully despatching someone ahead and making sure that there was a gun to watch his back. He had many enemies. He was in a fratricidal business that breeds enemies like dragon's teeth. Holy Writ tells us that they who live by the sword shall perish by the sword. Lew Cask lived by the nickel-plated bullet and he intended to avoid the one that was destined for him as long as he could.

He and his two companions would have liked to travel incognito, if one would use that semi-regal word in association with such men. But he had a nightmarish fear of being refused re-admittance to the United States if he were found with a false passport in his possession; his citizenship papers weren't altogether spotless. They should have been for the money they cost. He had been barred by immigration authorities in Brazil and Canada, and it would be insufferable if he were turned back from Paris; it would humiliate him in the eyes of his eminent fellow-players who had already humiliated him enough. He hadn't bothered to tell them that he would be arriving a day in front of them. He would have thought it the height of insanity to let anybody know where he was going and when he would arrive. Somebody could be waiting for him with one of those nickel-plated bullets. He had sent Vic Diamond ahead to look the Alcazar over, to ensure that there was nothing that could put his personal safety at risk. The poker-game would last at least a day and a half, probably running right through Christmas night with the occasional half-hour off for a nap. It would be a very tense and exciting game. Awaiting him in a Paris bank, provided by one of his numbered Swiss accounts, was a leather case containing a million dollars in thousand-dollar bills.

It was the entire week's revenue of the narcotics business. His *consigliori*, a cold dry Sicilian, thought the extravagance quite mad. He was too discreet to suggest it to his *padrone,* whose temper was vile.

Now let us look at the man. The animal. Call him what you will. There are not many photographs of him about; he avoided the press-camera like leprosy. The fewer who knew his face, the fewer there would be to identify him. He liked anonymity. Giulio

Tartozzi, a Don of one of the Chicago families, had let himself be proudly photographed at his daughter's wedding and had been shot to death before the second edition of the newspaper was on the street. Conceit was good for the funeral-parlour business; Lew Cask preferred them not to make business out of his body.

He would have needed an oddly shaped coffin. He wasn't very tall, barely five feet high, with a bull neck and a massively thick body. Seen in silhouette he looked like a stubby cylinder with a bulge in the middle; this being his growing belly. He was very fond of his food. He had given Vic Diamond explicit instructions as to what he expected to see on the buffet-table at the Alcazar when he arrived. Particularly *gelati*; he couldn't get enough ice-cream to slake his adolescent passion for it. He had had it since he left Taormina forty years ago. His face was dark, darker than most Sicilians, much darker than Vic Diamond's. He had a wide froggy grin that gave him a look of bland benevolence, until you saw that no trace of humour ever reached his eyes. They were very large and fixed, owl's eyes, and burned like hot coals when he went into one of his spectacular rages. He couldn't restrain himself during these spasms; he had killed six men during them, some of them for nothing, and his *consigliori* had warned him incessantly that the cops would surely pin something on him if they didn't cease.

He was in one of these stupefying rages now. He'd hardly been able to speak coherently since they'd left New York. '*Uno scandalo.*' He choked on the expression. 'That goddamned spick!' He was referring to Gregor Kassem, whose Levantine complexion was hardly darker than his own. He raved, 'I swear I will cut him up. I will have him . . .' and his *consigliori* pressed his hand: even in the VIP seats of a jumbo jet there were things that shouldn't be said.

The bile burned Lew Cask's throat. He had to relieve his venom in true Sicilian fashion; he spat disgustedly into the carpet. The hostess at the end of the compartment winced.

'*Infamita*,' he mumbled. The fire in his eyes leapt. He had suffered the infamy where it most hurt. What Lew Cask craved for was respectability. He had made enough money, he boasted, to buy out the Pope; what he now wanted was papal recognition. He hadn't a chance of being accepted by upper-crust society; his name stank in their nostrils. But he could speak the language of the ultra-rich and that was a kind of high-class society, too. He had heard that Gregor Kassem was pressing for a refinery in Seattle; the anti-pollution people, who were the curse of business, were raising hell. Lew Cask knew a couple of congressmen who could be bent. He had graciously offered his services to Gregor Kassem and got the refinery through. He now arrived for payment. When you sup with the devil you need to do so with a long spoon. There were strange rumours of the billionaires' Christmas Eve rendezvous: some kind of big, big poker. Beyond the reach of ordinary men. There was nothing ordinary about Lew Cask and he was good at poker. He would like, he told Gregor Kassem humbly, to play with them as the fourth in the club.

To rub shoulders with the great Parnassus and the industrialist Caesar Vinci . . . that would be making the top of the social ladder in one acrobatic bound!

Gregor Kassem suffered a minor thrombosis. For ten evasive minutes he refused to admit that there was such a game. But he'd had the service; he now had to pay. He pleaded with his friends Theo Parnassus and Caesar Vinci to let the man in. They grumbled ferociously. They really knew nothing about him; he just sounded vaguely repulsive. They should have listened to their instincts before they agreed. They were fond of Gregor and gave in. It took a month for the first shocking doubts to appear. Caesar Vinci, the Italian, made a few inquiries. The word Mafia began to be heard. It was chilling. Parnassus, a patron of the arts and a highly civilized man, blew up. Fond as he was of Gregor, Caesar Vinci upbraided him savagely. It was probably too late; Gregor Kassem was pledged.

He made a last painful effort to dissuade Lew Cask. He'd met him that very morning in his Waldorf-Astoria suite. 'My friend,' he'd murmured with Levantine delicacy, 'there are certain mental antipathies. Nothing personal, I assure you. We do not, perhaps, talk the same language . . .' and Lew Cask's eyes went red and for ten strangulated minutes he used language that turned Gregor Kassem's dusky complexion a dirty grey. For a moment of horror he wondered if he was about to see the animal's gun. He shrank. 'I shall not be despised,' Lew Cask said brutally, and spat at Gregor Kassem's feet. Yes, he did, in a Waldorf-Astoria celestial suite. He went out, slamming the door so violently that the windows shook.

Ten hours had elapsed since then. He still simmered like a rumbling volcano running out of gas. 'They look down their noses at me. I am not good enough for them,' he said. They were now circling Paris, a city he'd never visited and whose sophisticated pleasures he'd hoped to enjoy. They'd soured it for him. 'All right. So let them watch out.' He bared his big teeth. '*Guarda al cane!*'

Meaning: beware of the dog.

They touched down. There was a light flurry of snow. They passed through immigration without fuss; the festive rush was in full flood and nobody had much time for anybody. Vic Diamond was waiting for them in the lounge. His stomach turned over at the sight of his boss's face. He knew it too well. Something has happened, he thought. I hope to God it doesn't concern me. He came forward with a forced beam.

'You had a good flight, *padrone*?'

Lew Cask said tersely, 'It flew.' He had no time for garrulity. He stared heavily into Vic Diamond's face. 'Everything is all right? You have checked?'

'Everything is perfect,' Vic Diamond said. 'You are as safe here as you are at home,' and for the first time Lew Cask laughed. At home he needed an electrified fence, barred windows and three night-watchmen with dogs.

He turned to his *consigliori* who was about to return with the guard to the transit lounge: they were travelling on to London to negotiate a delicate deal over some gambling clubs. Lew Cask said to the guard, 'Watch out for him. See that he comes back in one piece,' glancing at the man stonily as if he didn't care if he came back in a casket in several pieces. He patted his *consigliori*'s back. 'Go with God.' He lighted a thick cigar and said to Vic Diamond, 'I am famished. Take me some place where there is good food.'

In the ride from Orly in the lush Renault Vic Diamond's mind began to churn. Lew Cask was aware of a tension; the odour of sweat. Something is going to be said. When I hear what it is I will decide what *I* have to say.

They had dinner at La Tour d'Argent. Have you ever eaten there? It is probably beyond your pocket. Come with me, just the same. You go up to the sixth floor in a tiny elevator that can give you momentary claustrophobia, but you step straight into the elegance of old Versailles; a penthouse filled with Aubusson tapestries, oil paintings and Gobelin-covered chairs. Only a peasant could fail to be moved by such distinction, but Lew Cask, that Sicilian *paisan*, wrinkled his nose. The huge windows looked down on the Christmas-snowy panorama of Paris as Santa Claus with his reindeer would see it, the cool shine of the Seine, the majestic contours of Notre-Dame, the glistening fairy-like cupolas of Sacré-Coeur. Lew Cask had to admit a reluctant thrill. They ate *quenelles de brochet*, which is a fish mousse cooked with button mushrooms. Already I can sense your saliva beginning to run. They had one of the great *entrecôtes* recommended by the *chef de cuisine*. It was like supping with the gods. The gods wouldn't have tucked their napkins under the chin, as Lew Cask did. He would have preferred to drink a plain Chianti, which he called *vino di compagna*, the wine of the country, but Vic Diamond whispered that it would offend the establishment. With the help of the *maître* who looked after the cellar they chose a fabulous Chateau d'Yquem. Don't ask what it cost.

When he had finished Lew Cask belched pleasurably and said, 'I've drunk better tipple, but the food went down well. It wasn't bad.' The *chef de cuisine* of one of the blue-chip restaurants of Paris would have flinched. Lew Cask lighted a thick Havana, thinking: something has happened here. Vic is not himself. He waited patiently for his bodyguard to give out.

In the half-hour between the fish and the steak Vic Diamond knew that everything had changed. His shirt clung to his body; he had to wipe the beads of sweat off his lip that he hoped the *padrone* hadn't seen. He had never realized how terrified of his boss he was. Until Lew Cask had emerged from immigration it had been his intention to proceed with the plan; that Casanova bastard was smart. It could work. Vic Diamond had run the whole gamut of women from Seattle waterfront hustlers to the expensive call-girls of Manhattan, but he'd never known anything quite like Joey, who began the sex operation with the soft blue flame of a spirit lamp and ended up with a paroxysm that scorched him like a blast of a furnace. He was consumed with lust for her; also with greed for the million dollars that would be his share. The pair of them could vanish for ever to some Caribbean playground. And he had only to look at Lew Cask's frozen froggy visage and his blood curdled.

Mamma mia, he makes me wet my pants.

'*Padrone*,' he muttered, 'I did not wish to disturb your appetite until you were finished. May I speak?'

'You have a mouth.'

Better to be forthright. Speak plain and honest. 'There is to be an attempt on the money,' Vic Diamond said.

I *knew* there was something, Lew Cask thought. His first anxiety was for himself. 'On me, too?'

'No, no, *padrone*. Not on you. Just the money. What I have to tell you is beyond comprehension . . .'

'I will have a little more coffee.'

'Yes, yes. A brandy?'

'We will finish the wine,' Lew Cask said. 'Go on. Whose money? Just mine?'

'The lot. The whole four million. Even now I cannot believe it. You should see the people involved . . .'

'One of the other *regimes*?'

'*Padrone*, these are not *mafiosi*. They are idiots. Crummy wrecks! Chief, I swear to you, they are pitiful. You have to laugh.' Vic Diamond struggled with some passion to make the point. 'They would rather die than lift a dollar from a beggar's can, and suddenly they want to walk off with four million because they object to the world.' He exaggerated a little here; what Papa Miche and Willie Tobias and Stefan objected to was the thin rich crust that lay on the pie of the world. 'They are not even worth a bullet. What they need is a big boot that will squash them like flies.'

'Vic, you are upset.'

'Angry.'

'But you are sweating?'

Vic Diamond said the one fortunate thing that saved his life. He was lucky. He said simply, 'You frighten me, *padrone*. You always have,' and Lew Cask nodded. It contented him. He liked the men of his *regime* to live in the aura of his terror, for scared men never started palace revolutions. It was the brash headstrong ones who had to be watched.

He said kindly, 'Drink a little wine, Vic. It isn't too bad. Tell me then. How did you come to hear of these crummy wrecks?'

Vic Diamond said with a disarming shrug, 'You know? I like girls.' Again Lew Cask nodded. He didn't mind; he liked girls, too. 'I met some kid in a night-club here, does some sort of Woggy belly-dance, and she spills the whole thing. These three dummies work there. See them for yourself! But it isn't that simple.' It never is, Lew Cask thought. That is why I am the supreme Don of a fat bunch of *mafiosi*; I take nothing for granted. It is a world full of traps. 'There is a man with a smart brain who has told them how to do it. And, *padrone* . . .'

'Yes, Vic?'

'It is startling. With luck it *could* be done.'

Lew Cask said calmly, 'Then we must take their luck away from them. Incidentally, you have not told me *how* it is to be done.'

Vic Diamond glanced about. The wine-waiter, like a rural mayor with his medieval chain of office, watched them covertly; there was something about Lew Cask, a hunched obdurate peasant, napkin under chin, that was totally incongruous in La Tour d'Argent. It brought back wartime memories of Gestapo generals supping at the Elysée Palace. But he was too far off to hear. 'I know it all,' Vic Diamond said. 'Every move. Joey has told me . . .'

'Who is he?'

'No, no. Joey is my girl.' And Vic Diamond, kneading the table-cloth into pleats, watching Lew Cask's face for the first ominous sign of incredulity, told him everything. Every detail. It was only when he came to Dr Auguste Benes and the capsule that Lew Cask jerked. The merest spasm. But his eyes went hot.

'For whom is this capsule?'

'Parnassus. Who else?'

And something loosened in Lew Cask's face. The hard wintry jowls seemed to melt in the warmth of some unexpected Springtime. He uttered a husky sound that could have been a chuckle. 'Finish what you have to tell me.'

Vic Diamond was suddenly bewildered. On edge. '*Padrone*, did I say something funny?'

'No. I just thought of something funny. Go on, Vic, *amico*. I am all ears.'

Vic Diamond finished with a breathless feeling. Things were happening he didn't clearly understand. He saw the shine in Lew Cask's eyes; he had seen it in the past, when it had usually been followed by something devastating. But there was none of the rage that normally convulsed the demon; it was a coarse amusement. His throat quivered. He was *laughing. Why*?

'Vic, permit your boss a private joke. I will soon share it with you.' His eyes now sharpened. 'This capsule. It really works?'

'It worked before. They took a man out of Hungary in a coffin . . .'

'Do not talk to me of coffins.' Lew Cask was superstitious. He crossed himself. 'So how is our good friend Parnassus to receive it?'

'He has made it simple for them. You know what he drinks?'

'I am not on intimate terms with him. What *does* he drink?'

'Mastika.' Lew Cask had never heard of it. His face remained blank. 'Some kind of Turkish brandy. Greek maybe. Christ only knows.' Vic Diamond shrugged. 'Like anisette, you dose it with water and it goes down like milk.'

Lew Cask said benevolently, 'He is well known for the milk of human niceness. Must be this mastika that does it,' and Vic Diamond remained ill at ease.

Strange; he preferred his chief's fury to this suppressed laughter. '*Padrone*,' he muttered, 'not to worry. I will have these dummies roughed up . . .'

'Why would you do that?'

Vic Diamond peered at him. 'To scare them off.' Did he want them killed?

'I do not wish them to be scared. It is a beautiful plan. Too good to be wasted. Let them proceed with it. Vic,' Lew Cask said, patting his hand, 'you are good with a gun, your loyalty pleases me, but thinking is not your brightest asset. I admire a good brain. This man who conceived it . . .'

'Casanova.'

'A lover-boy? Yes? He *must* be smart. If he has the right instincts I can use him.' Lew Cask suddenly blazed. It was now that the subterranean rage appeared. It bubbled up like lava. Vic Diamond gave a ghastly glance about; nobody made scenes at La Tour d'Argent. It would be like raising hell at the Vatican. The *padrone* said violently, 'These big rich *baroni*, these gentlemen of quality, they think they are the salt of the earth. It seems that I am not fit to associate with them.' Vic Diamond wondered painfully: what in God's name had happened in New York? 'I have been humiliated.' These were the mad moods that so convulsed Lew Cask; when he needed his *consigliori* to restrain him. His voice rose, 'They will learn to have more regard for me,' and a grey gentleman at an adjacent table, a *type diplomatique*, slipped a monocle into his eye and looked round with a whisper of reproach. Lew Cask glared back. *Dio Mio*, Vic Diamond gasped; his chief was capable of thrusting the monocle down that distinguished throat.

'Padrone . . .'

'Nobody humiliates Luigi Cascavagni,' which was the birth-name he'd brought from Taormina before Americanizing it to Lew Cask. 'It is going to cost them a million dollars each.' Vic Diamond stared at him. Suddenly he understood. His mouth opened soundlessly. Everything had got out of hand. 'Let these dummies of yours make their play. I think they will get away with it. But only as far as the street.' Lew Cask began to laugh. The pleasure of surreptitiously relieving his fellow-players of their stakes was almost more than he could bear. Pity that he would never be able to share the joke with anybody. He would have to laugh over it himself.

The time for jokes was past. He became coldly matter-of-fact. 'Let the money leave the building. But do not let it get out of sight. Not for an instant. Stay with it, if you wish to stay with your life. I will ring the *consigliori* to send Alfiero across to help you.' Alfiero was the guard who had accompanied the counsellor to London. 'Wherever the money lands out, Alfiero will go in and recover it. If he has to kill these people, he will kill them. He has the stomach for it.' Lew Cask studied Vic Diamond emptily. 'This is no reflection on you. Your face is known.'

'I understand, *padrone*.'

77

'You will not be offended if I now check on a few things for myself. These crummy wrecks of yours. Where can they be seen?'

'At the Kasbah.'

Lew Cask began to look suffocated again. 'What in Christ's holy name is the . . .'

'The nightclub where they work.'

'I think you are trying to make me mad. When?'

'Now.'

'Then why are we sitting in this antique flophouse? Pay the bill. The waiter has been staring poison into my back. Do not leave him a tip.'

'No, *padrone*.'

'You worry me, Vic. You are still sweating.'

Vic Diamond knew that he had to say something bold, outrageous even, to mask his guilt. 'God will forgive me for saying it, *padrone*, but when you are dead I will stop sweating. Not before.'

Lew Cask shrugged. It was an offensive thing to hear, but as good an answer as he could expect. They went out into the street. A *flic* was hovering militantly over their car. Before he could open his mouth to speak with the sardonic brutality of his kind Lew Cask shoved a flimsy note impatiently into his hand. He had no notion of exchange rates; the *flic* gave it a startled look and walked swiftly off. They got into the car. Vic Diamond said, 'You know what you gave him, chief? Five hundred francs.'

'It's just coloured toilet paper.'

'A hundred dollars.'

'*Bastardo*.' Lew Cask gritted his teeth. They drove off.

They drove slowly down Rue des Six Anges. Lew Cask peered through the window at the decrepit frontages, the pallid glitter of the strip-joints, measuring the worth and capability of the girls at the street corners if they could be organized. 'It is worse than Taormina,' he said. The car stopped at the kerb opposite the Kasbah. Lew Cask shook his head. 'This is the place?'

'This is it.'

A grim chuckle. 'It isn't exactly the Stork Club, is it? Take me in. You know how.'

Vic Diamond went ahead. He stopped in the dark lobby by the *vestiaire*. The young negro from Ghana recognized him. 'M'sieu?' He held out his hand for his coat. Vic Diamond slipped a hundred franc note into the receptive hand. 'We don't have more than a few minutes. My friend would like to take a look around.' He beckoned to Lew Cask behind him. Both pushed through the curtains into the stuffy *vestiaire*. There was a small window through which one could stare across the interior of the club. Vic Diamond motioned to the young negro to leave them; he slipped off. The Moroccan band blared out. Lew Cask came from a Mediterranean province facing the African coast and the familiar beat and wail of the music made him prick up his ears.

The pink and white floods swung wildly across the floor. Vic Diamond thought: we couldn't have come at a better time. It was Joey on the floor; down to the fifth veil, navel a-shimmer, and Lew Cask watched her steadily, the big eyes blank. Last but one veil departing; still no sound, no interest from the *padrone*, and when the last was gone and there was a ripple of applause from a thin audience, he had scarcely moved. 'That one . . . ?'

'That's Joey.'

'Young.'

'Yes.'

'Some belly. Now the others.'

'There,' Vic Diamond whispered, 'at the end of the bar.' A flash of light as the pink floods swung about; they stared at the obdurate old face, the thick academic mane of silver hair. 'His name's Papa Miche.' Willie Tobias leaned on the bar at his side.

'Looks a little crazy, yes?'

'Yes. The one with him's another.'

'Mother of God.' Lew Cask caught a glimpse of the sad facial twitch.

'Now follow my finger.' Vic Diamond pointed. 'There on the far side of the band. Look, Joey's just joined him.' She sat next to Stefan in her thin robe. 'That's the third.'

Lew Cask studied him for a long time. He said wonderingly, 'He is some kind of child. He keeps sucking his knuckles.'

'They got smashed. Now you've seen them.'

Lew Cask sighed with disgust. 'How can people be so pitiful?'

Vic Diamond could have said: it's a rough world that doesn't pity the weak. But he held his tongue. 'You've seen enough?'

'Too much. Come.'

They emerged, Lew Cask fumbling with his big hat behind the curtains, so that he just escaped brushing by Sam Casanova who now stood darkly silhouetted in the club entrance against the greasy shifting lights. Both turned their heads, glancing at each other in the dim lobby without recognition. But Vic Diamond was already half way across the street and Lew Cask followed him towards the car.

79

Sam hesitated. He was sure he had seen the *vestiaire* curtains swing. He moved back to the street doorway, keeping just out of sight, watching Vic Diamond usher his companion ceremoniously into the car. A short bull-like body, round owlish face. They sat murmuring for a moment before driving off.

The young negro was back in the *vestiaire*. Sam said to him pleasantly, 'How much?'

'M'sieu Sam?'

'What did they slip you to let them past?' He moved into the *vestiaire* himself, staring through the slitted window. His eyes ranged from Papa and Willie Tobias at the bar to Stefan by the band; the view even included Joey. All four seen in one swift photographic look. Worth how much? 'Fifty?'

The negro blinked. Sam gripped his thin wrist. The bones were as slender as a bird's. The lad grinned. 'Hundred francs.'

'Generous. Now you'll be out tom-catting tonight. Did they go into the club?'

'No, no.'

'What did they do?'

'Just looked through the window.'

'Put the money in the bank. Think of your old age. Don't let the wild women take it away from you.' Sam went back into the street and walked absently towards Clichy. He was in a faintly tremulous condition; he still hadn't recovered from the explosion of Joey. He shivered. In his overcharged mind he could feel the tender satiny body, the pulsating passion of an unbelievably skilled operator. Sybilla would have been blind with envy; she'd damn nearly blown him out of the bed. An alarm buzzed at the back of his brain. Who was the man Vic Diamond had brought into the *vestiaire*?

He entered Angus's American Bar, searching the evening mob for a particular face. He found it. He went across. 'Alan.'

'Hi, Sam.'

'Give me two minutes of your valuable time.'

'Cost you a brandy.'

Life gets dearer every hour. Sam nodded. He was talking to a very able Los Angeles correspondent. 'You ever heard of Lew Cask?'

Pause. Sam felt himself being studied. 'You just dipped your feet into some very muddy water, boy.'

'I never met him in my life.' Though I may have seen him half an hour ago. 'I'm worried over three of my clients who may get involved with him. Did you ever set eyes on him?'

'Once. He came up before a Grand Jury.'

'Would he be about this high?' Up to Sam's shoulder. 'Thick body. Moon face, big eyes, mouth stretching from here to here. Wears an old-fashioned hat with one of those Italian wide brims.'

'Rembrandt couldn't have painted a better picture of him.'

'Thanks.' So the alarm knew what it was buzzing about. 'No, Alan, I won't drink with you. I have to watch my figure.' I'm watching my dwindling bank-balance, too. 'Skohl.'

He took a *Métro* back to Sacré-Coeur. He looked in at Sybilla's apartment. She was home. 'Sam,' she said with sorrowful concern, 'how pale you are.'

'It's my anaemia.' An odd medical diagnosis of the scourge of Joey. 'Sybilla, could you give me a meal?'

'Is it that bad?'

'I tried Paul Getty for ten thousand dollars, but he didn't want to know.'

'Put your feet up. Rest your senile bones. I have a nice *pot-au-feu* on the stove. You need some good rich meat to set you up.'

They relaxed after dinner, watching television, stretched marital-fashion on the couch. Very nice. He could have closed his eyes. But she saw him glancing furtively at his watch. 'Sam,' she began to storm, 'not *them* again.'

'I have to be back at the Kasbah before midnight. They need a little help.'

'It is you who needs help. You are a fool. Your life is in pieces, you should be on your knees picking them up and trying to put them together again. And all you can think of is the boys!' Her voice rose. 'You owe them nothing. You deserve better.' Everybody kept telling him that. 'You carry them like a cross on your back.'

'Must be my sins catching up with me.'

'*You*,' she withered him. 'You never committed a sin in your life. You will come back to sleep?'

'If I can.' And he knew he couldn't. 'Tomorrow night for certain. Don't sit up.'

She was actually crying for him. He kissed her affectionately; there were still some good, if not over-moral, women about. He walked back to the Kasbah, arriving outside just as Papa Miche and Willie Tobias were preparing to leave. He stared at them. Shabby, down at heel, like featherless birds crusted with snow. It had started to fall. He said softly, 'Off to duty?'

'Yes.'

'I'll walk with you to the Alcazar. Get Stefan. I want him to walk with us, too.'

Papa Miche watched him. I'll get to look like that, Sam thought; all worn bone and eroded flesh. 'Has something bad happened, Sam?'

'Yes.' Sam nodded. When isn't something bad happening? Armageddon is coming.

Stefan joined them and they walked down Rue des Six Anges. Sam glanced at them sidelong; three discredited bums, engaged in dubious felony, heads bent against a chill blustering wind. Is that how God sees them? Better get it out. He said, 'Your coloured boy let two men into the *vestiaire*. They wanted to look you over. One of them was Vic Diamond. I think the other was his diabolical majesty, Lew Cask.'

Papa Miche stopped in the gutter with a shocked gasp. 'You cannot know that!'

'I saw him. I checked up on him. It was Lew Cask for sure.'

'That Vic Diamond,' Stefan cried strickenly. 'He has betrayed us.' He made a sound like a creaking door.

Sam heard himself say exasperatedly, 'What did you expect? He's a zombie. A wooden thug. He answers his boss's whistle like a trained dog.' Hideous thing to say. 'I think he meant to run out on his *padrone*, but the minute he showed up his guts fell out.' The language wasn't improving. 'Lew Cask's that kind of man.'

'You expected him to betray us?'

Another impatient shrug. 'I don't know what I expected.' If you want prophecy go to Isaiah. Malachi. Or Job. Sam said, 'I don't like him. But I thought Joey had her hooks well into him. Maybe she still has.'

'Yes, Sam.' Papa Miche nodded patiently. 'Go on.'

'There's nowhere to go.' They'd stopped outside one of the strip-joints; the *commissaire* appeared expectantly. Sam waved him away. 'Lew Cask isn't a man to trust anybody. He probably marched friend Vic straight off to the Kasbah to get a look at you himself.'

'So that . . . ?'

'Papa, for Christ's sake. You're an old Indian fighter. You didn't waste all your time in Spain.' The screech of recorded jazz from the strip-joint was making him raise his voice. He pulled them a little further along the street, but every other doorway was grind-and-drag. 'He'll be at the Alcazar later tonight to check if you're there. If you are, he'll begin to believe it's the truth.'

'Shall we be there?'

'You make your own minds up. I wouldn't be that mad.'

'But we are.' Papa chuckled gruffly. 'Quite mad. Sam, shall I tell you something?'

Oh, God. 'No, don't.'

'This Lew Cask is a very bad man. But very ingenious. He won't warn his colleagues to call off the game.'

Sam stared at him. Strange thing; the very same notion had been scratching at his brain. Perhaps it was because small crooked minds thought alike. He licked his lips. It lit up a whole different scene! Put yourself in Lew Cask's shoes. There wasn't much love lost between him and his fellow-billionaires; he'd been brutally snubbed. So Vic Diamond said. Only a Sicilian could savour the demonic pleasure of lifting the loot from these futile dummies (forgive me, Papa) once they'd pushed the thing through. A million dollars a head from Messieurs Parnassus, Vinci and Kassem for the snub. Something the *padrone* could split his sides over privately for life. Mother of Heaven, it's getting to be very dangerous. Don't let me give it another thought.

They trudged along the Champs—Elysées, growing whiter, up to wards the snowy mass of the Arc de Triomphe that promised only desolation for the mad. Sam could hear Papa Miche's heavy breathing, the faintest mutter from Willie Tobias who was talking to himself. Round to the Alcazar that glowed like a haven in a storm. They stopped outside the marble steps.

Papa Miche gave Sam a slanted look. His eyes were very bright. 'You think they'll come?'

'I hope they don't.'

'I think they will. Sam, this is the end of the road for you. Please go home.'

'Papa, there's still time. Don't go inside. Just walk away.'

'No.'

'Willie?'

He shook his head. Whom the gods wished to destroy . . . Sam stared at Stefan.

'No, Sam. Goodbye.'

'They'll eat you. Chew you up and spit you out.' He walked away, head down, very angry; now *he* was talking to himself. He stopped at the distant corner, then walked very slowly back. They'd gone inside. God help them. He looked at his watch; no need to, he could hear the distant boom of midnight from a clock. He backed out of the snow, across the street from the Alcazar, stamping his feet to keep them warm. I'll give them half an hour; no longer; then back to

Sybilla if my chilled body'll give her any joy. He waited. The traffic thinned out. My feet are . . . he suddenly stopped his sibilant grunt. A large car had drawn up outside the Alcazar. He shoved deeper into the portico that sheltered him, watching Vic Diamond and that blacksmith's stubby body get out. They went up the steps into the Alcazar.

Time that had no measure passed; a prolonged and frozen variety of time. Presently Vic Diamond and Lew Cask returned to the car. They really hadn't been inside very long. More discussion behind the wheel. He couldn't see their faces; but he caught the flap of excited gestures, and after a while the car rolled off.

He stood staring across the street. Sam, go home. You've carried their cross long enough on your back. It was like extricating yourself from quicksand; the harder you struggled, the deeper you sank. He went across the street, up the steps into that rich breathless warmth, momentarily regretting the plebeian slush he was leaving on the carpet. Papa Miche watched him calmly from behind his mahogany desk; Willie Tobias from his stool by the marbled elevator. They'd expected him. And here I am. More fool me.

'Sam, you shouldn't have come back.'
'I know. I saw them arrive.'
'It must have been cold waiting outside.'
'It was. What did they do?'
'They went straight to the lift. The boss hardly looked at me. Our friend Vic not at all. He just sweats. Sam, that is a very embarrassed man.'
'Go on.'
'They asked Willie to take them up to the Maharajah's apartment. The one that has been loaned to Parnassus. They told him to let them in. Sam, it is very beautiful in there. The banqueting staff from the Crillon have been here to set up the buffet. God wouldn't be ashamed to eat at it. If there are eight different kinds of caviare you will find all of them there. Champagne. Flowers . . .'
'Papa, you're just talking to kill time.'
'Yes. We are all very shaken. None of us thought we could be betrayed like that.'
'Then finish.'
'They came down in a few minutes. Now it was different. Lew Cask asked me to check the time so that he could adjust his watch. He didn't take his eyes off me. Sam, it was like being measured for one's coffin. He gave me a hundred francs.' It might help to pay

84

for the coffin. 'They went out. Willie watched them talking in the car.'

'I watched them, too.' Sam looked down at his fingers that had developed an unaccustomed tremble in the last few days. 'Papa, you're going to have to make a little change.'

'I know.'

'You know what to do?'

'I think so. I would like to hear it from you to make sure.'

Sam said softly, 'And nobody's to be told.'

'Not even – ?'

'Not even Joey.'

'What about Stefan?'

'Stefan has to know. Where is he?'

'Back in the service room. He doesn't work here. He shouldn't be seen.'

'Who's to see him?'

'You.' Papa Miche lifted his eyebrows. 'And her grace up there.'

'Have you ever seen *her*?'

'I wouldn't know she's alive if she didn't occasionally use the phone.'

A lush mausoleum. Sam glanced above. A near-empty shell. Somewhere high up, in her princely apartment, dwelt the solitary tenant, an aged duchess who refused to flee the snowy rigours of Paris; a stubborn sparrow that preferred its familiar nest. You could rise in that elegant lift, passing one silent floor after another, like an archaeologist penetrating the rich recesses of a pyramid to find that one of the Pharaohs was still alive. How lonely she must be.

I feel lonely, too. 'Papa,' Sam sighed, 'do you understand? It's for the last time. I can't do any more for you after this.'

'It would be wicked to expect it. Sam, how harassed you look. What are we doing to you? I don't think you're getting enough sleep.'

Who wants sleep? Who wants money, who wants bread? 'So long as you understand. Now get Stefan.'

'Willie, call him in. And you don't have to worry, Sam.' Papa Miche patted his hand sympathetically. 'Tomorrow night you'll be finished with us. It *is* for the very last time.'

They are pitiful, Lew Cask thought. This Vic of mine is right; they are not worth the price of a bullet, one should just tread on them like flies. And yet something will not let me be still. There is a little canary singing in the cage of my brain that our friend Vic sweats too much. I think we will have to stick a needle into him to see how he jumps. 'You are such a big Romeo,' he said puffing his fragrant Havana across the car.

'I?'

'You have been in Paris only a few days and you make such conquests at the drop of a hat. I ask myself, is it possible that you dropped a little more than your hat?'

'*Padrone*,' Vic Diamond cringed with horror, 'what are you saying?'

'This girl with the belly, this Joey, how forthright she is. So free with the information. She tells you so much. The bed is a dangerous place for confidences. I merely wonder if perhaps you did not tell her a little more than you should.'

'May God strike me dead if . . .'

'Why would I want Him to rob me of one of my best soldiers?'

'I would cut my mother's throat rather than let the breath of betrayal pass my lips.' The blood pounded in Vic Diamond's head. Joey had so convulsed him; he'd been more than a little indiscreet. He'd let his tongue flap dangerously in the bed. He said with passion, 'I have served you faithfully since I was a boy. Have I ever given you a moment's doubt . . . ?'

'Never. I honour you for it, Vic.'

'Have I not always been there to protect you with my life?' Lew Cask admitted it with a nod. There'd been times in the early days of *Cosa Nostra* when Vic Diamond had stood between his *padrone* and executioners who'd been sent to cut him down. Probably it is no more than natural shock; I am sometimes a little rough with my boys, he mused. He looked out of the window. They were sliding around Concorde. He peered up at the Egyptian obelisk and wondered what it was.

'I trust you implicitly, Vic.' If I didn't I would tell Alfiero, who is coming over from London, to slip his little nylon cord about your throat. 'It is just that a man's penis' – using a cruder anatomical expression – 'can be his worst enemy. In our trade we walk with death at our elbow. What is that?'

'The Invalides.'

'Some kind of hospital?'

'Where Napoleon is buried. I can show you round if you wish . . .'

'Let him rest in peace. I have no interest in the dead. Vic, this girl. I shall talk to her.'

Oh, God. I hope she is careful. She has my life in her hands. I must slip a word of caution to her first. 'Of course, *padrone*.'

'I like Paris. It is full of life. There are too many mouldering old buildings; they should knock them down and put skyscrapers up.' Lew Cask owned four major construction companies on the Pacific Coast that could do good business here. 'Do you know some bright nightclub? Not, for Christ's sake, like the Kasbah.' He opened the car window disdainfully to spit out.

Vic Diamond nodded. His heart settled down to an almost normal beat; the moment of danger had passed. 'Chez Eve.'

'Eh?'

'Champagne. Girls. Lots of tits. Yes?'

'Near here?'

'Pigalle.'

'Pick up your friend Joey on the way. I will talk to her there.'

Again the hammer of blood. '*Padrone*,' Vic Diamond protested, she has her show to do . . .'

'Buy the place. Burn it down. Vic, cannot we enjoy ourselves without discussion? Fetch her.'

'Yes. All right.'

They stopped outside the Kasbah. Lew Cask remained smoking in the car. He watched the scattering of tired tarts shivering in the snow. Pathetic; I wouldn't even use them in a topless bar back home, he thought. What *is* Vic doing? Collecting the Queen of Ethiopia? They finally emerged, Vic Diamond hurrying her across the road, opening the car door to let her enter the back. The first thing Lew Cask was conscious of was a breath of perfume. She *smelled* young. Then a faint warmth, a soft breath on his neck as she leaned forward and whispered, 'This is very wrong. I have left my audience . . .'

He twisted to look at her. Her face wasn't six inches from his. Their eyes met. She didn't flinch; she laughed. 'You have a better audience in me,' he said. She still had traces of theatrical make-up on her face; a lot of blue eye-shadow that gave her a lurid look, pink streaks about the delicate chin; she was aware of it and chuckled and sat back with a mirror and wiped it off. Lew Cask felt the slightest rigidity between his loins. He wondered if in her hurry she still wore Salome's veils under her coat, and as if she could look through his skull and see what was simmering there she opened her coat wide for him to see. Just a gown. Again she chuckled. Nothing is going to faze this girl. A kid. Is she, though? She peeled off the unnaturally long eyelashes and she was still very young, but no longer a kid. She now looked at him gravely.

'M'sieu, our friend Vic told me your name. But we should be introduced more formally. I am Joey St Claire.'

'Lew Cask.'

'*Enchanté*, m'sieu.'

'Fine with me. We'll be good friends.' Christ, she's a gem.

'Where are you taking us, Vic?' She pressed his shoulder.

'Chez Eve.'

'Can we not do better than that? I am sure M'sieu Cask is a gentleman of delicate tastes.' She saw him grin. 'M'sieu...'

'Lew.'

'Then I am Joey. Do you like gypsy music, Lew?'

'No.'

'Then we shall begin a process of education. Take us to the Romany, Vic.'

Vic cast a dubious glance at the *padrone*. He muttered, 'It isn't his thing. He wants to see...'

'I don't think he really wants to see anything. He fetched me out because he wants to talk to me. It will be too noisy at Chez Eve.'

Lew Cask nodded approvingly. It was going to be a practical discussion. It would save time. Vic Diamond sighed; he had become the spectator of a fearfully unpredictable comedy. He drove them to the Romany, which lies behind Georges Cinq. The name, of course, is shamelessly *schmalzy*. But it has a high standard of decor, nobody waters the champagne, and the food is as good as Maxim's. Well, not quite. But the music is authentic; the violinists are *virtuosi*. If you have a tremulous fibre of sentiment in you, if sobbing strings move you, as they do me, it is your place. If you can afford the menu. It is not cheap.

They ordered a light supper for Joey. She was famished. Lew Cask brushed aside the wine-card and said impatiently, 'Champagne.' He thought her eyes were faintly amused; she knew that he didn't care for the stuff, that he would have preferred the roughest *vino d compagna*. He felt the first stir of one of his sultry rages. I am evidently some kind of *paisan* out of the backwoods of Palermo. Before this night is out I shall have to slap her down.

She murmured, 'Vic, tell your *padrone* to watch his face. There are a great many people about.'

Padrone. Only his associates used the word; he glanced savagely at Vic Diamond. They *have* been talking about me, he thought.

'Do I amuse you?'

'Do you amuse anybody?' She sent the waiter back with the champagne and ordered a vintage more to her refined taste. 'No, m'sieu.

They were getting formal again. 'You do not frighten me, either,' she said.

'Jesus,' Vic Diamond said with a shiver, 'do we have to . . . ?'

'Shut up. You and I will talk later,' Lew Cask said. He watched her with animosity. He had a *bordello* in San Francisco; he'd broken damsels just as delectable as this. 'Now we'll talk.'

'But not too loud.' She nodded and munched. Caviare on toast. She'd been raised on nothing but the best. Like hell, he thought.

'So you know what goes on at the Alcazar tomorrow.'

'Tonight,' she corrected him. She showed him her watch. Midnight was past.

'But you know?'

Her mouth was full. Her lustrous brown eyes bathed him serenely. He thought: I'll either break her back for her or bed her. Perhaps both. She made the fleeting gesture of dealing cards across the table. She knew.

He said aggressively, 'It's supposed to be secret.'

'You cannot keep secrets from people who have sharp ears.'

Like yours I bet. 'How did you hear?'

'Would it be impolite to ask you to mind your own business?'

He said suddenly, 'Vic told you?' and thought he saw a flash of deathly fear cross his aide's face.

But if it was fear, or perhaps just angry offence, it vanished as she said disdainfully, 'Now you're being absurd.'

'I have to know.'

She nibbled a little cold pheasant. She watched him reflectively. 'You are only one of four players. Work it out for yourself. That is all you are going to be told.'

He burned her with his eyes. Could she have got it from Parnassus? That great patrician? Never! From Caesar Vinci? H'mm. Perhaps. From Gregor Kassem? H'mm h'mm. She'd left him in a maze of doubt. The waiter came across to the champagne bucket and poured a little in a glass for him to taste. It disconcerted him further. He glared up at the waiter and tasted it, making a face. It wasn't worth the money. He elbowed the waiter aside.

Joey said with the softest rebuke, 'A gentleman always studies the feelings of those who serve him.'

'There are no gentlemen at this table.'

'Speak for yourself.'

He bridled. I will hit her. Then he had to laugh. It was like the travail of a birth; the water suddenly burst, the baby emerged. It wasn't much of an infant, he didn't particularly like her, but you

D

had to regard her with begrudging respect. There was also that tightening of his flesh in the region of his crotch. He patted her hand. 'No more spatting. We talk like friends.' Businesslike now. 'Why did you tell it to the three crummies who work at your club?'

'They have suffered a great deal. I felt sorry for them. I thought they might make a little money to set them up in life.'

'You call four million dollars a little?'

'To you and Parnassus and Caesar Vinci and Gregor Kassem, yes.'

'They're not clever enough to take it.'

'But they have someone behind them who is.'

'This Casanova? The lover-boy, eh? You slept with him?' Lew Cask saw a spasm of outrage convulse Vic Diamond's face and he thought: this man of mine is besotted with her. It is something I will have to bear in mind.

Joey said calmly, 'If you are going to talk dirty I will kick you under the table and go.'

'Sit still. No hard feelings. A little rough language clears the air. What's in it for this man?'

'Nothing.'

'There has to be something.'

'For people like you, of course. You have your hands in everybody's pockets.' He glowered. If anyone's going to be kicked under the table it's her. 'There are some men who do things out of compassion for their friends.'

'They end up in the gutter.'

'Often. And where will you end up, M'sieu Cask?'

In a satin-lined casket, weighed down by eighty wreaths. He grinned sourly. He studied her with hooded eyes. He'd already decided to let the game go on; what he'd heard in the last few minutes had hardened his decision. Again his instincts vibrated, alert for danger. He glanced at Vic Diamond. This is my gun. Am I to trust him? I must. For what surged in him like gall, every time his mind reverted to it, was the slight that had been put upon him; his veins throbbed as he recalled Gregor Kassem telling him languidly, 'We do not talk the same language,' and he thought: I will talk to you in a language you will understand. He burned as only a disdained Sicilian can burn. Like Etna. What made it doubly enticing was that it would be vastly profitable; he would take a fortune away from them and guffaw revengefully behind their backs. Luigi Cascavagni, he thought demurely, you are about to spit and this is neither the time nor the place. You are in the presence of a lady; or so she thinks.

A trio of violinists were parading the tables and they draped themselves about him, the strings moaning a gypsy lament in his ear. He stared at them woodenly; he liked Italian music that bubbled with life. There would be time for tears when the inevitable bullet found him. He took out some notes to stuff into their hands and Joey made a little warning gesture: don't, her eyes said. She whispered, 'They play for love, not money,' and the warm brown eyes glistened with – could it be a personal message? Ever so faint.

His loins leapt. He said to her, 'We have a lot of things to discuss. Vic will take us back to my hotel.' He was staying the night before Christmas at the Ritz. They didn't know who it was they entertained.

It was late. The streets hushed, made white and somnolent by the heavy fall of snow. They reached the hotel and got out. Lew Cask took Joey's arm with significant possession and said, 'Good night, Vic.'

He saw his soldier's eyes go blank with shock. 'But Joey . . . ?'

'It is private in my room. We have things to talk about. She will be safe with me.' Your *padrone* has prior rights, Lew Cask thought.

She glanced ruefully at Vic Diamond with the slightest twitch of her lips. Something unforeseen, probably unavoidable, but certainly profitable, was happening and it would be foolish to swim against the tide. She let Lew Cask retain her arm and Vic Diamond's face went ghastly; he was also a Sicilian and knew what it was to have the sexual knife thrust into the heart. Tears wet his eyes as he watched his *padrone* and Joey disappear into the hotel. Now the tears came faster, and talking to himself in molten Italian he drove off.

V

A line of violins were pushing the reeds and they draped their bows upon him, the strings stopping a while, laments, his car.

'M'SIEU.'

'Oh, go away . . .'

Who was it banging on the door? 'M'sieu Sam.' It was one of the garage hands. 'There are three gentlemen to see you below.'

He sat up in bed. It was broad daylight. He rubbed his clogged eyes. 'What time is it?'

'Eleven o'clock.'

'Hell. I overslept. Who are they?'

'They did not say.'

'I'll come down.' No, he was only half-awake without his coffee. He got out of bed. 'Send them up. You won't forget to have the car ready for me, will you?'

'Our cars are always ready, m'sieu. You have only to get behind the wheel and drive off.' Hoping that you wouldn't forget to pay in advance.

He crossed the room to the washbasin. The sight of his face in the mirror revolted him; heavy with what looked like a four-day growth of beard. Gaunt as Lucifer after a brutal night. He sponged his eyes with cold water, wetting his pyjama collar. There was a tap on the door. It opened; watching it in the mirror he was surprised to see Dr Auguste Benes come in. He was accompanied by a plump, sleepy-eyed young man. He wore a coarse blue uniform and carried a peaked cap.

His mouth tightened. It was an endless assault on his privacy. He said nothing. He filled the kettle with water and put it on to boil. He prepared a pan with two heaped spoons of coffee, sprinkling in the pinch of salt that was reputed to kill the taste of chicory which he disliked. He always kept a few chips of eggshell to settle the grounds. Still not a word. He set a solitary cup and saucer on the table, hoping the gesture would be meaningful to them. Go away. There was a brioche and a pack of butter in the cupboard. The young man with the peaked cap glanced absently about the room as if he lived in better quarters himself.

Dr Benes began to fidget. The bitter bony face darkened; he took off his pince-nez to wipe them. It was symbolic of his rage. He burst out in a stifled voice, 'Have you lost the power of speech?'

'No. I still have it.' Sam peered at his furred tongue in the mirror. We have a doctor in the house; perhaps he can tell me what's wrong with me, apart from a broken spirit, a chronic hangover and total disillusionment with life. He spoke. 'What do you want?'

'There is the matter we discussed yesterday...'

'Who's this with you?'

'Jean-Baptiste. He is one of the ambulance drivers at the hospital.' The plump young man nodded. Sam thought the sleepiness was deceptive; the humorous blue eyes were very sharp. He looked as clean and shiny-faced as a junior surgeon who had just scrubbed up.

'They said there were three of you.'

'My nephew Stefan is too embarrassed to come up.' Dr Benes shivered. He seemed to burn with an uncontrollable venom. 'I have something to take up with you.' Sam poured boiling water over the coffee and stirred it. 'Are you listening?' Sam nodded. 'You compelled me to do something under duress. You threatened me with Inspector Massime of Marseilles.' The doctor's voice rose to a resentful shrill. 'I have since discovered that he has been dead for over a year.'

'Poor man.'

'You must have known.'

'It could have slipped my memory. I have a lot of things on my mind.'

Dr Benes said harshly, 'So you no longer hold anything over my head. We talk on a different basis now...'

'You're walking out on the business?'

'I did not say that.'

'Then what are you saying?'

'They told me in the garage you are leaving for Nice.'

'In an hour. You'd like me to drop you a postcard?'

'You are less amusing than you think. You are not going anywhere. You are going to stay and carry out your responsibility...'

'I don't remember having any.'

'You have it now.' Dr Benes blinked violently and sat frustratedly on the bed.

Jean-Baptiste said with a polite sigh, 'This is not a civilized way to talk.' He glanced amusedly at Sam. 'M'sieu, it is a cold morning. The coffee smells good. One hates to invite oneself...'

'Sit down.' Sam looked him over. One could grow to like him;

93

given time. And he had no more than an hour. He put out another cup and saucer. He turned to the doctor. 'Join us.'

'No.'

Jean-Baptiste said, 'As a medical man,' which he was in a very indirect way, 'I always carry a little alcoholic stimulent. In case of fainting fits, you know.' He brought out a small bottle of cognac. He held it invitingly over the coffee. 'May I?'

'It's too early for me.'

'My duties are very arduous. I have to keep up my strength.' He laced his coffee with the brandy and sipped it. The bland blue eyes brightened. 'Now we can discuss the matter in a more relaxed frame of mind.'

'What makes you think you're involved?'

'M'sieu, the good doctor has called me in. An ambulance will be required. I am a very alert and responsible man. I hope I shall be involved. The doctor has promised me a nice piece of the hundred thousand dollars he is to get . . .'

'He gets a quarter of a million dollars,' Sam said.

Jean-Baptiste stared reproachfully at Dr Benes. 'Doctor, that is not what you told me. I am surprised at you. It is not in line with your Hippocratic oath.'

Dr Benes said spitefully, 'You should not be too greedy. Your services are not as important as you think.'

'Important enough.' Jean-Baptiste's face became seraphic. 'It grows more and more interesting. I shall set myself up in business. I am a young man of ambition. It would make those four rich men proud to know how they have benefited me, should they ever find out my name. And they won't. By the way,' he said to Sam, 'are there any other secrets the good doctor didn't tell me?'

'Just one. It doesn't have anything more to do with me.'

'It has everything to do with you,' Dr Benes said. He rose unsteadily from the bed. 'It sprang out of your mind. You conceived it. You are the father of the plan. You cannot walk away from it and disclaim your child.' Sam watched him woodenly. He dunked his brioche. Dr Benes came across to breathe heavily over his shoulder. Sam averted his head; there were things the doctor's best friends hadn't told him. 'You twisted my arm yesterday. I would have got out of it if I could. This monstrous game at the Alcazar. Out of somebody's fantasy! I could not believe a word of it,' the doctor said. 'Then it occurred to me that to be a billionaire you must sometimes have a few monstrous thoughts. I have some private sources of information. You know what I found out?' He waited for some response from Sam. None came. 'Parnassus will be in Paris this evening. It doesn't mean much? Perhaps.' His eyes glittered. 'But by an odd twist of circumstance Caesar Vinci will be here, too. It is getting to look pretty solid. Now for the long arm of coincidence. Gregor Kassem, the oil man, will also be here. I do not believe in so much coincidence. I do not know about this Mafia man, Lew Cask . . .'

'He's already here,' Sam said.

Dr Benes's thin face suffused. 'You see? The stage is set. We are going to walk in on the play, exactly as you planned. With just one reservation . . .'

Jean-Baptiste said softly to Sam, 'You must stay with it, m'sieu.'

Sam shook his head.

'M'sieu, you must. These people of yours are not reliable. They are incompetent. They mean well, but they will stumble over each other's feet . . .'

'They'll cope,' Sam said.

'No,' Jean-Baptiste said strenuously, 'they won't. Something terrible could happen. They will go straight to their doom. I am no fool. I was taken to see them yesterday. The old man, Papa Miche, is an ageing bull. He will plunge in head down and break everything up. One of your friends goes like this.' Jean-Baptiste twitched an eye spasmodically. He meant Willie. 'If anything goes wrong he will fall apart. The one waiting downstairs chews his knuckles like a child.' Poor Stefan. 'He will never make it. M'sieu, they must have someone with them they can trust.'

'You,' Dr Benes confirmed to Sam. 'And you know why?' Sam waited to be told. 'Because you have been playing God with them. You said to them: do this and do that, just as I tell you, and you will go straight across Jordan into the Promised Land. They have no Joshua to lead them. It has to be you. If you are not there Jericho will not fall, there will be no Promised Land, no four million dollars, and some of us will end up in gaol.'

Jean-Baptiste said with a mild chuckle, 'I am too young to go to gaol.' He held the bottle of cognac again over Sam's cup. 'Yes? It gives coffee a little muscle.' Sam nodded. Jean-Baptiste laced it lightly. He whispered, 'Your friend is listening outside the door. The one with the knuckles.'

The door was ajar. Stefan pushed it open. Without looking at Sam he said furiously to Dr Benes, 'Let him be.'

'It's time he learned the truth.'

'He has done enough. More than enough,' which Sam took as an implied reproach. Stefan's eyes flashed with tears. 'Nobody should have interfered. We should have been left to blunder it through alone. Nothing could happen to us worse than has already happened,' and again Sam winced.

He said with a sigh, 'Stefan, sit down.'

'Don't let them force you . . .'

'I'm hooked.'

'That's right.' Jean-Baptiste watched him with pity. 'You should have known it from the start. You saw them jumping like idiots into the water and you put out a hand to save them. It's sometimes better to let people drown. All they have done is pull you in. Now we're all hooked,' Jean-Baptiste said breezily. 'But nobody should worry. It's the dream of a century. We are going to see this thing through.'

Sam said nothing for a while. He looked at Dr Benes. 'You brought it with you?'

'Yes.'

'Let Stefan have it.'

Dr Benes glanced hesitantly at his nephew. He took out a pill-box and removed the lid. A tiny pink capsule nestled in the cotton wool.

Sam said to Stefan, 'Take it to Papa Miche. Tell him I'll be round to see him. Now everybody get out of my room,' he exploded. 'This is my home.' Down in the garage they had brought in a truck for repair and the din of tearing metal was shattering. 'Let me have my breakfast in peace.'

By midday the snow had ceased. It left a dazzling pall that stretched from Avignon in the south to the Channel ports. The Christmas dusk seemed to creep in before the afternoon was gone. Theo Parnassus, Caesar Vinci and Gregor Kassem were now very close to Paris. It is time to take a harder look at them. We blame the rich for everything. But the super-rich, the great *colossi*, get to be mythological while they are still living and nobody wants to blame people who are so close to God. As in fact, they were. Caesar was a devout Catholic, Gregor an unswerving Moslem, and Theo Parnassus a strong upholder of the Eastern Church. It made their vast wealth, to use a rival religious expression, almost kosher. They spent millions on church renovations, in financing pilgrimages to Mecca, and can you get closer to God than that?

Caesar Vinci was already over Rheims, piloting one of his fleet of helicopters, so let us take a look at him first. He was very expert with

96

machines. He had the strong hands of a mechanic with a thick growth of virile hair up the wrists. He was in his early middle-age, a powerfully built man, beautifully dressed and healthily tanned. He gave joy to the best tailors of London and Rome. He let himself be barbered lavishly every day. You looked at him and saw the commanding features reminiscent of the busts of the Roman emperors; they all seem to go in for the high proud nose and the assertive mouth. Such men radiate power and semi-divine justice, and while Caesar radiated power he had to be a little more realistic where justice was concerned. He had ten major corporations under his command and international industry isn't run by being naive. He could be ruthless, explosively aggressive, and charming in the Latin style. As he was now. He had a passenger at his side and when the helicopter bucketed in a wild gust, the blades clattering like loose boards, he said to her delicately, 'You're all right?'

'Fine, fine.'

'Won't be long now.'

'Let it go on for ever. How beautiful it is below.'

He glanced down. The twinkle of lights in snow-bound hamlets. Everything pure white. God's colour. His eyes glittered. 'Beautiful,' he said. He'd just had a beautiful and meaningful confrontation with one of the princes of God.

Caesar Vinci was born a *ragazzaccio*. What a terrible word that is: it means ragamuffin. In Turin they sometimes apply it to the unwanted kids of the gutter. He had been dropped in one at the age of two. The priests picked him out of it and gave him his name. A wonderful gift. A wonderful name. They saw signs of an eruptive energy and apprenticed him to a garage when he was twelve. Noise. Oil. Fumes. He thrived on them. He adored cars. He learned to drive them as furiously as Jehu, that biblical son of Nimshi. They say that he was racing them before he had his first woman, which I doubt. When he won the Italian Grand Prix the Maserati people took him up. It was an epic rise; billionaires are made like moviestars. From the race track to the factory floor, then on to the boardroom, leaving him nothing to go for but control of the entire automobile industry. Italian, of course; he wasn't boss of General Motors yet. Only then did he have time to look around for a wife.

Something blue-blooded to match his wealth and princely tastes. He chose a daughter of the noble Orsinis, and there are few families that bleed bluer than that. What he wanted was a profusion of sons, and what he got was a limp sexless woman who managed to give him a dull loutish girl before drying up. Not much of a bargain. Well, one made the best of what one had. He had a towering position in Roman society and the respect of the Church; he was very close to a powerful Cardinal who would get him a Papal honour one day. He hadn't slept with his wife for two years, which didn't bother him a little bit. He had his private sexual refuge; a warm-blooded mistress in Milan who, with a bit of luck and assistance of his virile loins, would give him a son. He hoped. Anway, sex only occupied a few minutes a day. Business took up the rest.

But nothing stayed that simple. He'd just spent a few days in Vienna where he'd had to make a rather brutal choice. St Matthew said, 'Ye cannot serve God and Mammon,' but an arrogant man sometimes found it difficult to serve either. Just himself. He was floating a colossal loan through the Austrian treasury and when he entered the Minister's ante-room for his morning appointment he was surprised to see his old friend the Cardinal coming out.

His senses instantly sharpened. 'Eminence,' he said, making his obeisance. He kissed the ring. It gave him time to sort out some very curious thoughts. 'I wouldn't have expected to see you here.'

'My son,' the Cardinal said with a dim smile, 'Herr Hoechst,' who was the Minister, 'is a dear friend and a pious child of the Church. We have many wide interests to discuss,' and Caesar wondered suddenly: can these interests possibly include mine? Something put him on guard. He stared into the Cardinal's wizened face. He was a doyen of the Sacred College, well past eighty, but his eyes were as sharp as needles. Be quiet for a minute, Caesar thought; let him talk first. He's looking into my soul and he isn't sure he likes what he sees.

'Caesar,' the Cardinal murmured, 'step outside with me for a moment.' He drew him gently out of earshot of the secretarial staff.

'Eminence, I have an appointment with . . .'

'I asked the Minister to spare me a few minutes of your precious time.' So they have been talking about me. The Cardinal inhaled a little snuff. Caesar wondered emptily if that was what kept him going. 'The *marchese* called to see me yesterday,' the Cardinal said, and Caesar thought with a bitter shrug: so the old bastard's been complaining again. The *marchese* was his father-in-law, a dry overbred stick who'd transmitted that awful frigidity to his daughter, though he must have had a solitary spasm of sex to conceive her. 'My son, I am greatly disturbed by what I hear. Your marital relations . . .'

'Your eminence shouldn't believe everything he hears.'

'There are some things I have to believe. That there is a lady in

Milan who occupies the very special place your wife should share.'
Meaning the bed. The Vatican never referred directly to the bed; too
much sin occurred in it. The Cardinal searched Caesar's face and
said sorrowfully, 'Is she possibly *enceinte*?' Meaning pregnant. No,
she wasn't, though she was throwing out hysterical alarms every
other day.

The Cardinal went on with a sigh, 'The Church expects better of
one of its most successful sons.' The word 'successful' faintly stressed.
It was leading up to something and Caesar knew what it was. The
Church was preparing to dictate the rules. It was moving into the
citadel of his private life in which he permitted nobody to tread, not
even God. 'Render unto Caesar the things which are Caesar's . . .'
and he intended to keep it that way. For a moment his terrible will
blazed, but it was all inside. He knew how to control his face. 'I
shall be having dinner with the Minister tonight,' the Cardinal said
carelessly, as if it had nothing to do with what was in their minds.
'We have some private matters to discuss,' and I'm one of them,
Caesar thought. A little gossip over the sherry; the vaguest hint of
Papal disapproval . . . and *kaput*. The loan was dead. The old fox.
Something inside Caesar shivered. Two can play at that game. He
smiled pleasantly because the Cardinal was still watching him, but in
that instant they went their separate ways. The Cardinal said softly,
'I return to Rome tomorrow. May I express some kind thoughts to
your dear wife?'

Why not? 'But, eminence,' Caesar said agreeably, 'I was about
to express them myself.'

'So?'

'I have just put in a call to my home.' He would do it inside the
hour. 'I was hoping she might join me. The change would do her
good. Perhaps a few days ski-ing . . .'

'I am so pleased. If only I were young enough to be with you.'

'Your eminence is ageless.'

'So is the indulgence of Mother Church.' Just to remind him. 'And
the lady in Milan . . . ?'

'I think you are right. It is kinder to be cruel. My banker will make
her a generous allowance. It is time to pension her off.'

'Poor, poor woman.'

Poor, poor me. You nearly had me over a barrel. But never again,
Caesar thought. He wouldn't be too sorry to be rid of the lady. She'd
been getting very demanding lately, making false hints of pregnan-
cies to pin him down. It was an insult to his virility. None of them
ever came off. When he'd finished his business with the Minister he

rang his wife, phrasing the invitation so subtly that at first she grew excited, then confused, and finally said petulantly that she preferred to stay in Rome. Next he rang his father-in-law to complain bitterly about his daughter's behaviour. Let his eminence chew on that! He spent a few days ski-ing in Carinthia, where he'd picked up the ravishing Austrian blonde who now sat at his side. Not a bad exchange for Milan.

There was a sultry glow in the wintry sky. 'Look,' he pointed. 'There's Paris.' He brought the helicopter skittering round on course. She was thrilled. 'I have never been to Paris.'

'You'll love it.' He would park her temporarily in some hotel. He was looking forward to meeting his old friends Theo and Gregor. He hoped to enjoy their huge classic game of poker, though still faintly irked with Gregor for landing them with the barbarous Mafia man. His eyes gleamed. Perhaps we'll be able to take his ill-gotten shirt off him. He chuckled with anticipation and the ravishing Austrian blonde looked at him curiously, wondering what the joke was and why he couldn't share it with her.

Now for Gregor Kassem who had so irked his friend. Gregor the Iraqi. Given half a chance Iraqis will always make their way in the world. Certain parts of the world are more profitable than others, such as the vast areas of desert that produce nothing but sand, date palms and oil. Places like Abu Dhabi, Qatar and the twin Sultanates of Muscat and Oman. They sound as if they belong to the fantasies of the romantic Sheikhs, which they don't. They are much too brutal. Since the time of Mohammed they have been notable only for wandering Bedouins, camels and savage tribal vendettas. And suddenly they are bent double under the sheer weight of gold. Black gold. Oil.

Much of it passing through Gregor Kassem's hands without ever smearing a finger, but adding mountainously to his wealth.

The people who live in these primitive regions are unpredictable. To deal with them you need to understand the use of baksheesh, to have a facile tongue and a dramatic passion for prayer. Prostrate in the sand several times a day. Gregor had all these excellent qualities. He was a plump, smooth-skinned man with large glistening eyes and an air of benevolence that never left him until he was crossed. Then he could be dangerous, as he was now. He had made an emotional error when he was ten years of age and suddenly he was being called upon to pay for it.

He simmered like a shiny brown mole in the back of the huge

Rolls that was taking him to Paris. It wasn't one of Caesar Vinci's products. Gregor hoped his dear friend wouldn't mind.

He had been in Beirut, finalizing a tanker deal for one of the Trucial emirates. He had had an anonymous call to say that a certain person would be visiting him at his hotel. His hackles rose when his caller arrived. He was a thick-bodied, unshaven Syrian wearing the headcloth that had become the mark of the Palestinian guerrilla. He had carried a sub-machine gun through the hotel as casually as a gentleman in London carries an umbrella through the Savoy. He said peremptorily to Gregor, 'You know who I am?'

Gregor recognized him behind the dark glasses and the thick moustache. He nodded. He watched his visitor lay the sub-machine gun on the carpet, where it left an oily stain.

The Syrian said in a flat voice, 'You do not show enough enthusiasm for the cause. We now expect you to demonstrate it. The time has come to get rid of your Jew.'

Gregor grew cold. What had happened when he was ten years old, a street arab in every sense of the word, was now catching up. A Baghdadi Jew with the biblical name of Simon ben Manasseh had given him refuge; he was in the refinery business and he had taught Gregor the intricacies and opportunities of the oil industry, opening up a whole new world to him. It had become almost a father-and-son relationship; he and Simon ben Manasseh had co-operated ever since, not too obviously because of local circumstances. Gregor sighed. He wondered if he should deny it; but it would be disgusting. It would soil him for ever in his own mind.

He said, 'I need time.'

'You will have time. Two days.'

'I need six months.'

The Syrian rasped his unshaven cheek. He picked up his sub-machine gun and placed it significantly on his knee. Gregor looked into the barrel. The world has gone mad, he thought; I am sitting in a civilized hotel; how can such things be?

'Very well.' He shrugged. He said carelessly, 'Does anything happen to him?'

'By and by.'

I will warn him tonight, Gregor thought. He felt angry and defiled; nobody could do business with people like this.

'Remember. We will check up on you. Everybody has his bills to pay and yours are now due.' The man adjusted his headcloth, slung the weapon under his arm and went out, leaving his personal smell of sweat and mutton-fat behind. He would walk out of the hotel with the gun and the desk-clerk would avert his eyes, and if there was a policeman on traffic duty in the street he would pretend suddenly to be blind.

Gregor had been cold, and now he burned. What good was it to be rich as Midas, to have cultivated Europeans acknowledging you with a bow, if such bandits could walk in and intimidate you? In an hotel one *actually* owned? His self-respect would die. I will teach this ruffian the realities of power, he thought, if I have to spend a million dollars, and he rang three important people of a rival guerrilla organization who knew how to handle such things. The Syrian would have a finger chopped off; two if he howled. He would never know why. But I will know, and it will be good for my soul, Gregor thought.

It cost him a lot of money, expressly asked for in German marks. But that was what money was for; to buy satisfaction. The proof of it arrived in a small packet delivered to his hotel an hour before he left. It contained three fingers. The gentleman with the headdress would have to learn to write with his left hand.

He lay dreamily in the sleek scented upholstery in the back of the car. Its luxury elevated him mysteriously above the ordinary ruck of humanity he could see trudging through the snow. He would soon be in Paris. How nice to meet Theo and Caesar again. I hope they have forgiven me my little lapse; I did what I could to stall our Mafia friend off. His eyes twinkled. Wouldn't it be amusing if we could take his pants down for him? Speaking metaphorically, of course. He would hate to lose a million dollars. So would I. The prospect was so delightful that he threw back his head and laughed, and his chauffeur, watching him covertly in the mirror, thought: old Mustapha's got the chuckles. Somebody's going to be done down.

The third of the giants wasn't far off, but approaching over the Alps. Gregor Kassem had left his yacht at Cannes; Theo Parnassus had left his at Cyprus, and was flying in by private executive jet. It would be nice to relax. He hadn't had a holiday for months. He always looked forward to those big effervescent games with his friends, though this time it would be spoiled by that malodorous Lew Cask. He made a sound of disgust. God forbid that anybody should find out that I have associated with him. I would never live it down. He closed his eyes. He was very tired. But he couldn't doze; embers of anger still burned in his mind. He had just been through the most mortifying experience of his life.

It took a great deal to stir Theo Parnassus. He was of Turkish peasant stock, which made him impassive to begin with; and when one is fortified by a massive store of wealth, perhaps the greatest personal store of wealth in the world, one can take a very detached view of life. He had the crinkled brown face and placid hooded eyes of a Cherokee Indian. He was pleasant to talk to. A cultivated and philosophical man. Who would have suspected him of violent passions? He had the inborn pride of a great Medici and a patriarchal devotion to his family; attack either of these and he flamed.

He had been born in a little coastal village in the Turkish enclave of Cyprus with the name of Teos Parnaz. There is no point in describing his onrush to financial power; the galley-boy of a fishing schooner could have done worse. He modified his name a little to Theo Parnassus because so many of his interests were Greek. Parnassus was the name of a holy mountain dedicated to Dionysus, who was no mean god, and it pleased him. But he kept close contact with his roots and visited the village twice a year. His family had lived there for generations. Though he would have built them a palace if they wished, his venerable father and mother still clung to the house in which he had been born.

He had found them agitated. He could scarcely believe what he heard. They were to be evicted, the old house demolished and a sewage-farm planted on the site. There was something vaguely disgusting about the notion. He listened very calmly, but inside him that Medici pride began to seethe. A new local administrator had been appointed, an ex-army major, and this was his work.

'Father,' he said softly, kissing the aged stubbled cheek, 'do not distress yourself. I will see that this nonsense is forgotten.'

'Teos, this is a very haughty military man . . .'

'I can also be haughty. I carry no guns, but I have much power. I will talk to him.'

'You will go and see him now?'

'Father, I go to see nobody.' Through the window he could see the snowy glimmer of his palatial yacht. He could have blockaded the entire harbour with the merest fraction of his fleet. 'He will come to see me.'

He sent a polite invitation to the major and received the curt reply: I am available in my office. Theo Parnassus sighed; the mountain will not come to Mahomet; so be it. I will swallow a little pride and go to him.

He would never forget that meeting as long as he lived. He took the measure of the man within minutes. A frustrated officer; one of the fire-eating Young Turks. Probably left-wing and put out to pasture where he could do least harm. But he is harming my venerable parents and if he does not mend his ways I shall harm *him*. And savagely. The major was thickset, with the heavy slab of a moustache and cold wild eyes. Theo Parnassus stared at the shabby uniform, thinking: I know a few generals who could put you in your unsavoury place, which is in the vicinity of the sickening toilet I see inside that door. Flies buzzed in it. The major riffled through his papers. He beckoned Theo Parnassus to a seat as an afterthought. Then he uttered one chill word:

'Yes?'

'I think you know why I have come.'

'I know who you are. I know that that is your yacht.' A left-winger all right. He carried a full-sized chip on his shoulder. Am I going to have to knock it off?

'My parents are distressed . . .'

The major interrupted him rudely, 'So I hear. Do not expect me to weep. They have three days. They will have to go.'

God give me patience. 'They have lived their lives in that house . . .'

'Then they have had enough use out of it. You can afford to re-house them. You are a very rich man.'

'May I give you some advice?'

'No.'

'I shall give it to you nevertheless. You will not evict my parents. You will not demolish this house in which generations of my family were born. You will put your sewage-farm elsewhere. I speak to you with some restraint because I am rich, and therefore have you at a disadvantage, and because I have learned the wisdom of rational behaviour which you have evidently not. I beg of you, do not provoke me further.'

'You have finished?'

'If I have made myself clear.'

'You have.' The major's mouth snapped tight. 'Two days.'

Theo Parnassus leaned forward; he could scarcely believe his ears. 'You said . . . ?'

'Two days. That is when the housebreakers now move in.'

'And if I open my mouth again it will be twenty-four hours?'

The major said maliciously, 'That is right. I am not afraid of you and your wealth. I am not awed by your splendiferous yacht. I administer this village and I will do as I think fit.' He widened his lips into an ironic grin so that he could bite on his moustache. 'I may invite you to open the sewage-farm with due pomp.'

'You are too kind. One question, if I may.'

'What is it?'

'How long has the plan been known in the village?'

'A month.'

'And nobody complained?'

'Nobody. It would not matter if they did. I do not accept complaints. You may go.' In fact, the major went himself. He disappeared into the toilet, slamming the door violently. Theo Parnassus heard him relieving himself with a revengeful gush. He went out and looked up and down the sunlit street.

A few shopkeepers watched him covertly, then slipped out of sight. He glanced across the street at the local branch of the Ottoman Bank. The curtain in the window shifted; Zak Pahlevi, the manager, peered at him and hastily withdrew. Theo Parnassus's mouth twisted wryly. My charities to this village have been enormous, and not one of them raised a voice to protect my parents. Not one of them chose to inform me. He walked back to the house, straight-backed and seemingly serene, but his brain had not known such rage for years.

He sent a message to the bank-manager to call. He would be here in minutes; he had better. He knew that Theo Parnassus was vice-president of the mother bank in Istanbul. He brought the sour smell of anxiety into the house. Theo drank a little Mastika, of which he was inordinately fond. He offered his visitor nothing.

'Zak, why did you not speak up for my parents?'

'I did, I did. Strenuously . . .'

'The major says not. Not a living soul in this village desired to utter a word in their defence.'

'The man is wild. He is army. The whole village is scared . . .'

'Zak, I am the village. I am the fount of all your bounty, and I am not scared. I am merely grieved. The house in which I was born is to be demolished over my father's head. Zak, come to the window.' Through it they could see the long, surfwashed coastline stretching far into the distant enclave. 'You see the bay over there?'

The bank-manager shrugged. 'It is Greek . . .' as if Greeks weren't really people.

'It is where I am going to build a new port. Everything modern; a tanker terminal, fine wharves, first-class anchorages for a fishing-fleet. I shall make it the pride of the coast.' It will also reassert the dignity and authority of Theo Parnassus and that is what is important, he thought. These people are going to be taught the realities of power. Strange how the expression also dominated the minds of his brother-giants Caesar Vinci and Gregor Kassem. He saw the bank-manager's face seethe suddenly with sweat.

He stammered, 'It will be the ruin of us . . .'

'Should I be concerned?'

'I shall speak to the head-office. Instantly. Do nothing, I beg of you. This mad major will have to be withdrawn.' He rambled on, violently shaken, and Theo Parnassus watched him without emotion, sipping his drink; while his visitor was still speaking he walked out of the room, leaving him gasping with shock.

He drew his parents aside. 'We are leaving this place.'

They recoiled. 'Teos, these are our roots . . .'

'I shall plant you afresh. There is to be no discussion. We are finished here. I shall build you something wonderful over on the other side.' He looked coldly across the ancient huddle of roofs that the Parnaz family had known for three hundred years. He said, 'I am going to destroy this village,' but his parents were so stricken with grief that he didn't think they'd heard. No matter. It would happen just the same.

It wouldn't be a bad investment, either. He worked out the gross appropriation on the back of an envelope. It could pay off in cash as well as in pride. He felt his airplane dip. Lights flitted below them in the wintry murk. A momentary glimpse of what looked like the Etoile, and then they slipped down to the runway at Orly. He hadn't really been able to relax.

But now he could with Caesar and Gregor. We have a brotherly understanding of each other, he thought.

We have been taking a look at the kind of mental clockwork that made these super-stars tick. They weren't bad men; all three were great patrons of the arts. Nobody with a worthwhile charity ever had to appeal to them twice. They behaved like medieval barons because they believed that the world was still pretty medieval, despite rocketry and computers, and if you had to have commercial barons let them at least be efficient. They were. Not one of the huge complexes they controlled had missed a dividend in ten years.

They arrived at the Alcazar within minutes of each other. Caesar Vinci first. Gregor Kassem embraced him as he swept in. Benevolence radiated from them. Theo Parnassus came in, still looking tired, and the Cherokee Indian face instantly relaxed. Gregor kissed both brown cheeks. They gazed at each other like boys at a school reunion.

'Theo . . .'

'Caesar, how well you look!'

'I feel good. I have something special parked at the Plaza Athenée as my own Christmas gift.'

'Feminine?'

'Austrian. Dazzling blonde. Gregor, how *have* you been?'

Gregor patted his arm. Later he would tell them about the Syrian with the sub-machine gun whose fingers had been chopped off. He helped himself to a little pâté from the rich buffet. It is good to have such friends, he thought.

Then he saw Theo glance at him wryly. He knew why. He said with a faint sigh of hope, 'Maybe he will not come.'

'That type always comes,' Caesar said.

'He is some kind of animal,' Theo said, 'but we will be polite to him. However hard. Is he really . . .?'

'Mafia? Bestially so,' Caesar said.

'He will surely not come armed?'

'Theo, you cannot expect me to frisk him. He will probably have some gunman or other looking out for him.'

'How foul the world is growing,' Theo said.

And suddenly the door opened and the foulness walked in. He was alone. Gregor already knew him. Theo and Caesar stared curiously at the short stubby body with its pendulous belly, the round, almost inane, face, as dark as a Moor's, split by a friendly froggy grin. It wasn't quite what they'd expected; something lithe and magnetically devilish perhaps. It was only when they looked deep into the cold owl's eyes that they felt a stir of apprehension and had to hide their feelings behind empty smiles. 'My friend Lew Cask,' Gregor said. They couldn't avoid shaking hands. I must go into the bathroom and wash immediately, Theo thought.

He said courteously, 'You had a good journey, I hope?'

'I been looking around the town a couple of days,' Lew Cask said.

'Paris is nicer in the spring.'

Lew Cask said agreeably, 'So's Las Vegas,' in which he had a couple of decorative hotels that at least provided a little civilized sport. Dice and women. You could keep the frowsy museums. Though there'd been some mitigation in the form of that hot number Joey, who'd given him one hell of a going-over in bed. He continued to beam. Theo Parnassus was the one he watched. He went on amiably, 'I heard a lot about you.'

'I'm so pleased.' I wish I had heard less about you. I would feel easier in my mind, Theo thought. 'You stayed where?'

'The Ritz.'

'The chef is my very good friend. You must try his *poulet de Bresse* which he prepares specially for me,' and Lew Cask looked at him with mingled revulsion and disdain. I'd hate the goddam stuff. Give me a good pizza. He felt the first prick of annoyance. Is this high-hat bastard having me on?

'Sure, sure,' he said. He still maintained the grin. 'Business good?'

'We are here to enjoy a pleasurable game. We do not discuss business,' Theo said. Caesar broke the painful silence by opening a bottle of champagne. Gregor Kassem glanced at Lew Cask with a sigh. I have heard this man utter the vilest language that ever disgraced the human tongue. I hope he does not forget himself here. Caesar and Theo now began a fervent discussion about a sale at Christies; pure jargon to Lew Cask, who had never heard of Italian primitives. They could hardly be referring to aged women of a certain type. So all right; I'm frozen out, he thought. They don't like me. It's mutual. Give me another couple of years and I'm rich enough to buy any one of them out. This big, big Parnassus, this prince of men; what in hell was he, anyway, but a galley-boy? Heh? Some kind of Turk at that. This Caesar, who I hear chases women, was a *ragazzaccio*: a gutter-urchin. He don't have to look down his fine gentlemanly nose at me. This other is a Wog. This Gregor Kassem; he belongs to camels. I spit all three of them out with Sicilian disgust.

Lew Cask went across to the buffet, sought out a bottle of beer and drank it ostentatiously from the neck. He saw the three of them watching him over their shoulders with distaste. He'd meant to rile them, and he had. He now felt better. He had brought nothing with him but a flat leather case, and he opened it, as ostentatiously as he'd swigged the beer, revealing the packs of fresh thousand-dollar bills, smooth and green, prepared and accounted for him by his bank. How many people could afford to ask for a cool million in cash? These high-hats can? So can Lew Cask.

He took off his coat. He placed the case on the table, sat, and said arrogantly, 'So what are we waiting for? Thanksgiving Day? Let's play.'

VI

THE game of poker is forever associated with the motion-picture image of sweaty cowpokes sprawled about the table of some Western cattle-trail saloon, hips heavy with guns; you peer through the cigar smoke and you know that the sleepy-eyed gambler has a straight flush and a cocked weapon in his lap ready for a quick blast. Was it really like that in the old days? Who knows? Certainly nobody dies at the poker-table any more, though a history of cardiac thrombosis can still be as fatal as the blast of a gun. It is a fiercely eruptive game that sets the blood-pressure boiling and imperils the aged. Bluff is so much a part of the scene that the slightest twitch of a lip, the tiny throbbing of veins in the head as twin aces come up, can betray you. It can kill you. It can even bankrupt you.

It is not a game for gentlemen; certainly not for the dilettante, the academic Einstein who thrives lovingly on bridge.

Not being a gentleman, with a mental rating not much higher than that of a member of the Chamber of Deputies, the game fascinates me. How volatile it can be! As changeable as a woman. It seethes like a pan of rich stew. Players sit in for a hand, then drift out; new faces fetch new excitements, the pot fills up and empties; there is something endlessly refreshing about a game that starts on Saturday night and finishes with a few haggard insolvents and a heap of disputed IOUs on the table as Monday's cold grey dawn creeps in. I play with more discreet people, of course; we know our limitations and trust each other. But not too far.

And think of the amazing variations of the game! Five-Card Stud. Seven-Card Draw with Joker wild. Doesn't it conjure up visions of Jesse James in a smoky movie saloon? Spit-in-the-Ocean. (Yes, there *is* such a game.) Doctor Pepper. Who the good doctor was who gave his name to that variation I never found out. It is a dangerous game; strictly for chilled professionals. And when one comes down to it, that is what it is all about; the poker-addict has the immortal conviction that he *is* a professional. Cool, impassive, 007 with all his aces wild.

But this isn't the Middle-West of Jesse James; it isn't Dodge City, it is Paris, sophisticated, permissive Paris on a snow-blanketed Christmas Eve. And up in the hushed seclusion of the Alcazar a game is about to begin that would make history if the four players ever allowed a whisper of it to emerge; and they won't. There are some forms of human behaviour best kept hidden. The rich have to be forgiven a little unseemliness too. At least, everything seems set for a serene and enjoyable game! The Maharajah who owns the apartment spends more on its luxuries than he does on his tiger-hunts. Winter isn't permitted to enter; the place is as warm as the Costa Brava. The banqueting staff of the Crillon have furnished a buffet that wouldn't disgrace a royal wedding. The wines are all blue chips. And a distant bell tolls the advent of Christmas, spreading the eternal message of brotherly love and trust.

But Theo Parnassus finds it hard to love Lew Cask like a brother and Caesar Vinci would think it mad to trust him with a card out of sight. Gregor Kassem feels the weight of their disapproval and sighs to himself: this is going to be a veritable nightmare of a game.

He is right. It is. So they are all stripped for action, sitting about a table that was made for Napoleon, each with his personal leather case opened wide to reveal those flat packs of thousand-dollar bills. A million in this form takes up no more room than an overnight change. Theo Parnassus, as the senior citizen, the *doyen* of the four, will open up the game. He is Lorenzo the Magnificent who will not allow his civilized face to show his thoughts. Which are: this man is barbaric. I am soiled by his presence. These games are getting to be demeaning and this is the last I shall ever play. Caesar Vinci also thinks: watch this Mafia bastard like a hawk. *Madre mia*, look at those malevolent eyes. Gregor Kassem sighs again: it is only money and I would rather lose the odd million than lose my friends.

Listen to them. I can hear their brains humming, Lew Cask thinks. A man can split a gut hating them. So they don't love me. Who does? And who cares? I am rich, and when this game is finished I am going to be even richer. You hear that, Big-Pants Parnassus? I know what is going to happen to you tonight, and who is going to get all that money. I will split a gut laughing at you instead.

Theo Parnassus opens a fresh deck of cards and announces gravely, 'We play seven-card stud. Deal three cards, two down, one up. Dealer antes two thousand dollars. It is all right, Mr Cask?'

'All right with me,' Lew Cask shrugs.

'Caesar?'

'Perfect.'

'Gregor?'

'As usual, fine.'

'So we start.' Gregor Kassem has provided the chips. An ivory-worker in a bazaar in Smyrna fashioned them for him. Tilt the plaques to the light and you see the faint reflection of the heads of Roman emperors. Gregor Kassem isn't troubled by false modesty; he identifies himself with emperors. Theo Parnassus murmurs, 'Gregor, be so kind, the merest drop of champagne.' And so they begin.

Outside everything is still. The overnight fall of snow has muffled the city like a rug. The last rush of festive shopping is over; the traffic has died away; Paris is like a clock that has run down and will not be wound up until Christmas is done.

Go down in the lift and you have the uneasy sensation that you are disturbing the sleep of the opulent dead. The Alcazar is as silent as Pharaoh's tomb. Nobody is buried in it; but almost nobody breathes in it, either. Shout as you pass each floor and if you got a reply it could come only from the solitary senile lady in residence; she would probably ring furiously down to the desk to complain. The duchess likes the hush of the mausoleum. She no doubt expects to be in one very soon. She gets instant service from the temporary staff; Papa Miche and Willie Tobias have normally nothing to do but listen to the hollow creak of wood and marble, as if coffins are adjusting themselves to the night.

Tonight is different. Nobody should be in the tiny service room behind the desk, but intruders are gathering there, one by one. Dr Benes the first to arrive, wiping the pince-nez with nameless agitation. Stefan next. Pale. Very set in his expression. Somebody should tell him to leave his knuckles alone. Vic Diamond is expected with the lady Joey. She will at least light up the assembly with those youthfully exuberant eyes. Jean-Baptiste may be a little late; he has to slip away from hospital-call on his scooter. He will come, shiny-faced and sleepy-eyed; and don't be deceived for an instant. He is a determined young man. It sounds like the board-meeting of a raffishly enterprising business. But nobody is going to do any business until the chairman turns up. And, in fact, Sam Casanova is already outside.

He had just turned into Avenue Foch, sidestepping the slush spattered by a drifting taxi in bland disregard of the seasonal goodwill-to-all-men. The taxi-drivers of Paris bear goodwill to none. Dusk had fallen. He could hear the strains of a carol from a distant window. He should be decorating somebody's Christmas tree, wearing a funny hat, playing Santa Claus to somebody's kid, perhaps his own, and he recoiled with self-disgust as he approached the Alcazar, thinking dimly: when did I start to go mad? Too late to cut and run. He trudged by the parked cars, heavily shelved with snow, vaguely aware of one that was only thinly rimed with white, the hood steaming faintly catching the merest glimpse as he passed of a still figure behind the wheel, the gleam of a cigarette in the dark interior. It wasn't a night for dreamy contemplation. Two things registered with him: the wiped windshield and the clear view it afforded of the Alcazar. He shuffled on, head bent, slipping into the shelter of a portico as soon as he was out of the light of the street lamps.

He was early. He doubted if many of the others had arrived. He watched the car. He couldn't be seen, but he could grow both damp and abysmally cold. He looked up at the cynical stars. They must think him mad. He saw a car draw up by the Alcazar, nudge close to the kerb, and Vic Diamond and Joey get out. Then something happened. Vic Diamond froze, and not with cold, as he caught sight of the parked car across the street; he continued to stare at it intently, even taking a begrudging step in its direction; but Joey tugged at him with a whisper and drew him away. As he mounted the steps of the Alcazar he turned his head to look at it lingeringly again. Had he nodded in recognition? He followed Joey inside.

Well, now, Sam; do we spend our vacation here? The snow is so much cleaner and crisper in St Moritz. But who is the patient gentleman waiting in that car? And why? I think our friend Vic could tell us. An elderly couple came slithering along the messy street and Sam fell in behind, glancing fleetingly into the car as they passed. A thin Italianate face. A hatchet face. The man watched them emptily. A cigarette butt soared out of the window; a match spluttered inside as he lighted another. He was settling down for a long wait. Jean-Baptiste would be arriving from this end of Avenue Foch and Sam went on a little way, halting by the kerb. There was almost no traffic. Presently a hollow pop-pop sounded in the distance and Jean-Baptiste's scooter came sailing with a spray of slush out of the night, skidding close as Sam beckoned. He was fully uniformed for his ambulance; ready for a drunk, a seizure or an auto crash, whatever emergency Christmas Eve might bring. He might be spared for another emergency tonight.

He said cheerfully, 'M'sieu, my pony is not strong enough to give you a lift,' the grin fading as he stared keenly into Sam's face. 'Is something wrong?'

'Not yet. Walk along with me a little way. You see the seventh car parked over there?'

'The Renault? I see it.'

'I think it's there to watch us.'

'Has it been there long?'

'Not long enough to collect any snow.'

'What makes you so sure about it?'

'Do you trust your instincts?'

'Implicitly.'

'Then trust mine. It'll be hard behind us when the time comes for us to leave. It'd be better if it wasn't.'

Jean-Baptiste's face grew dreamy. He said with an understanding nod, 'I have a brother-in-law with a clapped-up truck. He is always ready to help a good cause.' As this one was. At least, for him. 'I think he would do it out of affection for me.'

'How much would his affection cost?'

'Could we say two thousand dollars?'

Brotherly love came dear. 'You'd pay him out of your own pocket, of course?'

'M'sieu,' Jean-Baptiste said reproachfully, 'we each have our own interests to protect. Would he have a long wait?'

Sam glanced at the lighted window high up in the Alcazar. 'It's in the lap of the gods. Why?'

'It is the eve of *Noël*. He would be parted from the bosom of his family. It would be a great wrench. Better say three thousand dollars. Shall I phone him now?'

'Yes.' Before he threw in the gasoline bill, too. Sam shrugged ironically. 'Have him here soon.'

'Guard my scooter for me, m'sieu.'

Jean-Baptiste vanished. He returned with a breezy nod. Sam wondered where he had phoned. 'At a *tabac* I know. My brother-in-law agrees. He has a charitable soul.'

And an eye for a lucrative deal. Sam beckoned. 'Go on in. I'll follow.'

He watched Jean-Baptiste putter ahead, prop his scooter on the steps of the Alcazar, and slip indoors without turning his head to glance at the car. The frigid wind skimmed a revolting surf off the slushy street; Sam shivered. Three thousand dollars for a clapped-up truck and not enough in it for me to mend these leaky shoes. Presently he walked briskly ahead and entered the Alcazar. Pity to defile the immaculate carpet. The warmth enveloped him like a tropical shroud. Papa Miche was bent over his desk. How worn he looked; the thick academic mane snowier than usual. He removed his shell-rimmed spectacles and whispered with an anxious glance at Willie, perched by the elevator, 'He is not too well.'

'What is it?'

'Nerves. The usual.' The ravages of Dachau catching up. Papa Miche, Sam thought, was beginning to look ravaged too. 'He'll be all right if he's needed.'

'They've all arrived?'

'In the back room. Willie,' Papa Miche called out.

'Yes, yes.' Willie came across. He said with a reassuring beam, 'Sam, don't look at me too hard.' The twitch was maniacal. 'It's just chronic. It doesn't mean a thing.' Sam heard himself sigh. He went into the crowded service room with Papa Miche and Willie, closing the door. And there they all were: the merchant adventurers.

Dr Benes glaring balefully about as if he despised the company he was in. Vic Diamond, burly and beautifully dressed, polishing his nails; but less assured than he seemed, for the hard muscled face had a glisten of sweat. Joey, peach-blossom Joey, with the dancing eyes. Always amused; perhaps when you were very young and luscious you could afford to laugh at life. Stefan tensely agog. Jean-Baptiste drowsing in the corner, his peaked cap tilted over his eyes. Papa Miche breathing heavily over Sam's shoulder, Willie Tobias twitching palpitantly behind. Are these my troops? This is the raw material of bedlam; I must be quite *quite* mad, Sam thought. 'All right,' he said. 'So now we wait. We just listen. We let it happen.' And he was praying: oh God, don't let it happen. He wondered if he had to wake Jean-Baptiste up. No, his hooded eyes gleamed. 'We can trust you to be on call?'

'Not to worry. Nobody dies on Christmas Eve. Tomorrow everybody drinks, they eat like gluttons, they drop all over Paris like flies. But tonight is going to be quiet.'

'Be ready.'

'My ear will be glued to the phone.'

'Stefan?'

'Shall I go now?'

'You'd better. You know what you have to do?'

Stefan protested breathlessly, 'Sam, you told me. The Garage Samaritaine you said. I'm to pick up the car you've hired. Is it so difficult?' They were sapping his confidence. 'It is really very simple. I *do* know what to do.'

'Park this end of the Pont d'Iéna and wait for us. That's all. Just wait. Flash your lights when you see us come by.'

'Sam, you told me that too.'

'And I'm telling you again,' Sam pressed his shoulder. There's no flesh on him; he's all bone, he thought with a pang. 'Stefan, *be* there. It's important.'

'Yes, yes.'

'So off you go.'

Stefan glanced at Papa Miche; the old man patted him encouragingly. Vic Diamond watched him go with unconcealed disgust.

'Goddam creep,' he said scathingly to Sam. 'You must keep your brains in your bum. You give that man a mission?'

'I trust him.'

'So do I. To foul it up. For Christ's sake, I wouldn't trust that ham-fisted crummie to find his way to the loo,' and Papa Miche said dreadfully:

'Hold your tongue.'

Vic Diamond turned to look at him with faint surprise. He stopped polishing his nails. Papa Miche glared back. 'You use that word too often. Crummie. It is not nice. *You* are not nice.' Here we go, Sam thought: I should have expected something like this. The old man panted, 'We thought we deserved something of life. Now I know what we deserve. Shame. That we should have to associate with people like you.' Dr Benes turned to Sam with a gasp of horror as if to say: what sort of talk is this? We are in business together. Stop him! Sam didn't think he could. 'Yes, yes, I know,' Papa Miche mumbled disdainfully as Vic Diamond stirred, 'if we were alone, if there were no witnesses, you wouldn't hesitate to, what is the expression? knock me off. I could come to terms with you if you were just an evil man. But you are incomplete. You are inhuman. There is something missing. You have no soul, only a cold substitute for one,' and now Papa Miche leaned forward with glittering eyes. 'I know where you keep it, too.' They all stared at him as if he were mad. 'I looked for the bulge in your coat, maybe in your belt. Not there. You know where it is? Your cold soul? Stuck in a strap inside your leg,' and Vic Diamond uttered the first soft growl.

'You've grown too many teeth. Maybe I should slap a few of them out.'

'Show them your leg where you keep your gun!'

'Gently, Papa.' Sam touched his arm.

The veined eyes filled with tears. 'He should not have called Stefan a crummie.'

'And he's going to apologize to you for it,' Joey said.

'Like hell,' Vic Diamond said.

'You are going to make an effort to behave like a gentleman. Just once in your life,' she said. She stood over him, ruffled and vivacious, like a windblown rose, eyes ashine. 'You will tell him you are sorry. And you will never call Stefan a crummie again.'

Vic Diamond said with a crinkled grin, 'I'll see him – ,' and the word he used was foul, though not by his standards. Probably not by Joey's, either. He must have been as surprised as Sam to hear her say vehemently, 'Wash out your grubby mouth,' as she slapped him stingingly across the cheek.

'Honey,' he said ruefully, 'that hurt.' He gave her a look of spasmodic rage. Sam wondered if he was going to hit her; he must have hit women before. He hoped he wouldn't have to do something about it. He was acutely conscious of the 'cold soul' strapped to the man's leg. Joey stood laughing at him. Vic Diamond's expression softened; he chuckled back at her, rubbing his cheek. 'All right,' he said carelessly to Papa Miche, 'call off the fight. I'm sorry.'

Papa Miche looked insulted. He went back to his vigil at the desk. Who knew? That solitary resident, the aged duchess, might ring down unexpectedly to wish him *bon Noël*, maybe to ask him what was going on in the outside world. Sam would hate to tell her. He went to the street door to peer out. The parked Renault was still there. Willie had returned to his perch by the elevator; he gave Sam a haggard look. This is a business for hardier souls, Sam thought. He went back into the service room. Dr Benes was pacing up and down in an agitated state; he still hadn't recovered from the shock of the affray. 'We are a rabble,' he burst out, fumbling with the pince-nez that were perpetually filmed. 'A disorderly rabble. I am mad to mix myself up with you. I am a highly respected physician, a man of affairs,' and he heard Jean-Baptiste chuckle softly. He glowered at him. 'There is nothing to laugh at. Go about your business.'

'Yes, *m'sieu le docteur*.'

'And stand by the phone. Don't stir from it. You are the one I shall call.'

'On guard.' Jean-Baptiste got up. He glanced curiously at Vic Diamond. He murmured, 'Do you really keep your gun inside your sock?' and Dr Benes made a muffled sound. He went out.

Sam sat in the corner. He drew a chair forward so that he could put up his feet. Dr Benes and Vic Diamond watched him fixedly. 'Nothing's going to happen for a few hours. I don't get enough sleep. Listen for the phone,' and he sighed off into the lightest doze, aware that Joey was studying him amusedly. She takes too many risks; one of these days somebody like Vic Diamond *is* going to hit her. I would like to be there.

The game was going badly. It had begun on a note of polite hostility; before they'd played many hands it had deteriorated sadly. By ten o'clock something so uncivilized had crept into it that Theo Parnassus was tempted to say to his friends, 'Let us stop it. This is enough.' In an active life that had begun in a Turkish slum and ended with more palaces than the ruling Medicis he'd rubbed shoulders with all kinds of men; government ministers, business adventurers and crooks. It wasn't always possible to distinguish between them. But never had he met a man as coarsely vindictive as this Lew Cask. He plays like a savage; he defiles the table, he thought. I shall have something terrible to say to Gregor when this unsavoury game is done.

Between deals Caesar Vinci watched Lew Cask as he might have watched an unbridled ruffian who, in an orderly society, would be behind bars. He is rich, he thought; he needs money like a hollow tooth; what puts him in such a rage? He and Gregor had been winning consistently. Theo Parnassus down somewhat; not too much. But Lew Cask was down a great deal and his face was grim. He counted out his shrinking stack of chips sourly, watching the massive pot with a disconcerting glaze in his eyes. Every time he threw in his discards he commented on the hand in Italian, which was Caesar Vinci's native language. And the epithets he used were vile. Caesar Vinci had to say to him at length, 'You do not sound very happy.'

'No.'

'Would you prefer to stop?'

'No.'

'We shall be glad to accommodate you if there is something you want.'

'I want you to hold your tongue. I raise you five thousand dollars.'

'As you wish.' Caesar Vinci was dealing five-card draw, deuces wild. He had a masterly hand. I do not want this man's money, he thought; but I would like to see him walk out of my life, stripped of his pants.

'You're too goddamned lucky,' Lew Cask said.

Caesar Vinci stiffened. 'What is that meant to imply?'

'Hold your horses. Christ's sake, you're so touchy. All I said was you're lucky.'

'How many cards do you want?'

'One.'

Silence. A sultry glow came into Lew Cask's eyes. He should not play poker, Caesar Vinci thought; his face talks too much. 'I up you another five thousand,' Lew Cask said.

'Your privilege,' Caesar Vinci said. He had the four aces. Unbeatable. He guessed from Lew Cask's lividly frustrated expression that he had four inferior kings. Too bad for the Mafia. He raked in the pot. He felt a sick tremor as Lew Cask crushed out his cigar and said carelessly, 'You play real rough. You and your chums give each other signals?'

'Yes,' Theo Parnassus said with a sigh. 'But not the kind of signals you think. Our eyes are saying to each other: what is this man doing here? He takes the pleasure out of our game.'

Lew Cask said with a tight sneer, 'You like me to dance? Make you laugh?'

'I will tell you what we would like. The gesture would be appreciated. We would like you to withdraw.'

'Something wrong with my money?'

'Money is of no consequence. It is an attitude of mind. We are not *en rapport*. You have asked us three times for a fresh deck of cards. I do not think it is because you are superstitious. The implication is distasteful. You make vague hints of cheating that in more elegant times would have had you called out. Thank God, nobody settles things with pistols any more. But if you cannot contain yourself, if you find it impossible to behave with refinement, it might be better to leave.' Well, Theo Parnassus thought, that is telling him; now he will surely spit. 'Have I offended you?'

'Yes.'

'So?'

'So play. I have a thick skin.'

Indeed he has; solid elephant hide, Gregor Kassem thought with a grimace. This is going to become an endless purgatory. But, for some inexplicable reason, it didn't. The whole mood of the game changed. Lew Cask began suddenly to play with an almost lustful recklessness as if he no longer cared how much he lost. The chips began a remorseless slide across the table; and not in his direction. It puzzled Gregor. When it was half an hour to midnight the *padrone* had lost a quarter of a million dollars and his eyes were very bright. For twenty minutes or so he played a more responsible game, taking in a nice pot with a very satisfactory straight flush. Then he was back on his crazy disaster course. It wasn't in character and Gregor Kassem was troubled.

But Caesar Vinci met his eyes with a shrug as if to say: maybe he's sick of it, too. The sooner he's cleaned out the better. Nobody's going to be saddened to see the back of this unpredictable oaf.

Don't worry, it's all coming back, Lew Cask thought. With a triple bonus. Now and again he darted a wolfish grin at Theo Parnassus. Wait and see what happens to you, my friend. But, of course, you won't see it; you won't be conscious. I'll see it and it'll be my pleasure.

At a minute to midnight he glanced at his watch with affected surprise. '*Madre mia*, look at the time. No wonder I'm hungry.' He threw in his discards and said briskly, 'How about supper? Let's eat.'

Theo Parnassus nodded tiredly. 'Of course.' He had had enough of these marathon games. They always left him with a queer prick of guilt; he supposed they were vaguely anti-social. He would never play another. This man, he thought, glancing at Lew Cask, has cured me of them for good.

But it wasn't quite all. Why was he so uneasy? Something had set the primitive Turk in him on edge. The display of so much money was barbaric; he closed his own leather case as if to shut its ostentation out of sight. At that moment he would have given the entire million to be back on his plane, heading for one of his villas in the sun. Corfu? Mombasa? Take your pick, Theo. First eat. The buffet looks good.

Breast of guinea hen. Glacéd pheasants, poussins in aspic, cold *boeuf à la mode*. A variety of delicate salads that Van Gogh might have yearned to paint. *Saucissons d'Arles*, tiny sausages that looked as if they wouldn't last seconds before they melted in the mouth. Compotes, strawberry tarts with whipped cream. And to crown them, hot-house grapes flown in from Belgium, bedded like dewy courtesans in ground cork. The Crillon people had done themselves well.

Caesar Vinci hastened to serve his friends. Gregor was an abstemious man; a little pheasant would do. All right then, if you insist; a glass of Lafitte Rothschild. An excellent year. Theo Parnassus had been made too fretful to eat much. A baby poussin in aspic. No more. So much that was luscious going to waste. Caesar's appetite, at least, was manly. And then they looked round. Where was Lew Cask? A penetrating odour issued from the tiny kitchen off the hall. Something hissed.

Gregor Kassem murmured wryly, 'What in God's name is it?' He sniffed.

Caesar Vinci was an Italian. He was familiar with the aroma.

'Pizza.' He closed his eyes with a sigh of despair. 'He has had his own fodder delivered. The man is mad on pizza and *gelati*,' he said.

Pizza and ice-cream. Gregor shook his head. It poisoned the Crillon's wondrous buffet with the smell. How could one enjoy the delicate flavour of pheasant with that burned haze of cheese and tomatoes and anchovies drifting in from the kitchen? Theo Parnassus put down his plate and went to the window with a muffled sound. What have I inflicted on them? Gregor shrank with guilt. 'It is an imposition. I think the man is enjoying it,' he said.

Yes, Caesar Vinci shrugged; I think so too. 'Theo,' he said gently, 'contain yourself. It won't take long. He plays so hideously, a few more hours and he will be gone.'

'Of course.' Theo stifled his disgust. 'I must be getting old. I let him outrage me.'

'Don't give him the pleasure of observing it. Suffer him. Here he comes.'

Lew Cask bustled in from the kitchen. The fumes preceded him. The pizza was effervescent; it still bubbled on the plate. In the other hand he carried a dish of his beloved *gelati*, a *Cassata Sicilienne*, studded with fresh cherries, that Vic Diamond had ordered for him. It was crisp from the ice-box. He propped himself against the Louis Quatorze bureau, chopping the pizza energetically like a hungry peasant. He watched the others blandly as he ate. 'Good,' he commented heartily, making smacking noises of appreciation, but nobody replied. You despise me? I despise you back, he thought. He would rile them a little more. He opened a bottle of beer, swigging it thirstily from the neck, and saw Theo Parnassus wince. Look at the afflicted aristocrat. How he suffers! Wait a while, *amico*; there's worse to come.

Barbarian. I mustn't let him molest me, Theo sighed. A glass of his favourite brandy would restore him. He went to the bar, searching the array of bottles; but everything was conspiring to discomfit him tonight. It wasn't there. Lew Cask, straining to listen, heard him mutter irritably, 'They have forgotten my Mastika,' and as Theo Parnassus reached testily for the phone to rebuke the desk the *padrone*'s heart seemed to swell suspensefully in his breast, his fork freezing half-way to his mouth. Pizza always gave him indigestion; but this time it made him belch with exultation. Now we're going to see a little action! The curtain is about to go up, he thought.

Midnight; well past midnight; and the phone rang at the desk, shattering the silence like glass. Gabriel's trump had sounded. It started a convulsion in the service room. Three hours of heavy nothingness had passed and Dr Benes came out of a doze with a shiver. Every bone was stiff. He reached blindly for the pince-nez that had slipped from his nose; without them he was undressed. The shrill insistence of the phone was terrible. Answer it! Vic Diamond lurched forward in his chair. Christ, there it goes. Had he dropped off? There was a bad taste in his mouth. He turned to Joey. She wasn't even aware of him. She was staring tensely at Sam Casanova lying loosely across two chairs. Vic Diamond muttered thickly, 'Wake the bastard up,' and the tired voice said, 'The bastard's awake.' Every joint rigid. Sam went to the door and looked into the hall.

The phone was ringing at Papa Miche's elbow. He sat watching it, frozen and fascinated, as if a hissing cobra had reared its head. It could have awakened the dead; and the Alcazar, as hushed as a sepulchre in the dead hours of the night, seemed a place of the dead. Willie Tobias stared at him tensely across the hall. Sam said softly, 'Answer it or go home.' Papa Miche looked round. Here's the moment of truth, Sam thought; he's started something rolling and he's wondering if there's still time to stop it. Not now, Papa. The others came crowding into the doorway. Sam was aware of the stench of animal fear; it came from Dr Benes just behind. Vic Diamond said brutally, 'Answer it, you goddamned creep. You want me to hit you?' and Papa Miche at last picked up the phone.

They could almost sense the dry scathing voice at the other end. Papa Miche nodded humbly as if he were looking Theo Parnassus in the face. 'Forgive me, m'sieu. It was ordered, of course. It arrived late. I will have it sent up . . .' and the metallic click of the phone chopped off his words. A very angry man up there.

Sam said, 'All right, Willie,' but Willie was gone. He was making himself ready. He emerged from the service room wheeling his trolley. Coffee for four, with the compliments of the house. Petal-thin cups, cream, sleek silver jugs, glistening trays of petits-fours, all on a great embossed dish. It couldn't *all* be silver? But silver was the meanest metal the Alcazar used. Willie had slipped into a starched white jacket. It made him look like a gentleman's valet, though no gentleman could endure that face in his valet for long. The upper part of it flickered as if the inner electric wiring had gone all wrong. And perhaps that was what was the matter with Willie; he had suffered enough at Dachau to ruin his electric wiring for life. On the trolley was the bottle of Mastika Sam had had ready for days. Glasses to help it to be drunk. 'Take it up, Willie,' Sam said, but Willie was already half-way across to the elevator. He turned and nodded. Willie, don't let us down. He looked dreadful. He went purring up.

Caesar Vinci opened the door for him. He glanced at the trolley; the smell of the coffee was fragrant. He beckoned coolly. 'Fetch it in.' Willie wheeled it into the hall. He would have gone farther into the big lounge, but Caesar peremptorily barred his way. Through the jamb of the doorway, as if he had been permitted a sliced glimpse of heaven, Willie saw a huge table littered with cards and chips. That celestial buffet, fit for the gods. But the man he knew as Lew Cask was eating off the bureau, and there was a curiously penetrating smell. Theo Parnassus came into the hall. He gave Willie an austere look; then his glance fell on the bottle and his face relaxed. Willie said breathlessly, as if he had climbed upstairs, 'It was unfortunate, m'sieu. Christmas, you understand. Everything is delivered late,' and while he was talking he was pouring out a glass of Mastika for Parnassus the god.

Theo said impatiently, 'It's all right. Just leave it.' He took the glass and the bottle. He saw the man staring at the tiny Raphael crucifixion that hung in the hall. The Maharajah who bought it was a Moslem who never let religious differences interfere with his artistic tastes. 'M'sieu, it is beautiful,' Willie whispered.

'Yes,' Theo nodded. That it was. He wished he owned it himself. But he couldn't take his eyes off Willie's palpitating face. 'Are you ill?'

'No, no, m'sieu.'

I am too harsh; I intimidate people, Theo thought. This man is afflicted. He pushed a few notes into his hand and ushered him out.

Willie descended in the lift. He returned to the service room. He said faintly, 'He took the bottle. I poured out for him.' Now something was going wrong with his voice; his face already felt fluid and totally out of control. I shall go mad, he thought. 'Two hundred francs,' he said confusedly, showing them the notes. 'You know how long it takes me to earn two hundred francs?' and Dr Benes gasped as if he was wasting time. Willie forced himself to go on. 'They are playing,' he sighed. 'Cards all over the table. They have stopped to eat. Such a strange smell. Is it possible? Pizza . . .'

'Yes,' Vic Diamond grunted. 'The *padrone*.' He shrugged.

And that was all. It was enough. Sam stared with anxiety into Willie's loosening face. He's done his stint; he's finished. We've squeezed what little vitality he had out of him like a sponge. He felt guilty. He said to Papa Miche, 'Open up one of the apartments for him. Let him lie down.'

'Sam, I can still . . .'

'Your part's done. I'll be back for you, Willie. Which one, Papa?'

'Number two at the head of the stairs. The Bolivian ambassador won't mind.' He might if he knew. Papa Miche led Willie upstairs.

And now it was just a matter of time. Only minutes maybe. There'd be a call from above; a signal of despair, and . . . Dr Benes couldn't stop whispering agitatedly to himself, walking up and down, so that Vic Diamond had to say to him coarsely, 'Will you for God's sake park your ass in a chair before you fall over my feet?' He had gone back to polishing his nails, that thick assertive man, but he was less confident than he seemed. There were beads of perspiration on his lip. 'Auguste,' Sam said kindly, 'settle down. You'll burn yourself out before you're needed,' and Dr Benes gave him an impassioned look. He's murdering himself with greed, Sam thought. And scaring himself to death at the same time. The combination could be fatal.

Sam now glanced at Joey. Her eyes brimmed with joy. Laughing girl. Not a frightened bone in her body; which was one of nature's primeval forces. Once handled, never forgotten. Papa Miche returned.

'He's blown out like a candle. He'll sleep a few hours,' he said.

Poor Willie. Sam put up his feet, couching himself for a nap. Dr Benes stared at him with bursting incredulity. 'How can you rest?'

How can I *not* rest? 'There's so much to be done.' But nobody was going to get any rest; the phone rang spasmodically. And quite astoundingly stopped. Silence. It held them with bated breath. Now it rang again; this time persistently. Sam said softly, 'This is the one. Let it ring a while.' He couldn't resist a shiver of apprehension: he rose stiffly, glancing at Joey, and she whispered, 'Not to worry. Everything is going to go well.' You guarantee it? She took his arm affectionately. 'I have great faith in you.' You and nobody else, Sam thought.

Willie's twitching face stayed with Theo Parnassus for a few moments after he had gone. He stood in the hall, holding the glass and the bottle, thinking: how does a man bear up under a shattering misfortune like that? Does it take a special kind of courage? Do I have it? He could see Caesar and Gregor chatting elegantly by the buffet, like two Roman senators at one of Lucullus's banquets, a glass of champagne in one hand, a morsel of caviare or pâté in the other, and he mused queerly: we do not know how lucky we are. They lived so securely behind the thick walls of wealth that no misfortune could get at them. Except death, of course. You couldn't keep him out for ever; in the end he broke through the walls. Though with all these spectacular medical advances a really rich man could hold him off for, say, five score years. By this time he had completely forgotten what had started this morbid train of thought. He dismissed it with a shrug. And that was the end of poor Willie.

He went into the lounge, nursing the glass, inhaling the pungent bouquet of the Mastika. What a rush of nostalgia it brought back! He had learned to drink it in Smyrna as a lad. It smells of anisette. You add a little water, which turns it milky; and that is as far as the resemblance to milk goes. It is not for children. It is for grown Turks and Greeks and Bulgarians with iron heads. The instant he entered the room Lew Cask's eyes rested on the bottle. He shivered with anticipation. It was almost like an orgasm; a gasping sweat, a trembling of the limbs, a sense of brutal satisfaction. Sex with Lew Cask was always brutal. Here it comes, he thought. Drink it, you bastard. Drink it! His eyes burned. I want to see you flop.

But as Theo Parnassus lifted the glass to his lips, Caesar, watching him indulgently, called out, 'Theo, we'll really have to start refining your tastes,' and Theo lowered the glass with a smile.

Shut up, Lew Cask fumed. Christ's sake. He glared at Caesar. Who asked you to butt in?

'Caesar,' Theo reproved him, 'They were drinking this when Alexander was born.'

'Alexander wasn't a gentleman. You are. Try a little of this Veuve Clicquot.'

'Woman's tipple.'

'Theo,' Caesar said, pretending shock, 'that's as near to blasphemy as you'll ever get,' and Lew Cask closed his eyes.

Jesus God, he thought frustratedly. Will you dry up? He felt suffocated. Let the man down it. Drink, you rich Turk. Drink, drink!

'You stay with champagne. I'll stay with my Mastika,' Theo said. 'It's food and inspiration, it's fire in my veins,' raising the glass, so that Lew Cask thought with tremulous relief: at last. Here we go. Just one quick slug, friend, again uttering a baffled gasp as Gregor Kassem, studying the scattered cards on the table, called out, 'Theo, that was a powerful hand you threw away.' Theo Parnassus put down the glass and went interestedly across.

Are they playing me for a sucker? Wog, shut up. No inquests. Let him take it, Lew Cask thought. He'd finished the pizza; he wiped the greasy crumbs from his mouth, reaching for the dish of *gelati*, spooning it up, crunching the delicate cherries, rumbling

abusively in his throat. He watched Gregor Kassem riffle through
the discarded hand.

'Look,' he was saying, 'two jacks up. Not bad. It deserved a call.'

'All it deserved was a busted flush. See what Caesar had. Pair of
deuces?'

'Yes.'

'King and a queen?'

'Large as life.'

'Gregor,' Theo patted him fondly, 'don't take up poker as a profession.'

'I won't.' Gregor grinned. 'Just the same,' he mused recklessly,
'I'd have risked a quick dive in at the deep end.'

'And finished up in an empty pool with a broken neck.'

Let me break it for him, Lew Cask thought. He hardly knew what
he was doing; they'd got him so much on edge. He champed wetly
on the ice-cream. One of the cherries split; it tasted bad; it seemed to
squirt bitterly in his mouth. Normally he would have spat it out,
but he was so engulfed with suspense and rage that he swallowed it
heedlessly, spooning away at the *gelati* with loud sups. He must have
been mumbling thwartedly to himself for he was suddenly aware
that they were watching him stiffly, as if he had gone out of his
mind.

As he had. They had got him really mad. And then he saw Theo
Parnassus lift the glass to his lips with a shrug, throwing back his
head to drain it in one swift gulp, and his mind flooded with joy. It's
done! Rich Turk, you have taken it, he thought. Now flop. He
watched him gloatingly; already he could see his features blurring;
and yet something was very wrong. It was his own vision that was
clouding. He put out his hands to make a violent protest; his elbow
sent the dish of *gelati* crashing to the floor, and as a great darkness
welled about him his mind screamed out with horror: it is me, me,
me. I am the one they have chosen! How can that be?

That Vic! I am betrayed. Vic, I will follow you to the ends of the
earth for this, and it was the last rational thought he had. He was
toppling. He fell heavily, but without pain, for he was unconscious
before he hit the floor.

What happened in the Maharajah's apartment that awful instant?
Nothing. Simply nothing. They froze. Use your imagination a little.
See for yourself. Theo Parnassus is staring with disgust at the *padrone*
gasping stertorously on the carpet as if he is indulging in some kind
of revolting joke. But there is nothing funny, nothing remotely

decent, about the gruesome sounds that are issuing from his throat. Theo detests the man as a moral obscenity; he shrinks from the mere thought of having to go over and touch him. For Lew Cask's eyes are fixed blindly on the ceiling; the spasms are terrible; and suddenly his body grows limp, there is still a lot of twitching but the dreadful gasping doesn't stop. What, in God's name, has pole-axed him? Gregor Kassem's face is a study in bewilderment. He murmurs, 'Nobody laid a hand on him,' as if it must be some ghostly influence that has entered the room. He doesn't quite know what to do. He glances uncertainly at Theo Parnassus. But there is no help there. His face is wrinkled with dismay. They are 'money men', of course; they are used to finance, not people; they employ hordes of aides to shield them from such ugly incidents and there is nobody here to turn to.

Only Caesar perhaps. He is the practical man of the three; he has come up through the factory floor. But his face is stark. One can almost hear him gritting his teeth. He stares at his friends with a sigh and goes over to Lew Cask and kneels by his side.

What can he do? He takes hold of one of the flabby hands that is flapping like a decapitated chicken's wing. It is cold and sticky; but that is only *gelati* from the dish he sent flying across the room in his spasm. The *padrone*'s face is going the blue-white colour of lard; as sweaty as a death-mask. And that is an awful association. Caesar gives his friends a haunted look. He lifts an eyelid, but there is no sight behind it; the eye glares at him emptily and he lets go of the lid at once. *Mamma mia*, he thinks, reverting to the vernacular of his childhood, we have a volcano here in this room. Ready to blow up. He has seen battered bodies on the racing track, he has seen dying men twitch and grunt like this.

And that is how it was when Theo Parnassus found his voice and said to him tiredly, 'How bad is he?'

'Bad enough.' Caesar Vinci shrugged. Didn't he have eyes? He found himself sweating. *Madre di Dio*, what are we going to do? He got to his feet.

Gregor Kassem muttered, 'What hit him?'

'Why ask me?' All I know is what has hit *us*. You. You are the one who unloaded this Mafia monstrosity on us. Caesar gave him a hard stare. You and I are going to have a little private quarrel tomorrow. Only God knows what tomorrow is going to bring.

Trouble. That's for sure. We may never live to see the end of this.

'Caesar,' Theo began painfully . . .

'All right. So I'm hot and bothered,' Caesar said. 'The man is sick. Some kind of seizure. See for yourself.' Listening to him was enough. 'Jesus God,' he whispered. 'He will go out on us.' The throat seemed to be passing air with the noise of a strangulated balloon.

And already they are blaming me, Gregor thought. Who could know that the malevolent creature had a tricky heart? All his evil life he has been avoiding bullets and he has to drop on us with a dish of ice-cream in his hands. Fate must be laughing her head off; the cynical bitch.

'Get him up off the floor.'

'No, don't move him. Let him lie where he is. A pillow and blankets, Gregor. Quickly.'

'Of course.' He hurried into the bedroom for them. Together they lifted the sweaty head and pillowed it. They tried getting a little brandy past the clenched teeth; it dribbled uselessly down the chin. Caesar had opened his shirt. What a hairy chest he had. They draped him with a blanket. What more could they do? They stood back distressfully, watching the human machine misbehave.

The gasping, at least, was dying down. Even the jerking of the limbs had subsided; it was as if Lew Cask was tired of the energetic performance he had been giving and was ready for a nap. He snored thickly. The gross Sicilian face had loosened; lying there like a stricken bull, the big cold eyes closed, so that one no longer had to flinch from the bitter glare, he didn't look much like the Mafioso chief that he was. Gregor could only think: how ugly he is. And then his head turned sharply. Caesar had gone to the phone.

He lifted the receiver. Before he could speak Theo Parnassus was at his side, pressing it back on to the hook.

This was when it rang spasmodically at the desk: just once. When Sam Casanova knew that the really important ringing was yet to come. And come it did. But first Theo Parnassus had to say passionately to Caesar Vinci, 'What are you doing?'

'He needs a doctor.'

'Caesar, think.'

'You know what could happen?'

'I know what could happen to us.' Who would recognize the proud, imperturbable Theo Parnassus? He didn't know how hard he was squeezing Caesar's arm. 'A doctor means questions. Perhaps . . .'

'The police?'

'Yes, the police. At least, the press.' No wonder he looked as if a hard fist had hit him over the heart. 'Nothing could stop it leaking out. Caesar, we are household names. We should be butchered to make newspaper headlines.' He averted his eyes from Lew Cask's livid face. 'To be found consorting with this social leper . . .' his voice thickening off. The word 'social' conjured up dreadful spectres for them both. Theo's wife was the daughter of a royal prince at the Shah of Persia's court. Unendurable! Caesar's face began to look like worn grey leather. His wife's family, the noble Orsinis, as proud as Lucifer, would publicly disown him; that revengeful old horror, the *marchese*, still stinging from his last rebuke, would give tremulous thanks to God. Gregor, Gregor, what have you done to me? I have spent a lifetime building a great arch of honour, and you have kicked away the coping stone and brought me crashing down. And, of course, I am going to be what the Americans call the fall-guy, Gregor thought. The same brutal fist that had hit Theo would now hit him. He was a member of a rigid Moslem sect that would look on the escapade – they would use a blacker word for it – as a moral affront. Oil revenues were involved! What could be blacker than that?

Had the figure on the carpet stopped . . . ? No, still breathing. 'The man is very ill.' Gregor licked dry lips. He thought Theo looked ill, too.

'You think so? He sounds better already.' He didn't. Much worse. 'Just listen. How quiet he is.' The dead were quiet, too. Theo struggled to speak. It was a losing battle. 'If we give him time to recover . . .'

Caesar said roughly, 'He needs a doctor.'

'Perhaps a few minutes . . .'

'A doctor. Now.'

'Of course, you are right,' Theo said with a sigh, finally admitting defeat. Caesar stared at him. The brown wrinkled face had aged ten years in as many minutes. I don't feel any younger, either. Theo, I'm sorry. The risk's too terrible. It has to be done. He glanced tensely at Gregor. As for you . . . but first the phone. He picked it up.

It rang at the desk. Persistently now. It was when Sam Casanova said with a shiver of apprehension, 'This is the one. Let it ring a while.' They let it ring. Caesar ground his teeth. It was late; perhaps even the night staff needed sleep. A husky voice finally answered. The old desk clerk with Einstein's professorial mane of hair. Did I wake him up? Caesar was too impatient to let him speak. 'Somebody here is ill. Get a doctor quickly . . .' while Theo and Gregor strained to catch the tinny murmur coming over the wire. Caesar cut it short, 'Don't mumble.' He was breathing hard as if he had

had to run a hundred kilometres to find a phone. *'Get* one. Fast.'
And slammed it down.

Now relax? How could he? 'It may be hard to find a doctor on
Christmas Eve,' he sighed. He looked at his watch; midnight long
gone. In fact, it was already Christmas Day. And nothing to do but
wait. He slumped into a chair. Nobody spoke. They were all watching the *padrone* lying under the blanket. It was like sitting in at a
wake, except that the normally silent witness was still terribly vocal.
The room throbbed with the slow snarl of his throat. He was probably the least worried man in the room. And in a little while, God
help us, even the few worries he had might be gone for good.

A tap on the door. Caesar sat up with a start. So soon? He went to
open the . . . *Mamma mia!* What am I thinking of? He froze. In
their preoccupation with the *padrone* they'd almost forgotten the
evidence of the night's foolish debauch. It littered the table like a
ghost at the feast; the cards and the poker chips, the four leather cases
stuffed with Midas's contribution to the megalomaniac splurge. He
shivered. Money makes you big-headed; how indiscreet we've been.
'Gregor,' he said harshly, and Gregor jerked out of his doze. He
hustled the leather cases into the Louis Quatorze bureau, locking it
and putting the key in his pocket. Four million dollars disappeared
as easily as they had been drawn from the bank. Caesar swept the
cards and the poker chips under a cushion on the couch, covering
them up. They looked at each other guiltily. Both too shocked to
speak. Caesar went hastily to the door.

It was the old desk clerk with the silvery hair. He said breathlessly, 'We have been lucky, m'sieu. A doctor will be here in
minutes.' He was making anxiously to come in. 'If there is something I can do . . .' and Caesar had to elbow him back. Rudely.

We want no unofficial noses poking into this. 'Nothing. Just the
doctor. Send him up the instant he comes.'

'I have rung the manager . . .'

'You have *what*?'

The old man shrank from the retort. He said humbly, 'M'sieu, it
was my duty. I have fetched him from a Christmas party. He is
coming at once. You can rely upon him to . . .'

'He isn't needed!'

But he was here; like it or not. The lift whined up. It stopped at
the floor and a man wearing a tuxedo under a light coat emerged.
Caesar thought savagely: we're going to be knee-deep in witnesses!
A solitary doctor is all we want. Especially one who is corruptible.
We shall have to tempt him sorely when he comes. He watched the

manager approach. He was yawning faintly; was he that tired? Christmas parties were apt to be a bore. He touched the desk clerk's shoulder lightly and said, 'Go back to the desk. I will see to things here,' and the old man bowed deferentially and went. Caesar looked him over as they waited for the lift to descend. Youngish for his job; he would have expected a place like the Alcazar to be run by a sleek old *boulevardier* wise in the ways of the world. Better tailored, too. Something vaguely unrefined about the man . . . what was it? The tuxedo didn't quite fit. Well, it was the way business was moving these days; everybody wanted accountant types. A sharp eye for a balance sheet and less emphasis on dress. Does he know me? I think he does.

The manager said briskly, 'Must we stand in the corridor, M'sieu Vinci?' and Caesar could have spat. I'm identified for a start!

'I'm sorry you were disturbed.'

A cool smile. Almost a gentleman. 'It was a very dull party. Don't be upset.'

'There was no need to call you away.'

'I would be angry if he hadn't. My staff have their orders. I'm to be kept in touch with everything day and night.'

'Just the same. I'm sorry.' How am I to get rid of him? Caesar turned to close the door. 'Now if you'll forgive me . . .'

But he was being detained by the lightest touch of his arm. 'The desk reported that you asked for a doctor. With great urgency.'

'Did I?'

'I may be able to stop him. Would you like me to?'

'No.'

'I have a record of your telephone message. Would you care to read it?'

'No.'

'Then what is wrong?'

'Nothing. Just a touch of colic . . .'

'Not M'sieu Parnassus I hope?' Oh, God. Caesar winced. He knows Theo is here. 'M'sieu Kassem perhaps?' Gregor, too. Caesar had the feeling that they were both listening uneasily behind the door. He planted his back hard against it. Nobody is coming in. How much more did the man know?

Enough. 'It is two o'clock in the morning,' he said with a sigh. 'Let us not waste time. We have called out Dr Benes for you. He is consultant registrar at the Hospital of St Germain-des-Prés. A very important man. He would prefer to spend the night of *Noël* with his family. I wouldn't like to think he has been called out at this hour for nothing.' A pause. No offence meant. 'Even for very rich and eminent men.'

Caesar bit his lip. I will have the man fired; but, of course, he wouldn't. Too much would come out. He said stubbornly, 'Good night.'

'I'm not sure it is. I wonder if it isn't going to turn out a bad one,' the manager said. 'M'sieu, with all respect, I have duties of my own. I have the amenities of the Alcazar to protect.' He was coming close. 'You are the Maharajah's guests. He would be very angry with me if I allowed anything to embarrass you.' Caesar felt the man lean on him. Belly to belly. God in heaven, is he pushing me out of the way? 'If somebody is ill . . .'

'Nobody is . . .'

'Then we shall see, shall we not?' And he had the door open. And he was in. Theo and Gregor waited stiffly in the hall. The manager said with dry relief, 'I am happy to see both of you well.' He went on into the lounge. And there stopped short, staring down at the *padrone*; not quite sure whether he was in the presence of life or death. Even Caesar was no longer sure. The manager turned to look at him with a sardonic twist of his lips. 'Not just colic?'

'No.' It was Theo who spoke. He sighed.

Caesar, he thought, signalling him with his eyes, tread warily. For God's sake, don't provoke him. He holds our lives in his hands.

He watched the manager kneel by the *padrone*. He flicked the blanket aside; lifted an eyelid, felt the probably chilled skin. He put his ear very close to his mouth and now he was the one who sighed. He looked up grimly. 'His pulse isn't good.'

Theo muttered, 'But he's . . . ?'

'Alive? Only just. The doctor will soon be here. I hope he will be in time.'

He rose. Theo thought: now he's going to ask, 'Who is the gentleman?' and nobody's going to tell him. Not right away. Not at all if we can avoid it. First of all we have to know: is he going to be our friend? Meaning 'bribable'. I doubt it, Theo thought. He had the impression of a rough careworn face, shrewd eyes, a suggestion of something peremptory . . . as if the man would put up with nonsense for just so long. Theo took a light shivery breath. He's going to have to be patient. He can have no idea what is involved.

Sam thought: they're weighing me up. Wondering if I can be bent. Friend Parnassus would offer me one of his shipping lines if he could slip out from under. Caesar Vinci, who likes direct action, would prefer to have me banged up. Fatally if need be; but of course there isn't time. Gregor, the Levantine, would draw me aside so that we could haggle tenaciously like traders in a bazaar, settling for say . . . two hundred thousand? In gold. All of it untaxed. I hope they won't tempt me too far. In the meantime they're waiting for me to ask:

'Who is the gentleman?' And Sam asked the question.

He got no response.

'You don't *know* him?'

Caesar looked at him coldly, woodenly, wiping the sweat off his fingers behind his back. You'll sweat a lot more copiously before dawn comes, Sam thought. And there'll be no chance to have me banged up.

'A friend of the Maharajah?'

Theo grimaced. Parnassus, your wife will kill you. What have you done? You have destroyed yourself.

Sam said dryly, 'A vagrant walked into the Alcazar? Is that what you expect me to believe?' They didn't. But they were mute. We'll have to make a little conversation, Sam thought. He moved idly about the room.

He picked up the spattered dish of ice-cream. 'Messy.' He glanced meaningly down at the *padrone*. 'Our friend?' And still nobody spoke. He sniffed at a plate on the bureau. 'Pizza,' he murmured disbelievingly, wrinkling his nose. He turned to look at the Crillon's sumptuous buffet. 'How odd.' He removed the plate from the bureau as if it were an offence to a lovely piece of Louis Quatorze. I know the man who makes these things, he thought. I also know the man who cut a spare key for Papa Miche. And it's all in there; every dollar of the four millions. His instincts vibrated sympathetically as he passed.

He paused by the couch. A card protruded between the cushions. He lifted one of them and gazed thoughtfully at the sprawl of playing cards and chips. He held one of the embossed chips up to the light. Beautiful. 'Poker?'

'Why not?'

'With a stranger? A man with no name?'

'Yes,' Caesar said savagely. 'A vagrant off the streets.'

'Who is he?'

'It isn't your business.'

'The Maharajah is my friend. Anything that involves him is my business. If it threatens the good name of the Alcazar that makes it my business, too.'

Nobody could see any immediate threat to the Alcazar; but the man had keen eyes, probably an even keener nose for a dubious

132

situation, and something was beginning to smell perceptibly here. Caesar, Theo thought with anguish, be still. Do you have to be so militant? We are close to the precipice; one nudge from this man and we are all over the edge.

The manager said evenly, for the second time, 'Who is he?'

Caesar stared at him. The hollows of his eyes were very dark. 'Don't push us too hard.'

'Better me than the others.' Meaning the police? Theo thought he did.

Dear God. 'Caesar,' he begged, 'let it be . . .' but Caesar was beyond control. His arrogance was monumental. He'd risen to stupefying wealth from the gutter of Turin, and now and again, under terrible stress, he reverted to the language of the gutter. They can really make the air smoke in Turin. I remember hearing him, years back, at the Siena Grand Prix, cursing insufferably while his crew changed a wheel and they all stopped to listen to him with awe. It was a long time since anybody had goaded Caesar like this. He stared white-gilled at the manager, abusing him softly, and the least offensive word he used was *bastardo*. Theo recoiled.

Stop it, stop it! Can't you see that the man is trying to help?

The manager glanced at him with faint surprise as if he expected better of the elect of the earth. He stooped again over the *padrone*, his fingers slipping quickly through his pockets, and Theo leaned close to see. What would he find? An airline ticket, a wallet roll fat with bills, a passport. American green. The manager riffled through it pensively and glanced up. Theo was the one he spoke to. Presumably he thought him a civilized man.

'The name's Lew Cask. A citizen of Seattle . . .' his eyes narrowing. Theo heard him mutter, 'Now why should the name ring a little bell?' He was struggling to think. 'No, of course,' he said to himself, 'it isn't possible . . .' but he rose, still holding the passport. There was a tap on the door. He went into the hall. 'Come in, doctor,' Theo heard him say, and a thin pasty-faced man wearing old-fashioned pince-nez entered; agitated and maybe angry, certainly out of breath. They had brought him out in such a hurry so late at night. 'This is Dr Benes,' the manager said, glancing with faint disdain at Caesar as if to say: behave yourself. You may need a doctor, too.

Dr Benes peered about. Beaky and petulant. He stripped off his overcoat and a thick muffling scarf; underneath the jacket Theo could see striped woollen pyjamas. The emergency hadn't even given him time to dress. His eyes rested with astonishment on the buffet. He glared at them, one by one, as if disgusted with so blatant a display of wealth. A Communist. Let him get the *padrone* up off his back, Theo thought, and I don't care if he's as Red as Karl Marx. The doctor got down. He straddled the *padrone* with his knees. He began a quick professional process; the bony hands tested the pulse, the cold skin, lifting the eyelids; then out with the stethoscope. While he listened he stared glassily into Theo Parnassus's eyes. Does he know me? Perhaps. So many people do. The doctor grumbled heavily under his breath. Worried? Who wouldn't be? Theo felt his own blood begin a convulsive beat; he may soon be looking me over too.

The doctor finally said, 'It was sudden?'

'Very.'

'No scenes? No excitement? Nothing to provoke it?'

If spite and vindictiveness were excitable, yes. The kind of scenes only a vicious poker-player would create. The less said about that the better. 'We were eating,' Theo said.

'His condition is bad.' The doctor opened his bag. A hypodermic glinted. Gregor flinched. He was a very sensitive man. The manager, observing it, beckoned to the bedroom. 'It would be better if you waited in there.' The three retired next door. Theo left it slightly ajar.

He could just see the doctor stooped over the blanketed *padrone*. The manager bent beside him. They were whispering together. Theo couldn't hear what was being said. It was fortunate that he couldn't. He would have been very confused. Sam was murmuring to Dr Benes, 'He's all right?'

Dr Benes mumbled testily, 'He isn't in the best of health.'

'But it's going the way you said?'

'Yes, yes. Don't raise your voice.' The doctor panted, wiping the dampness from his pince-nez. 'The breathing's shallow. It'll soon be almost imperceptible.' Hardly a flutter now. Sam looked into the empty babyish face of Lew Cask. What mother wouldn't want to disown him? How much better a place the world would be if the baby monster had never been born. 'He's a very strong man. He's slipping into a deep coma but it won't last as long as I thought.'

'How long?'

'Two hours.'

Sam caught his breath. 'It doesn't give us much time.'

'It's as much as you're going to get.'

'And then?'

134

'He'll wake up with a raging headache. He'll be a very bad-tempered man.'

'What's that you're injecting?'

'Glucose. Are they watching? It'll do him no harm and it won't do him much good.'

Sam rose. 'Don't sweat so much. Nobody trusts doctors who sweat.' He was aware that the three men in the bedroom were watching. He would give them something to hear. He went to the phone, ostentatiously studying the passport, and dialled. He guessed that the strain on their scruples would be insupportable; one of them would listen in on the bedside extension. It was Gregor, the Levantine, who did.

He entered the beginning of the conversation. An irate sleepy voice was saying, 'Jesus God. You know what time it is?'

'Eddie, I wouldn't ring you if it wasn't important.'

'What in hell's important on Christmas Eve? It's blasphemous, goddammit. Sam, I'll put a curse on you if you don't let me get back to bed.'

'Is the name Lew Cask familiar?'

'You're kidding, of course.'

'I am?'

'Oh, come on now. Where were you raised? Mafia, man. Big chieftain, big West Coast clan.'

'Yes?'

'What do you want?' A sneeze. 'His police blotter?'

'Briefly.'

'Two gaol terms. Extortion and bodily assault. Maybe three. Hell, my mind's mushed. Ducked an arraignment for murder. Grand Jury impending. Don't introduce friend Lew to your mother.' Another sneeze. A woman was complaining frustratedly. 'Keeping strange company, aren't you?'

'I'm not involved. There are others.' Which of them was listening in? Sam had caught the faint click as the conversation began. It was all for their benefit. 'Eddie, go back to bed.'

'Do me no favour.'

'Do her the favour. I can hear her screeching behind.' He put down the phone. He could imagine the ferment going on next door. He gave the guilt and the distress time to intensify. Then he went into the bedroom, closing the door quietly behind him. He tossed the passport grimly on to the bed.

'You listened, of course?'

Caesar said between his teeth, 'Did you think we wouldn't?'

'I don't know. I don't know what goes on in the minds of people like you.' Did anybody? Except super-billionaires? Sam looked them over scathingly, as if lost for words. And he wasn't; he had to be careful. Too many words were bubbling to his lips. 'What sort of people *are* you? Sick? Perverse? Wilful?' He said, almost wearily, 'To defile the Maharajah's hospitality,' glancing back at the door behind which Lew Cask lay. 'It's the ethics of social bandits. What possessed you?' but it was like talking to ghosts. No sound but a husky creak from Theo Parnassus's chest.

'A friendly game of poker with the Mafia,' he said with a sigh of distaste. 'To fetch a criminal obscenity like that into the Alcazar.' It was the major crime. 'A murderer. An extortioner. The Christmas Eve touch makes it nice. What were the table stakes?' he inquired wryly. 'Police graft? Protection money?' Piling it on a little; never mind. They'd been caught, as the Parisians would say, *tout nu*. With their pants down. Caesar made a belligerent move, but the sweat on his face was from anxiety, rather than rage, and in any case Theo Parnassus clamped a hand on his arm and said harshly, 'Enough.'

Almost. But not quite. 'The Maharajah won't forgive you. You've brought the Alcazar into disrepute.' Unforgivable, too. 'And I *still* don't understand you,' Sam said. 'You're such eminent men. You're top brass. When you're not running world economics, you can't pick up a social glossy but one or other of you's dining out or ski-ing or basking in the sun.' Yachts like destroyers. Who could understand them? 'Didn't you *care*?'

Theo Parnassus cared. He stared at Sam. Gregor Kassem also watched him intently. He was thinking: let him work off his head of steam. Then we'll begin to talk. In terms of money. It's the great healer. But the manager was shaking his head with a faint cold smile, as if reading his intention, and Gregor wondered with a chill of horror: is it possible that we have come up against an incorruptible man?

'No excuses,' Theo Parnassus said wearily to Sam. 'But nothing happened quite the way you think.' He glanced sidelong at Gregor. It didn't, did it? You sprang the *padrone* on us. 'We mustn't overdo it,' he went on to Sam. 'He has a good doctor with him . . .'

'The best.'

'He will recover.' And a voice behind them said, 'No, he will not.' The doctor stood in the doorway. His face glistened with perspiration. He was wiping his pince-nez passionately, glaring at them as if they were asking more of him than they would ask of God. He said harshly, 'He will not recover. He is dead,' and Caesar recoiled as if he had been hit in the face. Gregor sucked in his breath. Sam couldn't see Theo's face; he had turned away; but he knew that in that moment of distress he was wishing that he, too, was dead.

VII

DR BENES now held the stage. It was a terrible predicament for
him, for he was quite a terrible actor. A very good doctor, mind you;
I still let him treat me for such minor ailments as migraine. The odd
cold in the head. You can trust his medical judgment, if not his
professional ethics, once you get over the slight nausea induced by his
physical presence. Apart from being the most dishonest, he is quite
easily the most excitable man I ever met. Agitation throws him
into a panic. Panic makes him sweat. In torrents. And he smells.

It develops certain nervous peculiarities. He brandishes his pince-
nez wildly. He can suffer an actual trauma. He glares about accus-
ingly as if he is being robbed. In all the years I have known Dr
Benes nobody has ever succeeded in robbing him of a sou. Money
obsesses him. He clings to it like a leech.

Still an excellent doctor. And when for the second time he bent
over Lew Cask, checking the thready but regular pulse, the almost
imperceptible whisper of his breath, he could gauge exactly how
long it would be before the *padrone* woke up. With that anticipated
insufferable headache and the attendant spasms of rage. No more
than two hours; and it wasn't enough. The man had a fearful
reputation. Murder was his least fault. Dr Benes's eyes glazed with
anxiety. Time was running out on them like water through a sieve.
Too much remained to be done.

He had just rung Jean-Baptiste for the ambulance. He had got
through in thirty seconds; but every one of them, as he clutched the
phone with perspiring hands, weighed on him like lead. He was
aware of the drum-drum of his heart. Answer! Then Jean-Baptiste's
voice said softly, 'Speak up.'

'What?'

'I just answered you. Twice. What's going on?'

'It's done! Now for God's sake . . .'

'Doctor, are you sweating again?'

'Don't speak to me like that!'

'Control yourself. Everything's going to be all right. Is the
patient . . . ?'

138

'He's ready. Waiting. Get out to the ambulance and be here fast.'
'I'm on my way.'
'We're short of time . . .'
A chuckle. 'Look out of the window.'
'*What?*'
'You hear the siren? It's me parked outside.'

Humorist. I hate him. Dr Benes put down the phone. He had forgotten to flick the blanket back over the *padrone*'s face. The semblance of death. He did it; and that was when the premonition of doom overwhelmed him. The passionate certainty that everything was going to go wrong. Organized chaos! He had been left alone in the room with the presumption of death. And standing there, surrounded by antiques that museums could scarcely afford to buy, with that fine Utrillo hanging in the corner (who but a tiger-hunting Maharajah would use a Utrillo as a casual piece of decoration?) he thought: I should never have done it. His pince-nez misted. He had to physically resist the impulse to pick up his bag and run.

Something held him. He couldn't take his eyes off the Louis Quatorze bureau; it froze him. Not ten paces away from him lay wealth, negotiable wealth in hard currency, on the scale one usually associated with national budgets. Many an undeveloped country would regard four millions as a windfall. All in four leather cases, behind those delicately veneered doors. Locked, of course. If indeed it was there. And his mind said: I know it, I know it. It is! He found himself approaching the bureau hypnotically. There was no-body to watch him but the *padrone*, and he was deeply preoccupied with his coma. Dr Benes touched the bureau, holding his breath, tugging gently . . .

And could have died of a nervous tremor; there was a hard rap on the hall door. Another. Quite sharp. His lungs emptied with a childish ululation; a gasp of shock. He drew back shudderingly, mopping his face, as Sam Casanova came swiftly out of the bedroom and whispered, 'Auguste, go away from the bureau,' as he went to the hall. Theo Parnassus, Caesar Vinci and Gregor Kassem had followed him into the doorway. They were staring with intense horror at the *padrone*. It was the first time they had seen him with his face covered up.

What was Papa Miche doing outside? His face was creased with alarm. Dr Benes caught his hasty gabble, 'She is coming up . . .'
'Who is?' The doctor was surprised to hear himself cry out.
'The duchess.'

What was he talking about? 'What duchess?' Sam listened gravely. He let Papa Miche speak.

'The Duchess di Ravenna. She lives in the apartment below. Something is going on, she says. It woke her up. A commotion. Banging. The lift going up and down. She keeps shouting, the Maharajah is away, nobody should be here . . .'

But we *are* here, Dr Benes sighed. It was bound to go wrong; I knew it. My instincts never lead me astray. He stared distractedly at Sam. Do something! The three tycoons were listening distressfully by the bedroom door. Sam turned to them and said softly, 'Please go back. There's no need to be seen,' and they retired, making husky sounds of gratitude, closing the door.

The lift was whining up. Papa Miche went along the corridor to meet it. Now I must un-involve myself. I must separate myself from this business quickly, Dr Benes thought. We're in deep trouble. He gave Sam a frantic look. I'm leaving the baby in your pram; I'm getting out as fast as I can. Papa Miche was returning, accompanied by a strident feminine voice. The duchess. And Dr Benes's jaw almost fell out of its sockets.

I must be going mad, he thought confusedly. What are they doing to me . . . ? It was Joey who walked in.

And now began the charade that would stay with Dr Benes as long as he lived. Even longer; I will take this monstrous farce into the grave with me, he thought. He took no part in it, of course; how could he? He was so dumbfounded that nothing but a vague mumble came out of his mouth. But in the privacy of his brain, that awful devious brain, his resentment screamed: why didn't they tell me? I should have been warned. Look at her. The duchess! She came sweeping along the corridor ahead of Papa Miche, brushing him off as if he were a senile fly, the screech of her complaint loud enough to reach the three distracted tycoons behind the bedroom door. Which was exactly what was intended; the whole purpose of the play-acting, as Dr Benes was shrewd enough to guess, was to keep them off-balance; to give them no time to reflect. They had already been conditioned by the sight of the *padrone* lying under the blanket in eternal repose.

The doctor forced himself to look round. For a moment he thought he saw the blanket twitch; no, the corpse was breathing peacefully. It still had an hour and a half of simulated death to go.

She pushed impetuously into the hall, like an outraged dowager, no, more like a snarling virago, her voice thick with the roughest

Italian accent he had ever heard. Where did she pick it up? 'What is going on here?' A fearful squawk. She was dishevelled. She flung her hair out of her eyes. There was a sleepy bloom on her face as if she'd been torn from her bed. She wore a silk robe and nothing else; either by design or accident it had worked loose, revealing, if not her vital parts, at least the full cleavage of her breasts. Dr Benes stared at her glassy-eyed. He was seeing for nothing what the patrons of Le Kasbah paid good money to see. I know him to be a dry stick of a man; he never had much use for sex. It was such an unprofitable business. But for the first time in years, he told me, he felt a physical stir. Some disused gland in him began to jump. Another piercing cry. She was glaring at Sam. 'Are we no longer safe in our beds?'

'Madame la duchesse,' he murmured pacifyingly . . .

But she wouldn't let him speak. 'What has happened? I demand to know.'

'Nothing of importance, madame.'

'Not important? Am I mad? I heard it with my own ears. A scream. A terrible scream. Voices. Running about.' She stabbed a sudden finger at Dr Benes as if she had never set eyes on him in her life. 'Who is this person?' He couldn't get hold of himself, he told me. The whole world, he felt was going mad.

'A doctor, madame.'

'The Maharajah has come back ill?'

'The Maharajah is on vacation. He is perfectly well. He has a guest. It is he who is ill.'

'He has been assaulted?' She leapt on it with a howl.

Again Sam tried patiently, 'Duchess . . .'

And still she wouldn't let him speak. 'There has been a burglary. Of course,' She had pushed far enough into the hall to see the *padrone* lying on the carpet. She whispered, 'May God have mercy . . . have they killed him?'

Dr Benes wondered if the men in the bedroom were watching; probably not. Listening to her was enough. Sam said gently, 'Nobody has been killed. Don't distress yourself, madame,' his eyes narrowing to a cynical glint. She was overplaying the part. He was signalling her: cool it down. She suppressed a joyous chuckle. She was enjoying every moment of it. Her face shone. Horrors. I hate them both, Dr Benes thought. He wished she would fasten up her robe. It was hard to be clinical about what was being so carelessly revealed. Sam led her deferentially to the door. 'Please go back to your apartment, duchess. An ambulance will soon be here.'

'What is the Alcazar coming to?' She flung up her arms. 'You are the manager. I hold you responsible for my safety, m'sieu.' She let him lead her along the corridor. Bitch-pussy. What a performance. Dr Benes felt drained. While they were still within hearing distance of the bedroom she cried out, 'I shall complain to the governors. The Comte de Valois is my very good friend...' dropping her voice as they reached the lift. She whispered exultantly to Sam, 'Was I good?'

'A little rich,' he said with a dry smile. 'But good.'

'I'm so glad.' She patted his hand. 'I told you, didn't I? You and I were made to get along.' Papa Miche opened the lift gate for her; she chuckled again and entered duchess-fashion. It took both of them down.

Dr Benes peered along his nose. A drop of perspiration had collected at the tip. 'I should have been warned,' he muttered.

'Auguste, it would only have worried you. You're such a sensitive man.'

'Next time tell me.'

'Next time,' Sam said gravely. He took the doctor's skinny arm. 'Now let's go in and do what has to be done.'

They returned to the bedroom. I remember Dr Benes telling me, 'It was the worst part of all.' He put on his usual pompous show. 'I am a man of principles.' Laughable. 'One has one's professional ethics,' though they'd never troubled him much in the past. The simple truth was that he was a badly frightened man. A terrible actor who didn't know what to do about the guilty outpouring of sweat.

And the moment they entered the room everything changed. It was startling. The three men waiting for them so patiently were as frightened as he was; more so in fact. They had infinitely more to lose. Theo Parnassus lifted his hooded eyes. They said plainly: do you know what this scandal will do to us? He is used to shaking the world with his dictates, Dr Benes thought; and now he is shaking himself. Caesar Vinci, the great industrialist, was busy manufacturing excuses. Evasions. It wouldn't get them off the hook. Only Gregor Kassem had given it clear, direct thought. Middle-Eastern thought. He was studying them critically with a measuring tape in his eyes. Dr Benes guessed that he was thinking: what will it cost to buy these people off?

Sam guessed so, too. He said with a shake of his head. 'M'sieu, I hope you are not going to offer me a bribe,' and Gregor looked faintly disconcerted. Everybody accepted bribes.

'This has to stop,' Sam went on with a sigh. He still looked very angry; but as he stared at them, one by one, disdainfully almost, it seemed to Gregor that there was a gleam – no more than a gleam, mind you – of compassion in his eyes. Let it grow! We need all the compassion we can get, Gregor thought. The manager said with a wry mouth, as if he had been personally soiled, 'It's not you I'm concerned about. It's the Alcazar. You're newsworthy people. You've involved yourselves in something disreputable and you'll bring us into disrepute, too.' Was he softening? Another sigh. Caesar Vinci was flexing his hard fists tensely. Theo's heavy-lidded eyes now closed. The manager finally turned to the bony doctor with the pince-nez and said, 'Doctor, what happens when the ambulance comes?'

It was time for Dr Benes to play his part. He barely turned his head; just enough to see the *padrone*'s feet projecting from the blanket. 'He will be in the morgue in half an hour,' he said with a shrug.

'And then?'

'I have to prepare my report.'

'Why?'

'Why?' Dr Benes appeared confused. 'It is mandatory. The police ...'

'The police are only interested in what they are told. Doctor, do you know who these gentlemen are?'

Dr Benes gave Theo Parnassus a fleeting nod. 'Him I know. I have seen his face in the papers.' A quick glance at Caesar Vinci. 'Him, too, I think. I am not sure.' He hardly looked at the third. 'That one I do not know,' which was an implied insult to Gregor, though he didn't mind. He was in a business that thrived better out of the glare of publicity.

'His name is Gregor Kassem,' Sam said. 'He is deep in oil.' Deep in baksheesh. In two per cent off the top. 'They are very important people. Doctor, I don't want their names to appear in your report.'

'What are you saying?' Dr Benes had to express agitation. It wasn't hard. 'You expect me to ... ?'

'I expect you to protect the good name of the Alcazar. The chairman of our board is a heavy contributor to your hospital. We could bring a lot of pressure to bear. Is it necessary to twist anybody's arm?'

'No.' Dr Benes shrugged. His shirt was wet. He grumbled reluctantly, 'But they had better not be here when the ambulance comes.'

'They won't be.'

Theo Parnassus began huskily, 'We cannot thank you enough. If there is anything we can offer . . .'

'Nothing,' Sam said brusquely. 'It wasn't done for you.' He was watching Dr Benes obliquely. The doctor's agitation had suddenly become very real. He kept looking at his watch. What was keeping Jean-Baptiste? The ambulance should be here by now. If anything has stopped him . . .

And when the phone rang it jarred him to the bone. That's him! The worst has happened! He cannot come . . . He felt quite faint. He let Sam Casanova pick up the phone.

It was Papa Miche at the other end. His voice oddly muffled. Didn't he want it to be heard? 'The police are here,' he said.

'Where?'

'Two of them. At the desk.'

'And you?'

'In the bar. Sam, they are coming up . . .'

'What is it?'

'The duchess.' Momentarily Sam could only think of Joey. Papa Miche blurted out to correct him, 'Not her. The real one. The old lady below. The commotion frightened her and she rang the *flics*.'

'Stall them.'

'Sam,' Papa Miche's scared voice mumbled, 'nobody stalls *flics*. These are very unpleasant . . .'

They were all unpleasant. 'Hold them for five minutes. Tell them I'm coming down.'

'I'll try . . .' but not too hopeful. Sam heard the old man's throat creak with despair. He put down the phone.

It had to happen, of course. It was all going too well. Everything would now start falling apart. This was just the first joint cracking. Something of his starkness must have communicated itself to the others for they watched him with dread. 'It isn't going to be so simple. The police are below,' he said.

Gregor Kassem voiced his distress audibly. 'Why?'

'There's been a complaint.' No time to explain. 'You mustn't be found here. Please come with me.'

He led them straight across the corridor to the opposite apartment. He opened the door with his bunch of master keys, ushering them in. It was as elegant as the Maharajah's apartment, in a strangely womanish style. Some striking masculine nudes hung on the walls. Only a man of a certain type would want to own them. 'This belongs to Baron Hoechfer,' he said. Somebody or other *diplomatique*.

Caesar Vinci muttered, 'He is a friend of mine.'

'Then he won't mind you sheltering here. Please be quiet. And don't come out.'

To make sure he locked them in. Dr Benes hung behind him. He looked into his pale wild face. 'Auguste,' he said softly, 'don't be absurd.' The doctor was glancing up and down the corridor, seeking the fire-escape. There is a time to stay, and a time to run. It is the sensible rats that leave the sinking ship . . . aware suddenly of the lift humming up. The pang of fear almost stopped his heart. They are here? *Already?* But it was Joey who emerged. She hastened along the corridor towards them, hampered by her loose flapping robe. She whispered to Sam, 'Papa told you?'

'Yes. Did they see you?'

'I left as soon as I saw their car.' She was far ahead of them, already into the apartment, staring down at the shrouded *padrone*. Her eyes were unnaturally bright. She clutched Dr Benes's arm. 'Can he be moved?'

What was she talking about?

She repeated passionately, 'Can he be moved?' squeezing the stick of his arm so fiercely that it hurt.

'Of course he can be moved. He will soon have to be moved anyway.'

'Then get him into the bed.'

Which of us is mad? Dr Benes peered at her stupidly. Was she laughing again? He was sure that she was. He turned to Sam Casanova for enlightenment. He was watching Joey wryly as if he understood. Something in his eyes . . . a lost bitter gleam. What was it? Pain? Sorrow? Disgust? Dr Benes couldn't tell. When he finally spoke the doctor could hardly hear his strained voice. 'Auguste, help get him into the bed.'

'What for?'

Joey said vibrantly, 'Stop asking questions,' striking him lightly, almost playfully, across the cheek. Between them they lifted the *padrone*'s flaccid body, carrying him across to the bed. They inserted him between the sheets, covering him so that only his head was visible. 'Switch out the lights. The curtains quickly,' Joey said.

Sam switched out the lights. Drew the curtains. The room was now shadowed; eerily silent. Lew Cask slept without sound. They could just make out his face, the greasy black hair, on the pillow. *I am the one who is going mad*, Dr Benes thought. He saw Joey strip off her robe. She was stark naked; the gleam of her body was elf-like; she slipped into the bed beside the *padrone*, who was in no condition to savour her. It was a horror situation; it was too much for Dr Benes; for the second time in ten minutes it almost stopped his heart. He wasn't much for sex; it was the chilling sexuality of the performance that filled him with revulsion. What happens now? She whispered, 'Now get out fast,' an excited face, glimmering eyes, bare breasts lustrous in the dark. She was almost incandescent.

Sam Casanova watched her . . . just watched. Dr Benes heard his heavy sigh. They went out of the bedroom, closing the door, out into the corridor where the doctor saw the sheen of sweat on his face.

Sam said to him, 'Auguste, get away from here quickly. Anywhere. I have to go down.'

'Yes.' The doctor fled along the corridor. Miraculously he found the fire-escape; he went down the stairs, flight by flight, whispering his terror to the night lights; and when he came out into the narrow street at the side of the Alcazar he leaned against the wall, catching his breath. The snowy air chilled his hot sodden face. Not ten paces distant the ambulance was parked at the kerb. Jean-Baptiste sat behind the wheel, peaked cap tilted over his eyes, smoking a cigarette. Dr Benes went across to it and got in.

He gasped, 'What are you doing here?'

'There is a police car out in the front.'

'Then drive off fast.'

'Why?'

'I cannot begin to tell you . . .'

Jean-Baptiste said calmly, 'But you're going to try, aren't you, before you sob yourself to death?'

Insolent. Dr Benes glared at him. He shouldn't be smoking. It was forbidden on duty; doubly forbidden in the cab. The ambulance smelled pungently of formaldehyde; it smelled of the vomit of the endless drunks it had picked up. Jean-Baptiste fumbled in the first-aid box over his head. He brought out a flask of cognac and filled the thimble cap.

'Doctor, let me prescribe a little sedative. It'll settle you down . . .'

'You know I don't drink.'

'It's a cold night. I do,' Jean-Baptiste said. He drank it off. 'Now tell me what happened.'

Dr Benes told him. He licked his lips when he came to Joey's part. Jean-Baptiste's eyes glinted. 'He isn't dead, is he?'

Lew Cask? 'God forbid.' Dr Benes cringed. 'Are you trying to drive me mad?'

'She's got some nerve.'

'Too much. It's all over. Now drive off . . .'

'Not yet. We're going to see this thing through,' Jean-Baptiste said. 'I have great faith in M'sieu Sam. He'll work something out. Talk something up,' and he would have, too, if he'd had a little luck. Unfortunately luck doesn't belong to people. It belongs to fate. And fate, as Gregor Kassem said – it was him, wasn't it? – is a bitch. She likes to get the threads of life all snarled up and laugh like a thing possessed.

What was going on? Vic Diamond wished he knew. He had heard Papa Miche gabbling on the phone, and he sat in the tiny service room behind the desk in a state of intuitive shock. *Flics*? Why? It was like sitting on a bed of nails; there was no comfort whichever way he turned. Why had the *padrone* sent for Alfiero, the contract man? Alfiero made 'hits' for an agreed price. Nothing was put on paper. Nobody actually paid for the bullet; but the money found its way into a private account and the victim found his way into a coffin. Usually lavishly adorned with wreaths. Vic didn't want to enter such a decorative coffin. Alfiero now sat in the Renault across the street, watching and waiting ... for what? For the ambulance to arrive? For Sam Casanova and his idiot-gang to emerge? Or was another 'contract' involved?

Alfiero could have told him. He wouldn't, of course; there was a principle involved. *Omerta*. Nobody speaks. In fact he had two contracts. One was to recover the money; the other was personal. It wouldn't dismay Alfiero, for he didn't particularly like Vic. He squatted patiently in the car, wiping the misted windows frequently, for he needed a clear view of the Alcazar, smoking ... listening to the car radio blatting out carols in a language he didn't understand; and suddenly stiffened like a mongoose observing a snake. A police car had just rolled up. He sank very low in the seat, feeling instinctively for the comforting presence of his gun.

What was going on in the building? Did the *padrone* know?

No, he didn't. The *padrone* was aware of nothing; nothing would stir in his comatose brain for perhaps an hour and a half. An hour, at least, before he would be conscious enough to spit fire and brimstone. Joey lay dreamily by his side. Two minutes ago she'd had a palpitant shock that almost startled her out of the bed. She'd stolen a look at her sleeping companion, expecting to be secretly and illicitly thrilled by the sight of the great Parnassus's face; and what was it she saw? The open-mouthed visage of Lew Cask, whose gross features she'd seen in a similarly intimate position the other night. For a moment or two she couldn't catch her breath. Then she understood. What a switch! Vic will go out of his maniacal mind. She began to laugh. Laugh and laugh!

That Sam; you need an extra eye to watch him, she thought.

Willie lay dozing in the Bolivian ambassador's apartment. He watched nobody. Nobody watched him. Papa Miche had taken him into the opulent bedroom, saying, 'Rest, Willie. Sam will be back for you,' and he nodded gratefully. He *was* exhausted. He drifted off to sleep on the vast bed, the guest of a hot-blooded diplomat who didn't know he was there, one thin arm thrust out so that he wouldn't see that distressful tattoo on his wrist even in his dreams. He didn't hear the police car arrive.

Papa Miche was frightened of *flics*. Who isn't? I never observe a uniformed member of that hooligan race approaching but I get a tightening of the bowels. And I am as law-abiding a man as you will find in France. Within reason, of course. Most civilized peoples regard their police as guardians of the community, even as their friends. Not so in Paris. Ask around Pigalle and they will tell you that the *flic* is a squeezer of small shopkeepers, a sadistic waver of clubs. Exaggeration. He is a meagrely paid individual whose chief reward is the petty power the uniform gives. It is hard to like him. Ask a *flic* the time and you will think he is rolling spit in his mouth. He isn't; he is merely rehearsing a scathing reply that you are old enough to carry a watch.

The pair who arrived at the Alcazar in the patrol car were no better and no worse than their class. A little heavy with liquor perhaps; it was a snowy night and they'd stopped at half a dozen bars to collect their usual Christmas tribute. They looked about the elegant foyer with disdain. Socialists to the marrow. To show their political independence they left the slush of their boots on the carpet. They approached the desk. 'You now,' one of them said roughly to Papa Miche. See the kind of wage-slave they have here. A professor to boot. 'So what is going on?'

Papa Miche's habitual terror of *polizei* froze him. He had had some very bad experiences. He licked his lips.

'You have a tongue?'

Papa Miche nodded dumbly.

'Then use it.' They stood there, overpowering in their leather coats, breathing the mixed odour of pernod and vin ordinaire, shedding snowflakes, leaning on the desk to leave wet blotches on the fine veneer. The day will come when the masses occupy these places, *flic* number one thought. 'We have a complaint. A serious one. Terrorism is going on here,' he said.

'Terrorism?'

'You *can* speak, eh? Some old scrag is in a panic.' What a way to refer to a lady of breeding. 'The duchess of – what, Georges?'

'Ravenna.'

'The salt of the earth. Scratch her and she bleeds blue. She says murder is going on over her head. Who lives up there?'

'The Maharajah of Gabour.'

'Another of them, eh? This place reeks of Versailles.' He stared truculently at Papa Miche. 'Why are you so scared?'

Papa Miche whispered, 'It is you, m'sieu.'

'Have I lifted a hand to you?'

'I dislike uniforms.'

'We have an anarchist here, Georges. We shall have to look around. Which is this duchess's apartment?'

'Number eight on the fifth.'

'Georges, go up and talk to her. See if she makes sense.'

Flic number two went up in the lift. Papa Miche muttered, 'I must ring the manager,' hurrying into the service room behind.

'Ring God if you like.' *Flic* number one called after him, 'There is a phone on the desk.'

'I have a direct line to his apartment in here,' Papa Miche said. He was desperate to warn Sam before the *flics* went up; he didn't want them to hear; for insensitive men they had uncannily sensitive ears. He was glad Joey had managed to escape as their car drew up. He beckoned to Vic Diamond to crouch in the corner well out of sight. *Flic* number two was back when he returned to the desk.

He was saying, 'She complains of shouting. Bodies falling. Much running about. She must be twice as old as Lot's wife.'

'Something is wrong, you think?'

The *flic* said cynically, 'Everything is wrong when I am separated from a woman on Christmas Eve,' and stopped as the lift gate opened.

A man in a tuxedo approached. Another plutocrat? No, the manager. Burly. 'Messieurs,' he said crisply, and halted four paces off to stare at the defiled carpet with bitter disgust. He said softly, 'This is not the lobby of one of your police *postes*. If ever you come to the Alcazar again you will be careful to wipe your feet.'

The *flic* reddened. I will wipe his face with my knuckles if he talks to me like that. 'M'sieu, I would watch your tongue . . .'

'No, it is you who will watch yours. It is two o'clock in the morning and you will keep your voice down. M'sieu Laporte, the Minister of Culture, sleeps directly above.'

The *flic* stared at him, thinking: I am not a cultured man. I would like to have him in my car for just ten minutes. Five would be enough. 'We are here on official business,' he said.

'Then behave with propriety. We are not accustomed to the gestapo here. What is this nonsense about the Duchess di Ravenna?'

'Didn't your serf tell you?'

'My *what*?'

'Your desk-clerk,' the *flic* said, glancing at Papa Miche. 'I have been up to talk to the old crow . . .'

'I will not warn you again.'

'The duchess.' Name of Christ. He thinks everybody went to finishing school. He will have me talking like a kindergarten teacher yet. 'She is in a great twitter. She heard violence in the apartment above. Murder perhaps. The old lady swears . . .'

'She is eighty-two years of age,' Sam interrupted him with a shrug. 'She is a recluse. She suffers from senile dementia. We have two complaints from her every day. Either the airplanes are threatening her with the noise, the windows rattle or there are burglars under the bed. We treat her with compassion. We do not necessarily take her seriously.'

'Some Indian potentate lives up there.'

'The Maharajah of Gabour. A gentleman of international repute. He and the Maharanee must be fast asleep.'

'With all that row going on?'

'It exists only in the duchess's imagination,' Sam said with a sigh. 'If you will forgive me, it is you who are making all the row.'

The man annoys me. I don't know why. 'We shall have to look into it,' the *flic* said.

'I would advise you not to.'

'You are too free with your advice. We are going up.'

Sam studied him thoughtfully. 'The Maharajah is a close friend of the President. Disturb him at this hour of the night and you will find yourself on the prefect's mat in the morning, having the uniform torn off your back.'

'Which would give you pleasure, eh?'

'Which wouldn't worry me a jot.'

Bastard. 'Lead on.' Too late to back down now. He saw his comrade glance at him uneasily. We are in this together. Understand? So stuff your twitters up your back.

'This way.' Sam beckoned with frigid courtesy to the lift. He urned fleetingly to Papa Miche. His eyes said ambiguously: wait. Papa Miche wondered why he looked so pale. Something had shocked him. It couldn't be Joey . . . could it? The lift ascended; and there was nothing one could do but sit here tensely and wait.

Sam led them quietly along the corridor. He lifted a knuckle to tap softly on the door, but the *flic* shoved him roughly aside. 'No warnings,' he said. He was in a very great temper. He didn't quite know why. I am not a policeman for nothing; something is going on and I want to see what it is. 'Do you have a key?'

Sam stared at him. 'For the last time . . .'

'Don't argue with me. You have a key?'

'Yes.'

'Then open up.'

Sam slipped the key into the lock and slowly pushed open the door. The light from the corridor flooded into the hall . . . the *flic*'s torch poked about. Silence. Nothing. Nobody. The beam went poking on into the big lounge and both *flics* followed it in. Sam stood well back.

The beam rested on an insanely luscious buffet. Mother of all Mercy. Just look at that array of food. *Flic* number two's elbow bumped an occasional table in the darkness and a lamp rattled. He sucked in breath. His hand reached up to the light switch . . . and froze. The bedroom door was opening slowly.

The beam of the torch reached across. It caught a woman blinking in the doorway; she stood there bewilderedly, young, clutching some kind of shift, a robe perhaps, to her breast. Behind it she was naked. The *flic* with the torch saw a soft shoulder; sleek limbs. She whispered with shock, 'Who is there?'

Sam moved forward. 'Your highness . . .'

'You?' She was still bemused with sleep. 'What are these men doing here?'

'They are police officers, madame. They want to look around.'

'At this time of the night?'

Flic number one, still uneasy, stared at her stupidly. He muttered, 'There has been a complaint. Some kind of disturbance up here . . .' and it seemed to ignite her.

She hissed fiercely, 'Get out, get out. The Maharajah will kill you if you wake him.'

'Won't take a moment.' *Flic* number two, the stubborn one, went blundering ahead. He pushed past her, entering the bedroom. She blazed, 'You are mad. I will have you stripped for this,' and now he was frightened himself; he'd gone too far to retreat. The beam of his torch flicked across to the bed. He caught a glimpse of a dark greasy head on the pillow; fast asleep; and before he could go further the woman, the Maharanee, now panting with rage, slapped him violently across the face. The fury of her response made her drop the robe; as the torch fell from his hand he saw her naked, breasts to toes, eyes distended, and then the beam went out, and now he was blundering to the door.

She was half screaming, 'The Maharajah will speak to the Commissioner of Police. You will suffer for this,' following him across the lounge, distraught, still naked he supposed; he didn't dare look back. Sam draped her with the robe in the doorway and said, 'Highness, they are gone. Forgive me. There was nothing I could do.'

The *flics* were waiting in the lift. He joined them. They descended together. They sweated profusely in their leather coats.

'They really know the President?'

Sam said coldly, 'You were warned.'

'But the noises the old woman heard . . .'

The *flic* who had shown anxiety said lewdly, 'Wouldn't you make noises, doing your trick with a woman like that?' Who wouldn't? thought Sam dryly as he saw them to the door. Had he made the appropriate noises when his turn arrived? He watched the patrol car drive off, then shifted his head to see if the Renault was still parked across the street. It was. He turned to look into Papa Miche's grey face. He's got about an hour of endurance left in him; and then he's finished. It'll wear us all out. The ambulance slid like a snowy phantom up to the door. Nicely timed. Sam went up in the lift.

Joey waited for him in the apartment, wrapped slimly in the robe. A little pale, perhaps? Hard to say. She searched his face sadly. 'You look disgusted.'

'Nothing disgusts me any more.'

'I did it for you.'

'Of course.'

'Only I didn't expect it to be him,' she said, glancing back at Lew Cask. She smiled wryly. 'I almost fell out of the bed with shock.'

It would take a lot to shock her out of a bed. She said reproachfully, 'You should have told me.'

'It was an afterthought.'

'Now Vic is going to be terribly upset.'

'Pity.'

'Sam,' she said earnestly, 'you mustn't trust him any more.' She pressed his arm. 'He will live in terror of that man,' glancing again at Lew Cask, 'when he finally wakes up. He is wild. He is capable of anything. You must take care of yourself, Sam.'

'You're worried about me?'

'Always.' Again touching his arm; pale face still sad and wry. He patted her reassuringly.

'They'll be up in a minute. Be ready,' he said.

He crossed to the opposite apartment, rapping on the door to announce himself. He came face to face with Theo Parnassus as he went in. The others stood by the window, staring down into the street. 'The police have gone,' Sam said.

'Yes,' Caesar Vinci muttered gruffly, 'we saw them.' Adding after a moment's hesitation, 'Thank God.' What a lot they had to thank Him for. They'd escaped social defilement by the skin of their teeth. He rasped his face. He needed a shave. His shirt had been soiled by perspiration. But they all looked grubby; like rich bums recovering from a dissolute night. And how dissolute it had been! Very nearly fatal. They were common flesh like everybody else. Wealth just polished them up.

'Be patient,' Sam said. 'Won't be long now. The ambulance is here.'

He crossed to the window. The world slept through the unholiest hour of the night. The snowy slush gave the silent street a metallic sheen. Was the Renault still there? It was. A long cold wait. The rear door of the ambulance was flung wide; a dim glow in the interior. Nobody stood by it. They'd already removed the stretcher, the wheeled trolley Parisians called the 'salad basket' because of the human vegetables it usually bore to the hospital. It was probably on its way up. Gregor Kassem came behind him. He smelled; it was more than sour sweat; fear had its own distinctive odour. Sam's ears were pricked for the sound of the lift ... There! The softest whine. The tinny clash of the gate; then the muted whisper of voices in the corridor. The stretcher was going in.

Gregor Kassem's head turned stiffly in its direction. His macabre mind was picturing what must be happening in the apartment across the way ... but Sam's imagination was more perceptive. He could see through two thicknesses of door and know *exactly* what was going on.

Joey holding the door open for them. No more laughter. Laughing Girl was very serious now. The steely rattle of the 'salad basket'; Jean-Baptiste wheeled it in professionally, flicking a glance at Joey

F

as he passed. There is a lot of good shape there, he thought. But he had more important things to think about. They had reached the holy of holies and his bland young face was flushed. Papa Miche, that elderly ambulance attendant, close behind him, as grey as Job suffering the strains of an unpredictable world. Now they were all staring at the fine Louis Quatorze piece. It seemed to freeze them. Move, Sam thought. It was as if a film of the action was running through his mind. Papa Miche fumbling for his key . . . two feeble attempts to unlock the bureau. Joey took the key from him gently and opened the door.

Was it there? Joey uttered the faintest sigh. Her face delectable; how it shone. Her eyes rested on four leather cases tossed in loosely as if they weren't of much account. And perhaps they weren't.

Ten seconds to pack them in the stretcher; another thirty to nestle Lew Cask on them like a vast floppy sack of grain. The first thick mumble issued from his slack lips. It shocked them. Five more seconds to blanket him out of sight. The *padrone* was about to depart with more wealth than he had brought in.

Sam's ears caught the creak in the corridor; the tinkle of the 'salad basket'. Time to leave. 'I have to go with them,' he said with a sigh. Am I sweating? His chest felt tight. 'I may be back. I don't know . . .' He wasn't too certain himself. 'I'd wait here till dawn if I were you.' He stared at them with a little wrinkle of pity between his eyes. 'Has it been bad for you?'

Theo Parnassus's shrug was expressive. Dreadful.

'You were so very foolish,' Sam said. He went out. Gregor Kassem followed him impulsively into the corridor; just in time to see the rear end of the stretcher entering the lift, a uniformed attendant wheeling it in. Sam pushed him back with the gentle warning, 'No,' and closed the door.

He joined them in the lift. Jean-Baptiste nodded excitedly. Removed his peaked cap to wipe his face. Joey stole closer to him; Sam felt her cool hand slip into his. A tiny squeeze. But for some unaccountable reason Papa Miche began to cry. Sam looked at him. A little late to repine now.

They came out into the foyer. Vic Diamond was waiting suspensefully by the desk. He watched them approach. Something took him as the stretcher slid by; some strange Sicilian whim: he reached down and twitched the blanket from Lew Cask's face and uttered a convulsive cry. He glared at Sam, words bubbling meaninglessly to his lips. Sam had never seen such stark fear in a man. The stretcher rolled on, down the steps, across to the ambulance; one quick shove and it was in. Papa Miche joined it behind. Sam got into the driver's cab with Jean Baptiste. It suddenly occurred to him. 'Where's the doctor?'

'*Fini*. Thrown in his chips,' Jean-Baptiste said. 'All the stuffing's out of him. He'll be waiting for us at the club.' He would always have enough stuffing to see that he got his share. A roar of the motor. Jean-Baptiste slipped into gear. The ambulance slid off, riding the ridge of snow at the kerb.

Vic Diamond watched it frustratedly from the steps of the Alcazar. He hadn't stopped talking to himself in embittered Italian. He glared across at the Renault as if willing it to follow. What was Alfiero waiting for . . . ? But at last the car was coaxing itself away from the kerb. An awful lot of sodden mush. Alfiero had forgotten to switch on his lights; he did so now, watching the tail lamp of the ambulance as it skated off in the direction of the Etoile. If he had concentrated on it less he might have seen the truck overtaking him, though when he came to think of it later he had his doubts. It swerved in. It took the side of his Renault with a crunch, fenders interlocked; there was glass all over his lap, and he was lying under the seat, the car flung like a crumpled leaf back into the kerb.

He couldn't get out. The door was jammed. The truck driver descended ponderously. Alfiero heard himself screaming abuse at him through the window. A big man. I should shoot him dead. The *padrone* will do as much to me, Alfiero thought. Lifting himself enragedly he glanced across at the Alcazar and saw Vic Diamond standing on the steps, hunched as if he had been physically battered too.

And now he was being distracted by the truck driver. 'Animal,' Jean-Baptiste's brother-in-law addressed him through the window in brutal tones. 'You are not fit to be on the road. Look what you have done to my truck.' Not that anything short of a howitzer could do much harm to that clapped-up wreck. And not that he was really angry. He sucked a grazed knuckle. Three thousand dollars wasn't bad for a night's work.

Joey came forward with a faint smile. That Sam; he thinks of everything, she thought. She shivered in her thin robe. She took Vic's arm, surprised that he should have such emotional tears in his eyes, and led him inside.

From the high window Theo Parnassus, Caesar Vinci and Gregor Kassem watched Lew Cask enter the ambulance, the driver shut the door on him and drive off. Never had they been so glad to see anybody depart from their lives! Only now could they feel really safe. They drew away from the window with indescribable relief. I must write to the manager of the Alcazar and thank him, Theo thought. A courteous man, and curiously helpful. But not just yet. It may take a little while to make sure nothing leaks out. And then the screech of brakes, the crunch of metal, drew them back to the window with shock. Not the . . . ? No, no. Thank God. A truck and a car were locked in collision; the snowy roads were death traps. They could hear screams of recrimination below. The tail lamp of the ambulance was a distant red speck and vanishing fast. Even as they watched it swung about Napoleon's triumphal arch and was gone.

Follow them for a while. The roads are very tricky, but Jean-Baptiste is one of the best drivers in Paris. Straight down Avenue Kléber, and fast. As fast as the snow-crusted streets permit. Jean-Baptiste looks sidelong at Sam. Why so quiet? He himself is tremulous with excitement and so eager to talk. He glances swiftly into the back where the stretcher is locked on its ramp. A faintly audible whisper is now beginning to issue from Lew Cask's lips; Papa Miche, sitting beside him, finds his haunted eyes fixed on that terrible face, and as often as he switches them away they are drawn inexorably back.

'Forty minutes to Orly,' Jean-Baptiste says confidently to Sam. 'We'll do it nicely in time.'

But watch it! The back of the ambulance waltzes over a snowy patch . . . he turns into the skid. No trouble. All is in hand. I never met Jean-Baptiste, but he is probably an estimable young man. A little inclined to felony, but one has to make one's way in a very hard world. The urgent thing now is to disembarrass themselves of the four leather cases lying in the shelf over Papa Miche's head. If they should be stopped with them aboard . . . but that is why Stefan is waiting for them at the Pont d'Iéna with the car he has collected from the Garage Samaritaine.

And here's the Pont. And there he must be; parked this side of the Seine. And he isn't. The ambulance drifts to a stop. The first cold suspicion that all is not going to go well grips Jean-Baptiste's heart. What has happened to Stefan?

There are people who come to a kind of hopeless understanding with fate. The Americans call them 'losers'. The Greeks knew about them too; there is the story of Sisyphus who was endlessly condemned to pushing a stone uphill, always to see it go rolling down.

He was a loser, too. So was Stefan. Between exile, mangled hands and a ruined career, his life had been an endless loss. He had been sent to pick up the car; it wasn't a very difficult task and this time, at least, he meant to succeed. But when he arrived to collect it he found the iron gates of the garage locked, the place in total darkness, and not a soul about. Because of the bad weather Christmas had started a couple of hours earlier than usual at the Garage Samaritaine.

He was too stunned for a moment to do anything but rattle the gates. Then tears of frustration came into his eyes. He found himself uselessly shouting at the top of his voice. It brought some harridan to a window across the street. 'Closed for the holiday,' she screamed. 'Pagan. Don't you know it's *Noël*,' and he looked at her distressfully. Was it always going to be like this?

He walked off. He knew that the car was important; Sam had said to him gently, 'Stefan, we need it,' and the thought of meeting Sam's eyes, though he would be very kind about it, was harrowing. The garage was in the dingy warren of streets behind Gare Montparnasse. He grew curiously sullen as he trudged along; he no longer felt like accepting defeat so meekly. His coat was threadbare ex-army and his feet were cold. He found himself staring at the cars parked nose to tail. Even peering through the misted windows to see if the keys hung inside. God knew what he would do if he found one.

Nervously he tried a door. It opened. But keyless. And it was then that fate, that ruthless bitch, seemed to relent. He backed breathlessly into a dark doorway. A car turned the corner, bumping towards the kerb. People got out tipsily; merrymakers returning from a Christmas party. Still guffawing in the silent street, a man escorted two women into a house. What could a man want with two women? Stefan could be very naive. He moved across to the car. The hood steamed; the lights glowed; he could see keys dangling from the dashboard, and between panic and desperation he opened the door and got in . . . or half got in.

His collar was seized. The man had seen him and pelted back. He was in a rage; if he had been sober he could have hurt Stefan badly, but half his pummeling missed. Stefan tore himself away and ran dementedly down the street. '*Voleur*,' the man yelled after him, but Stefan was no thief; he had only meant to borrow the car for a few hours.

He stopped in an alley. He was sick with distress and tears of humiliation. He leaned his hot face against the bricks. And then he saw it. A huge dark vehicle. He watched it numbly. He knew what it was and he shrank from approaching it. He forced himself to go across. The lights were on; who would leave such a thing with the keys inside? He slipped in quietly. He had to nerve himself insufferably; the very nature of the vehicle chilled him to the soul. Finally he started the motor. Nobody ran out this time. He drove it away.

Papa Miche said defensively, 'He must have tried!'

'But he isn't here,' Jean-Baptiste said. He stared tensely up at the leather cases in the shelf over Papa Miche's head. What he had hugged so exultantly a few minutes ago could get to feel like hot coals in his lap. All the way to Orly; an airport thronged with the army of officialdom, especially on a traveller's Christmas Eve; police, checking clerks, excise men. They might even have to pass a customs barrier. He didn't know if he looked pale; but he felt it. He turned to Sam for a miracle.

Sam said drily, 'You still want them?'

Is he mad? 'Of course.'

'Then suffer for them. Unless you want to take them back. There's always time.'

He *is* mad. Jean-Baptiste stared across the Pont at the ice-cold Seine. I'd sooner jump in there with them and try swimming to America . . . 'Let's move,' he sighed. 'Time's running out.'

He swept a last glance about for Stefan. No sign of him. Probably fainted from hypertension on the way.

'I'll tell you what's happened to him,' Sam said as they drove off. 'Life's kicked him in the teeth. It's been doing it for years. He's its favourite whipping boy. It'll do it to him once too often, and then he'll just run away from it and die.'

Papa Miche looked at him with horror. 'Time is running out. You've got thirty-five minutes,' Sam said. 'Now *move*.'

And how they moved. Past the Champ de Mars as if the hounds of hell were at their tail, sometimes sliding side-on with a spatter of snow, disdaining the gleam of traffic lights in the empty night, bounding over beslimed cobbles so that Papa Miche, staring into the *padrone*'s face, thought ridiculously: you'll wake him up. Jean-Baptiste clamped his mouth. How volatile youth is; we've had a bucketful of luck, he thought; now there's a hole in the bottom and it's all running out. Away on their left was a dark wilderness peopled by ghosts. The windy cemetery of Montparnasse. It signalled a grim warning. Not without cause. A torch flashing ahead. He didn't know what to do; he was tempted to beat it; then he glimpsed the white armlet of a motor-cycle policeman flagging him down. We've had it. He whispered to Sam, 'Should I . . . ?'

'Just stop,' Sam said.

They slithered precariously past the policeman and stopped. He came across. We're being persecuted by *flics* tonight, Jean-Baptiste thought. A weathered red face, topped by the white dome of a crash-helmet, protruded into the cab. 'It could only happen on Christmas,' he said. 'Out of the blue. I need you. I am waiting for the local ambulance and you turn up.'

Jean-Baptiste stared at him. His heart needed a few seconds to recover its natural beat.

'Round the corner. Two doors down,' the *flic* said. He removed his helmet to mop snowflakes off his face, wiping the plastic dome absently; it was as if he were caressing his own bald head. 'I have a customer for you. The woman is in labour and if we don't hurry she will litter before we get her to bed.'

Someone is laughing somewhere, Jean-Baptiste thought. He muttered despairingly, 'M'sieu, we mustn't delay. We have an urgent case for Orly airport. We are already late . . .'

'Hardly five minutes to the Hospital des Enfants Malades,' the *flic* said. He leaned impassively into the ambulance, flashing his torch from Papa Miche's face to the stretcher containing Lew Cask. 'Sleeping peacefully enough. We won't trouble him.' He beckoned authoritatively. 'Back round.' Jean-Baptiste looked at Sam. He nodded. The *flic* went on to Sam, 'You are the doctor?' Again Sam nodded. This is a small beastly joke, Jean-Baptiste sighed. 'If your man wastes much more time you'll be delivering her in the cab,' the *flic* said. He banged peremptorily on the side of the ambulance. He was a policeman asserting himself. '*Vite!*'

He roared his motor-cycle round the corner ahead of the ambulance, sounding his horn twice. Lights came on swiftly in the surrounding windows. Parisians in this area knew a police klaxon when they heard one. A protruberant woman issued from a house. Jean-Baptiste glanced at her belly professionally; any moment for her, he thought. She was followed by her husband, presuming he'd given her a marriage certificate, which couldn't be guaranteed round here. He carried a suitcase. The *flic* took it out of his hand. He flung open the rear of the ambulance and ushered them in. 'M'sieu,' he called out to Papa Miche, 'if you would be so kind,' and Papa Miche moved up to make room. 'Do not disturb the stretcher case,' the *flic* warned the couple. There wasn't much space for their suitcase. He reached up to the shelf and tossed the four leather cases carelessly under the stretcher. Jean-Baptiste felt a wry shudder; I shall laugh over this one day, but only when I am very old. The suitcase went up in their place. The *flic* returned to his motor-cycle and led off fast.

Jean-Baptiste followed his tail light. He knew the hospital well. He looked grimly at his watch. He leaned close to Sam to murmur in his ear, 'We're not going to make it. You know?' and thought he heard him say, 'Does it matter?'

No, he couldn't have said it; I must have imagined it, Jean-Baptiste thought. But he *did* hear him say softly, 'Can you deliver a baby?'

'I make them. I don't deliver them,' Jean-Baptiste said. And he'd probably made a few in his time. A last bitter glance at his watch; every second's delay a useless hour of purgatory. He was very close to the motor-cyclist ahead. He had a violent inclination to run him down, to cut and run for it, woman and emergent baby and all. Mad. They swept up to the hospital portico. The *flic* dismounted and called over his shoulder, 'Wait here.' He paused for a moment and came back. He took off his great leather gauntlets, flexing big fists. He leaned into the cab. 'What plane did you say?'

Nobody had said anything. 'The New York flight,' Sam said. 'In from the Lebanon.' He gave the departure time and flight.

The *flic* nodded ponderously. 'Don't go away.' He entered the hospital. They heard him shouting; presently two Algerians in white coats came out for the woman. She stepped down bulkily and went in. The husband, if that was his status, followed. He said courteously, '*J'en offre mes remerciments*,' and Jean-Baptiste looked at him woodenly. You will never know what that act of kindness cost. Papa Miche was replacing the leather cases uneasily on the shelf. The *flic* was coming back.

'She will be all right.' He looked pleased. 'I am a married man. I have three children of my own. At a pinch I could have handled her myself.' Then he said something astounding. 'One good turn deserves another. I have rung the airport. They will hold the plane for you.' He flung a gaitered leg over his machine. 'I will escort you myself,' and he was off with a roar that shook the hospital windows, beckoning to them to follow.

They almost lost the thunder of his exhaust; there was nothing to hinder them but a treacherous surface, the occasional cobbles that loomed out of the night, shaking the stretcher and its occupant so roughly that Papa Miche had to hold him in place. They caught the glow of the airport a long way off; the endless glitter of the approach path, spidery pylons tipped with orange spots. Something droned lonelily in the night.

They entered the airport through an unfamiliar maze. The motorcyclist rushed them past loading bays, past silhouetted aircraft in dark parking stands. Suddenly they were on the inner perimeter, blasted unmercifully by the wind. It seemed to come off a vast prairie split by long runways fringed with dazzling fences of light. The *flic* swerved and pointed; a security truck with a flashing beacon was waiting to take over. He waved a benevolent farewell and was gone.

The ambulance slid across to the truck. The driver leaned out. 'Hurry. There she is.' An airplane on the runway approach, shuddering with the strain of its engines, windows aglow. 'The captain is impatient. He is fifteen minutes late.' He had to shout to make himself heard. 'There is someone in attendance?'

'The Pasteur Nursing Service. Everything's arranged.'

'Over there.' The driver pointed to a glistening white car under the airplane's wing. 'Follow me.'

He led them across the tarmac. A white-coated attendant and a nursing sister waited by the car. A big woman. She might be needed. Two men stood with a stretcher ready to take the *padrone* aboard.

'You are late,' the white-coated attendant said with breathless reproach. 'Another two minutes and they would have gone.' They could hardly hear him above the howl of the engines. There was an air of suspended activity, of baffled annoyance. The captain watched them blackly from the cabin. It was an airliner of Air Liban; a swarthy hostess was poised at the gangway door. A gang stood by the mounting steps, ready to slide them off. 'You are Dr Benes?'

'His associate,' Sam said. The attendant wasted no time. He entered the ambulance. A small man, Gallic, very precise. Sam watched him lift an eyelid, peering into the *padrone*'s pupil with a pencil torch. He tested the pulse. 'The sedation seems deep.'

'There are symptoms of mild paranoia,' Sam said. 'You may find him confused when he wakes up. Even restless . . .'

'We will know how to keep him calm,' the attendant said. He beckoned to the men with the stretcher to remove the *padrone*. Someone was shouting. 'Yes, yes,' he called up. Then to Sam, 'Ticket? Passport?'

Sam handed them over.

'No boarding pass?'

'The police fetched us straight across.'

'Of course.' The *padrone* was safely aboard. A steward was waiting at the gangway door. 'We shall report to you from New York,' but the nurse was already up the steps; he followed hastily. The door slammed on him. Jean-Baptiste watched dreamily as the steps were slid off.

'Move.' Sam squeezed his arm. 'This isn't the place for a vacation.' The ambulance swung across the tarmac, caught by a hot careless blast as the airliner crawled on; they raced along the perimeter. 'Only a minute,' Jean-Baptiste breathed. He stopped by a cargo ramp. 'For my own peace of mind I have to see.'

The airliner crept like a glistening bug about the runway approach; it took a long time to find its final stance; they could hear the engines whining. The whine grew suddenly to a gritty roar. The bug moved; faster, rocking, taking an endless time to spread its wings; and when it all seemed a pointless exercise in din and belch it took to the air, soaring steeply as if mounting a staircase into the sky. Lights flicked in its belly. It made a slow turn. Its bulk had vanished. The flicking lights were like red points in the night; then they too vanished. The din softened. Lew Cask's adventurous game of poker was done.

They came back very fast, very quiet, wholly subdued. Past the *cimetière du Montparnasse*, now over on their right, which probably chilled them; it is a gloomy place at the best of times, and at night under snow those pious stone angels have a mournful dignity I can do without. Sam Casanova told me that Jean-Baptiste, that normally phlegmatic young man, began an ecstatic chirruping. Something hysterical came into his voice; then he became aware of Papa Miche's stark silence and Sam's impassive face, and he fell silent too. But he remained terribly conscious of what was thudding with every bounce in the shelf over their heads.

He drove with care. No accidents now. It would be monstrous. Silence all about them. It was as if some malignant plague had swept Paris clean of life. Bearing left now for the Seine. You know the Avenue de New York? A good address. Very handsome. You come on it over the Pont d'Iéna, which isn't an address but is very handsome too. Napoleon threw it up to celebrate one of his albums of victories. The river glistening like chilled mercury. They swung hard about the decorative parapet and for the first time – it shocked them – discovered signs of life in that empty world. A kind of life uncomfortably connected with death. A huge black hearse stood at the kerb. A patrol car parked alongside; two policemen haranguing somebody. A glimpse of a white scared face as they sped by. Were the *flics* actually getting to be suspicious of the dead?

Jean-Baptiste averted his head, straightening up, threshing snow. He was startled to feel a hard hand clapped on his knee. 'Stop.'

'What for?'

'Go back,' Sam said. He'd recognized the scared face. 'It's Stefan.'

Jean-Baptiste said nothing. Licked his lips. He put on speed.

'Go back for him,' Papa Miche cried.

Jean-Baptiste stared stubbornly ahead as if he hadn't heard. Suddenly everything was in jeopardy all over again. You had to sympathize with him; a man could go a little mad. They'd managed to achieve so much, despite these three defectives. For a bleak and bitter moment he actually hated them. Papa Miche mumbling in his ear, Stefan cringing inexplicably back there with a hearse – a *hearse*, for God's sake – Willie, that tattooed relic of an old holocaust, sleeping off his exhaustion in one of the Alcazar's beds. He tried to get Papa Miche off his neck; he was panting, 'Go back, go back.' And Jean-Baptiste felt his hot stale breath on his cheek, then the drip of something warm and wet. The old man was weeping with aggravation. He seized one of the leather cases in his despair and whipped it across Jean-Baptiste's head. It really hurt; the buckle was almost lethal. Perhaps there is something vaguely sacrilegious about being clouted – if I can use the Anglo-Americanism – by a million dollars, for Jean-Baptiste flinched, making a skidding U-turn to go back. He drew up alongside the patrol car. Sam whispered to him reprovingly, 'I'd have hit you much harder,' as he got out. Much, much harder, Jean-Baptiste didn't doubt.

He watched Sam move briskly across to Stefan brushing aside one of the *flics* who had turned with surprise as the ambulance approached. Heard him say in a crisp appreciative voice. 'We've been searching for him all evening. Don't distress him,' again pressing back the *flic* as he tried to intervene. He stopped just short of Stefan, shaking his head. He said chasteningly, as if addressing a child, 'It was very wrong of you, Stefan,' taking hold of his arm. 'We trusted you. You know the rules. You should not have left the ward,' and Stefan stared palely into his face: wholly confused. Both *flics* feeling vaguely slighted, now moved close.

Surly as always. One of them began, 'M'sieu. . . .'

'Doctor.'

'*M'sieu le docteur.* Can you imagine what this man did?'

'Of course. He stole a hearse.'

It seemed to perplex them. 'You *expected* him to?'

'It is the third he has stolen this year. He has a morbid preoccupation with the trappings of death.'

Both watched Stefan narrowly. 'He is mad?'

Sam said sharply, 'You are not to speak like that in his presence. There is some maladjustment. He is not a dangerous man.' But you are, Jean-Baptiste thought; you put your head into a noose every time you open your mouth. One way or another it never seemed to tighten. He must have some private insurance with God.

It was very cold; very dark. A snowflake or two drifting down from a bleak sky. One of the disgruntled *flics* rasped his face. They'd wasted several minutes that might have been spent dozing in a warm car. He grumbled, 'You should take better care of him in your hospital.'

'They are entitled to some relaxation. There was a Christmas party. He slipped out through a lavatory window,' Sam said. Enough, Jean-Baptiste thought; don't push your luck. It was such a useless exercise in compassion. With so much at stake. He wasn't particularly callous; he merely thought Stefan expendable. He felt a spasm of added despair as Sam cupped Stefan's face in his hands and turned angrily on the *flics*. 'He is agitated. Have you been abusing him?' I am sure they had.

'We have a job to do.'

'It is not to harass the sick.' Sam beckoned to Jean-Baptiste. He got out and led Stefan into the ambulance. He went shiveringly, without a word, still staring hurtfully into Sam's face.

The *flics* never let anyone escape unscathed. 'We shall have to make a report.'

'So shall I.'

They leaned sourly into the cab. 'It mightn't have done him any harm to spend a couple of nights in the cells.'

'It isn't prescribed medical treatment.' Sam pushed them off. '*Bon Noël.*' They watched the ambulance depart. I am sure they spat.

The Seine at last behind them. The Eiffel Tower vanishing into the murk. Stefan said passionately, 'Sam, I am not mad.'

'Nobody thinks you are.'

'I tried so hard.' He was near to tears. 'The garage was shut. It was all I could get . . .'

'Stefan, we managed. Let it be.'

'You still take too many risks,' Jean-Baptiste said. His fingers twitched electrically on the wheel.

164

'A lot too many.' They swerved into Avenue Foch, pulling up at the Alcazar. It still stood. They sat in silence, stiffly, as if their muscles ached from running. 'There aren't any risks left,' Sam said.

He got out. It seemed an age since they'd driven away hastily from this door. The Renault, bathed softly in gathering snow, lay askew across the street in a glitter of showered glass. 'Wait here while I collect Willie,' Sam said.

He went into the foyer. Warm. Hospitable. And deserted. He glanced into the service room behind the desk, not really expecting Joey and Vic Diamond to be there . . . and they weren't. Glasses on the table. A bottle of Bourbon emptied. Vic's thirst was ferocious. Sam climbed the single flight to the Bolivian ambassador's apartment and looked in. The bedroom door was open. Inside a solitary lamp glowed. Something moved the hairs on Sam's scalp. He didn't know why; he was over-sensitive tonight. He moved in. Willie slept. Pity to wake him; he'd never sleep in so luxurious a bed again. But who could sleep in a posture like that? Sam bent to touch him. He hadn't been dead for long; his cheek was still warm. Willie's twitch, that memento of the old holocaust, was finally stilled. There was a dark blotch on his temple, edged with a corona of blood, made perhaps by a big fist, belonging to somebody as revengeful and maniacal as Vic Diamond. It had cracked his fragile neck like a stalk.

Sam loosened his mouth that had frozen into a grimace. He stood for a while, listening to the slow exhalation of his breath. Presently he went out, closing the door with the faintest snap. He didn't go downstairs; he pressed the button for the lift, and when it appeared he went up in it, not down, moving along the corridor to the all-too-familiar Maharajah's apartment.

VIII

HE found them aghast when he returned to the ambulance. Stiff with alarm. 'What kept you so long?' Jean-Baptiste gasped.

'Have I been long?'

'Twenty minutes. The night is swarming with *flics*.' The night was empty. Nothing moved this snowbound Christmas Eve, not a stray cat, not a pre-dawn water-cart. 'What could you be doing?'

'Cleaning up after us.'

'Do you have to be so fastidious? Where is Willie?'

'Asleep. Pity to wake him.' Nobody could. 'I'll collect him later,' Sam said.

He made no effort to enter the ambulance, his feet in the slushy gutter, staring absently down the street. 'Sam,' Papa Miche reproached him uneasily, 'the night won't last for ever. You should have fetched him.' And he wasn't even listening. 'Is something wrong?'

'What could be wrong? Everything went so well.'

'You look ill.'

'I'm tired. I'm old.' He felt senile. 'I could do with a long, long sleep.' But not as deep as Willie's.

Still staring fixedly along the street. It should be here any moment. And here it was; a long way down. The twin lights of a small truck nudging into the kerb. Why should I feel like Judas's brother? Jean-Baptiste said exasperatedly, 'This isn't the place to carry on a debate.' They were terribly conspicuous. 'Hurry, for God's sake. They're waiting for us at the club.' No response. He leaned out of the cab to peer up at Sam. 'Are you coming? Or is this where you walk out on us?'

'I'm coming,' Sam said. He stepped back a pace to take a last nostalgic look at those lighted windows high in the Alcazar. A man could live comfortably up there; even with splendour. But it isn't for me; the burden of great riches might cramp my individual style. He got into the ambulance. Jean-Baptiste barely waited for him to be seated. He jolted violently away from the kerb.

Now very fast. The last lap; like a tired horse straining for the tape. They were in Pigalle within minutes; a jerk and a rolling skid into the primeval gloom of Rue des Six Anges. The sidewalk lamps feeble, the strip-joint neons out. How quiet it was; it took the holiest of nights to quench the growl of bump-and-grind music that normally vibrated the clubs. They drew up outside the Kasbah. Nothing said for a moment; the motor still running. Jean Baptiste unclenched his tense fingers from the wheel and switched off. He looked at Sam with a shuddering laugh. He seized the leather cases from the back and got out, pausing to glance at the lights of the truck that had slipped round the corner to park at the tenement end of the street. He said to Sam with a frown, 'It didn't follow us, did it?'

Sam shook his head. He had been aware of it all the way. 'The whores are doing road-haulage business tonight,' Jean-Baptiste said and went into the club.

Papa Miche and Stefan halted in the doorway, waiting for Sam. What was the matter with him? He stood irresolutely on the wet sidewalk. 'Sam, are you coming?'

'Be with you in a moment.' He waved them inside. He'd caught a glimpse of high polished lacquer and massive chrome; one of those vast American sedans. It rolled lazily into the street, parking outside Le Sex Hot. The place was closed. Nobody emerged. The lights went out. Sam turned to look back at the truck. Neither was interested in the whores of Rue des Six Anges.

And now he stared at the Kasbah with a sigh. He had a terrible reluctance to go in. If he had a particle of sense he'd knock up Garfunkel and say, I'm so cold, I'm tired and depressed; if you have a spark of Christian feeling in that good Jewish heart of yours you'll give me a bed for the night. But he wouldn't do that. He'd been born a fool and he'd go into the club.

He moved into the lobby. He would always remember its pungent smell with disgust. Dubious North African cooking, assorted kebabs, spices that corroded the stomach; mixed with these odours was something headier. The resinous haze of hashish the Moroccans smoked after the club closed. Ghastly. No sound but the creak of grubby canvas scenery; the place very nearly as silent as a morgue. Tables stripped, chairs piled one on the other. A solitary lamp glared in the ceiling. It splashed a cold circle of light below. All around was mice-haunted darkness. When they pulled the building down, and they might within a century and a half, a massive population of rodents would have to find new premises. Dr Benes sat under the lamp.

The four cases lay on a table before him. One of them opened wide to reveal the pure green sheen of paper. Few people ever got to see a thousand-dollar bill, and only men like Parnassus were used to seeing them in bulk. Dr Benes stared wryly at the open case as if an operation he had never had any faith in, a thoroughly dangerous piece of surgery, had actually worked out. Jean-Baptiste watched him brightly. He would remember that moment of awe as long as he lived. Only Papa Miche wanted to forget it. His mouth drooped. He never really wanted it, Sam thought; it was just the last spasm of an assertive old man trying to extract a little meaning out of life.

He heard Dr Benes mutter, 'And the others?' He wanted to draw all four cases into his embrace.

'All the same,' Jean-Baptiste said.

Papa Miche looked round at Sam. 'I am frightened.'

So am I. With better reason.

'Sam, I have known you a long time. Something has happened. I see it in your face. Why didn't you come down with Willie?'

'He . . .'

'He is dead?'

'Yes.'

And the senile eyes gushed. 'God forgive me. What have I done?'

You'll see in a minute. Maybe less. 'Papa,' Sam whispered, 'take Stefan and go and sit by the bar.'

'He is really dead?'

Deader than Nebuchadnezzar. 'Papa, hurry.'

'Yes.' He drew Stefan across to the bar. They were almost lost in the shadows outside the pool of light. Dr Benes was saying irritably, 'They are not here.'

'They must be.' Jean-Baptiste turned to Sam. 'What can have happened to the girl Joey and Vic?'

'They're here,' Sam said.

Dr Benes bridled petulantly. 'I have been waiting an hour for you and nobody else has turned up.'

'They were here before you arrived,' Sam said. 'They're still here.' He saw Jean-Baptiste's face wrinkle. He glanced about the desolate club. Maybe in the band-room? No, not there. Back of the bar? Not there, either. 'In the *vestiaire*,' he said aloud. He was sure of it. It had the tactical advantage of blocking the exit from the club. As if he had uttered some magic 'open sesame' the *vestiaire* curtains rustled and Joey and Vic Diamond came out. Sam glanced at her only fleetingly. The gay demure face, eyes aglow with something more potent than mischief. It was the other he watched. There was a gun in his hand, pointed unwaveringly in his direction, and Sam knew that Vic Diamond wanted desperately to kill him.

'Didn't I tell you?' Joey said banteringly to Vic. 'He'd produce us like rabbits out of a magician's hat.' She looked at Sam with a smile. 'And here we are.' Yes, here they were. Fitted out with a professional gun. Sam licked his lips. He was shocked by the depth of his panic. Nobody had ever pointed a gun at him in his life.

'Vic, you'll be careful with it,' Joey said.

'Bastard,' Vic Diamond said. Mouth slanted as if he'd bitten on a bad tooth. And he had; I'm the bad tooth, Sam thought. He'll never forgive me for switching Parnassus and Lew Cask.

The sick thoughts he was having! A man should have more friends; there'd be nobody to mourn him but Sybilla. He did me an injustice. He would have had me. Joey said to him gravely, 'You're angry with me, Sam.'

'Yes, I am.'

'And disillusioned?'

'That, too.' he said.

'I wish you weren't. I told Vic I liked you. Sam, you don't know how hard I've tried to get him not to kill you. He works at killing. It's a profession.'

One wonders what his professional kill was. Something frightful. I remember asking the security officer of an insurance company I have an interest in, and he said calmly, 'Give him fifteen years of working life with Lew Cask. He'd do three a year. Count them yourself.' Forty-five. Not even the bad sheriffs of the old West notched up figures like that.

'Papa?' Joey looked round into the shadows. She could hardly see him. 'Where is Willie?' she asked. As if she didn't know.

That foolish Dr Benes fumbled blindly with the pince-nez, making a throaty noise. He got up abruptly, knocking back his chair. She said considerately, 'Doctor you know the sight of money always upsets you. Please shut the case.'

He shut it. Jean-Baptiste rubbed his face. It must have been distressing to see a young man so near to tears.

'Joey, you talk so much,' Vic Diamond said.

'Yes. It's a kind of release.' It made her happy. Her face shone. 'Then take them.'

She bundled the four cases together. Quite heavy for a delicate girl. She touched Sam's shoulder as she went to the door. 'I was so sure you'd understood. Could I have made it plainer? The terrible life I had. So corruptive. You should never have trusted me, Sam,' and

169

she was gone. They pricked their ears to the street. A car door slammed. Vic Diamond remained bulkily in the doorway. He switched out the light. The darkness was petrifying. They heard his voice, 'I'll kill the first of you who moves. All of you if I have to.' They never knew when he was gone. Sam thought he heard him breathing but it was the whisper of the ice-box in the bar. They heard the car drive off. After a while, long enough to be sure, Sam rose and switched on the light.

In the abrupt dazzle he saw Dr Benes sprawled brokenly across the table. He looked up at them blearily. His cheek left a wet imprint on the wood. He said huskily, 'They have betrayed us.'

'Yes.'

'Thieves.' It was the ultimate in condemnation. 'They are nothing but thieves.' He, of course, was a man of impregnable honesty. He mopped his face, dislodging the pince-nez on his nose. He let them sit there crookedly. 'And you.' He had trouble with his breath. 'You are bunglers. You bungled it from beginning to end.' He took a tiny pill out of a silver case and swallowed it dryly; something to tranquillize him. But nothing pharmaceutical would do that. 'All for nothing. So much suffering . . .' Of the five people in the room he had suffered least of all. He got up unsteadily and went to the door. He looked back at them with detestation. 'I wish I had never set eyes on you. Never speak to me again . . .' They heard him still mumbling in the lobby. Then nothing. He was gone.

Jean-Baptiste got up, too. He was more resilient; he had youth on his side. It was still very bitter and he sighed. 'Did you trust them?'

'No.'

'I did. I will never trust anybody again.' He shrugged heavily. 'I must take the ambulance in. They will soon have an alarm out for me,' and went to the door.

Sam said to him gently, 'Then come back.'

It stopped him. 'What for? It is finished.'

'Come back. There may be a call before dawn.'

'Yes?' He shrugged again. He would never believe in anything. 'All right.' But he never came back.

Papa Miche heaved himself erect. 'Now if we can go . . .'

'Sit.'

He peered incredulously at Sam. 'There *will* be a call?'

'Yes.'

'Sam.' The old man shivered. He had missed a shave and the

stubble was white. 'I am so tired.' He was indeed gaunt. But mostly afraid. Racked with guilt. He pleaded thickly, 'I would rather...'

'No, Papa. You began it. You have to see it through. Rest a while. I'll wake you.'

But the phone woke him. It woke everything that crept and crawled in the club. A good hour before dawn. Papa listened tensely; he had dozed crookedly across the bar and was frozen stiff. All he heard were a few brief non-committal words. Sam put down the receiver. He looked a little gaunt, too. He glanced compassionately at Stefan. He had slept through it all.

'Leave him here. He'll come to no harm. Pick up your old bones, Papa,' he said briskly. 'We have to go.'

What happened to Joey and Vic Diamond when they drove away from the Kasbah? Very few people know. And the few who do are not given to idle talk. I managed to get a pretty good picture of the action nevertheless. Some of it given to me first hand. I have my sources. A few drinks loosen the tongue. Some of it frankly hearsay. I have a fertile imagination and it knows how to fit the missing pieces of a jig-saw puzzle into place. I see the pair driving off with exultation. What an easy triumph! I see Joey's entranced face; much easier than she'd thought. They were watched, of course, from the moment they piled into the car. So I know the route they took.

They were heading east, making for Lille I think; probably to get quickly out of France. They had a fast warm car. They might have made the frontier in a couple of hours, depending on the messy condition of the roads and the benevolence of God. I don't think God was with them that night. A rush down from the hill of Montmartre towards the old Halles. It would have taken them out of Paris by Bastille. A sinister omen to begin with. They never got past the Halles; they never even reached Bastille.

Before they were clear of Montmartre they were aware of a clinging phantom. A presence behind. It didn't exactly hug them, but it didn't go away. A taxi? At that hour? A vast American sedan. All glittering chrome. Vic Diamond, driving, tilted his head curiously to the mirror; he didn't know if Joey was aware of it. She was. Very much so. No longer entranced. She touched his arm and pointed. He broke off the street and lost it. And a small grubby truck took its place.

Disturbing? The night was so empty, so soundless, that anything on wheels in the vicinity was odd. Joey said softly, 'Slow down. Let it pass.' They could dispense with its company. The truck *did* pass them. But that American sedan reappeared conspicuously, and they had company again. It now rode ahead, swerving gently from side to side, so that nothing could slip by its great bulk. And the truck fell back to sandwich them from the rear.

The scenario of the action now became rather brutal. They were being hustled in a certain direction; it was done quite expertly. Every time they tried to break away or double back the American car baulked them and the truck swung out to cut off their rear. An observer might have thought it a cynical game, played without humour. Dangerous, too. It seemed so to Vic Diamond, for a light sweat suddenly appeared on his face. Joey could hear his hard breathing. How did they get into the Rivoli? They didn't know.

The Rue de Rivoli is at least wide. There is room for manoeuvre. There mightn't be another opportunity; Vic Diamond wrenched violently at the wheel into a skidding dash. And almost made it. Both cars brushed. Bumped. Metal rasped. Weight counted, for the sedan somewhat smaller than a tank, if sleeker, pushed hard. Ruthlessly indeed. I picture the sweat gathering on Vic Diamond's face. I picture both lurching along, the way children's cars recoil from a buffeting in a dodgem-rink. Joey leaned across to get a glimpse of dark foreign faces. It was no longer a game. Glass tinkled; the truck had come up like a persecutor to harass their back. How did Vic manage to writhe out of their embrace? I think they let him; this wasn't where they wanted him. He peered blindly about; he wasn't familiar with Paris. He didn't know where he was.

Joey did. She knew every alley in the warren between Notre Dame and Bastille. So do I. There are sleazy restaurants behind the *Cité* that serve the best onion soup in France. There are also narrow streets in which it is hazardous to pursue anything larger than a cat. Vic had to be reassured. She could hear him panting obscenely. She pressed his arm and said, 'Vic, do as I say.'

'Yes, yes.'

'Be ready to turn off. I will tell you when. It will be a squeeze. You will hit things. Don't stop.'

'Just tell me where . . .'

'Any moment. *Now*. Here on the left. Quick.'

Hurtling into an ill-lit thread lined with noisome garages, drab *charcuteries* and the caves of dark hotels, in which one needed iron nerves to spend a night. It was probably Rue Henri Baume. It was named for an undistinguished savant who wrote a paper on disease-bearing fleas. He must have found much material for study in the street. Vic Diamond hammered along it with a blacksmith's clamour ripping at congested cars. One sickening impact sent a projecting motor-cycle through a shop window. Before he was half way down a blinding dazzle at the far end warned him that the way was closed. A brief flash behind told him that there was no retreat. He was now whispering to himself in unintelligible Italian. He managed to break out at the next intersection into that tight warren of streets. They criss-crossed limitlessly. And at every corner a quick flicker lit up the night; as many as three simultaneously. They were being hemmed in like lambs for the slaughter. A quick shove on. This way, that way; then back. Trapped.

A car bleated softly. Another, taunting them. How many were there? Too many. Joey sighed. She was a realist. She was surprised by the terrible froth of Vic's sweat; she wouldn't have thought him capable of such panic. He was squirming like any of the victims who had fled from his gun.

I think it was then that she decided to ditch him. I imagine her taking a lingering regretful look at the leather cases behind. It was finished. *Sauve qui peut.* Everyone for himself. She'd had the feeling all along that they were being nudged towards a certain quarter. She thought she could guess which one, and why. Well, she would help things along.

She touched Vic's fingers. 'Listen carefully. Straight on.'

'What?'

'Don't talk. We have to get out of this.' He nodded. He drove blindly; he was lost in the maze. 'Now right.' A hard swerve. 'Right again,' and suddenly a bitter wind was blowing about them. Where had she brought him? They were running along one of the industrial quays fringing the Seine. On one side was the shimmering river; on the other a fenced wilderness of dark warehouses. Barges loomed.

He looked at her stupidly. 'What have you done to me?' That familiar dazzle of headlights in his eyes jolted him to a stop. The wing mirrors glinted; other cars were drawing up behind.

Men emerging. He pulled out his gun with a passionate gasp. 'Vic, you mustn't,' she rebuked him softly. 'This is Paris. You will make it very hard for yourself,' taking the weapon out of his nerveless hand. He slid wildly out of the car, grabbing one of the leather cases. He would get something out of it, at least. He ran for the nearest warehouse fence, scrambling over the top. She heard him cry out. It was heavily laden with barbed wire. She could understand his terror as he struggled to free himself. A man had issued from the truck with dogs, and they came snarling forward, leaping for his legs. I am sure she watched the scene with detachment. She heard Vic calling out, not a word distinguishable. He was fearfully hampered by the case under his arm and he had to let it drop. The man in charge of the dogs picked it up. Others approached from the waiting cars. Nobody interfered with Vic; they had what they wanted and they waited indifferently while he ripped himself free and dropped on the other side. Nobody attempted to follow. Joey heard the thud of his fall; then the soft rush of feet into the darkness. She knew she would never see him again.

The man who had picked up the case came across to her car and leaned in. A hard sallow face. Greek or Turk. Before he could speak she said gravely, 'I took the gun away from him. I thought it would be better,' and put it into his hand. He gave her an impassive look. She pointed humbly to the three remaining cases in the back. 'I kept these for you, too,' and now he showed his teeth with a sardonic grin.

'That was very wise of you.' He beckoned her out. 'You have saved us a great deal of trouble, mademoiselle.'

I will not tell you the name of the hotel Sam Casanova visited. It is overwhelming. The *crème de la crème*. Spend a few days there if your bank manager thinks you can afford it; you will discover what gracious living really is. Nowhere will you eat better. Nowhere will you find staff so ready to assume that its patrons spring from aristocratic stock. I have experienced the thrill myself. The foyer was hushed in the dark early hours of that Christmas morning as Sam Casanova and Papa Miche trudged in from the snow. Eyes followed them tautly. Examined the imprints of spongy shoes, Papa Miche's frayed ex-army coat. They were obviously not *crème de la crème*. I imagine the traditional courtesy of the desk was strained when Sam asked that M'sieu Parnassus be called.

To disturb the deity at that hour? There was a whispered conversation with the *maîtresse* in charge of the floor. Next a check with the *chef de rang* who prepared breakfast. It had already been served in M'sieu Parnassus's suite. Only then did the *concierge* have the temerity to ring him. The upshot was surprising. He beckoned to the lift attendant curiously and said, 'Show the gentlemen up.'

They entered the suite. Perhaps they felt like pygmies in that overpowering environment. It was certainly a bitter moment for them. They stood inside the door, still muffled against the cold, waiting to be recognized. And nobody glanced at them, much less spoke to them. It was then that Sam heard Papa Miche's chesty sigh.

It troubled him; the old man's stubbled face was wan. He'd walked much too far and was near to collapse. And still nobody spoke.

Those three very powerful men were at breakfast. They had left the Alcazar during the night. It had embittering associations. In the months to come they would recall the affair with sweat, perhaps with traumatic shock; Caesar Vinci, who was particularly volatile, with a savage grinding of the teeth. But for the moment it was past. They were now in a hotel that delighted in them. Even venerated them. Each had a suite suitable to his princely style; it was a normal expectation. Each nestled in the bliss like a pearl within an oyster. Because they had been so shaken, and needed consolation, one from the other, they were having breakfast together in Theo Parnassus's suite.

No hotel will give you a better view. After all, you pay for it. Look out of the window and catch the snowy vista of Champs-Elysées. Hushed. The distant clanging of holy bells. A saintly Christmas day. It hadn't been a very saintly Christmas Eve; disreputable in fact. Forget it. In here it was warm. The service discreet. Silver on the breakfast table. The mouth-watering fragrance of warm croissants and coffee, the faint sizzle from the chafing dish that contained those tiny succulent Milanese sausages that Caesar Vinci liked. Pork. Gregor Kassem averted his head. Anathema to a good Moslem. Nobody offered anything to the two men still standing by the door. I like to think that Gregor, whose heart had a few soft edges, would have given the old man a drink. He looked ghastly. But Theo was in a frosty mood. And Caesar might spit.

Finally Sam spoke. He said in a wry voice, 'Are we disturbing you?'

'Yes,' Theo Parnassus said chillingly. 'You are.' For the first time he looked straight into Sam's face. His bitter eyes said: I would like to ruin you. But who could ruin a man who had so little? You couldn't even prosecute him; the Paris police would make a field day of the affair. He simmered with frustration and baffled guilt. He took one of Caesar's sausages on a fork, staring at it emptily as if it smelled bad. It was the weight of his guilt that smelled bad. A man lay dead in a room in the Alcazar. He'd gone below to check for himself. Some pathetic, emaciated creature with the horrid decoration of a concentration camp number on his wrist. Theo had never seen such a thing in his life. He would never forget it.

He needn't have been so upset. Never is a long time. Money in bulk is a great tranquillizer for helping people to forget.

He ate the sausage. Fatty. It would give him heartburn. It was so

175

unjust. Why should he be condemned? As if his mountain of wealth had taken a diabolical hand in that ill-fated game of poker, playing for its own evil ends. Mad. So all right, he shrugged; we are human, we sin, we do foolish things. But I am a civilized man. It was Gregor who saddled us with Lew Cask. He turned away from Sam with an offended mutter. The things he'd said . . . something about 'money being irresponsibly used'. What did he know about money? He'd never had any in his life.

What really incensed him, of course, was that for a few panicky hours this sad, ironic man had reduced them to life size; he'd made them feel small and ineffectual. They would never forgive him for that.

How he wished he'd never seen the decorative tattoo on that thin wrist. May God forgive him. He was a religious man. He hoped piously He would forgive Caesar and Gregor, too. Already he was getting to be practical. There is nothing like reducing the burden of guilt by sharing it out.

Sam said softly, touching Papa's arm, 'Could he sit down? He's very tired. He's come a long way.'

Theo was tempted to say testily: let him stand. That professorial hooligan. He began it. Look at those broken shoes. That ludicrous coat. It was a long time since Theo had associated with people who wore ludicrous things because they were cheap. The old man looked ill. We had one man dying on us; I don't want *him* on my conscience too. He pointed to a chair with a shrug and Papa Miche made a grateful sound and sat.

He was hungry. He had to avert his head from the table. The smell of the food was making him sick. It drew his eyes across to the sideboard. The four familiar leather cases lay on it ostentatiously and he uttered a thick gasp. He'd last seen them departing from the Kasbah in Joey's hands. He turned bewilderedly to Sam. How had they come here?

They're going to tell you, Sam thought; and they're going to rub it in with salt.

Theo Parnassus pointed to Papa Miche. He said roughly, 'This is the old man who began it?'

Sam said nothing.

'You are a fool,' Theo Parnassus went on brutally to Papa Miche. 'Did you really think you could get away with it? For how long?' He was tired and restless; he hadn't slept a wink. 'We are not revengeful men. We do not deal in emotions like that.' Didn't they, though. Every day of the week. 'But you demanded us. We have feelings.' And now they were on edge. 'We have people in high positions whose job is to divine our feelings and act as they see fit. Somebody would have said: find these men and punish them. And then you would never have had a moment's rest. It would not have taken long. We have banks and agencies all over the world. It could have turned out very bad for you.' Bad for himself, too. He was talking himself out. He repeated harshly, 'You are a fool. And you are an even bigger fool,' stealing a sour glance at Sam. 'You would have had nothing out of it if what you told us last night is true.'

Papa Miche said convulsively, 'He *told* you?'

'Of course.' It gave Theo a little savage relief. 'He came and told us.' Why should I feel sorry for the man? 'He betrayed you.' He saw a thin sweat forming on his face.

Papa Miche turned to Sam with whispered horror. 'But why?'

Still nothing.

'Because you are mad. It was the best thing he could do for you,' Theo Parnassus said. 'No matter where you hid, Cuba or Fiji, you would have been found. I could not stop you being killed. I do not control everything that goes on in my empire.' It had become too vast for even a man like Theo Parnassus to watch.

Stealing another curious glance at Sam. He looks wrung out. I feel like that, too. It would have surprised his intimates, his wife included, who thought him a cold unflappable man. Ah! He threw up his hands. He had had enough of them. 'Now go.'

Papa Miche rose creakingly. Perhaps it was his bones; perhaps his chest.

'Wait,' Theo Parnassus said. He went to the sideboard. He slipped one of the leather cases aside. 'Mine,' he said possessively. He tossed another at Caesar Vinci's feet. 'That is his.' The third on the carpet by Gregor Kassem. 'And that is his.' They barely glanced at them. How many people drawing breath could toss millions about like that? One case was left and they knew whose it was. 'That is Lew Cask's,' Theo said with a grimace. 'It is dirty money in there. Its presence soils me.' He hadn't particularly recoiled from it during the poker game. 'It is narcotics money, prostitution and extortion money. Everything foul. You took it out of the Alcazar. Now take it away. Get rid of it. I do not care how.' He looked at Papa Miche with dry meaningful eyes. 'Nothing will persuade Lew Cask that Vic Diamond does not have it. Give it back to him if you wish.'

Papa Miche shivered. He turned to Sam. Sam gave a sharp, but pitying, shake of his head. Papa Miche sighed and went shrunkenly to the door. That was as far as he got. He looked round. The case lay solitarily on the sideboard. He came fluttering back like a bat and seized it, clutching it to his chest like a lost child, and hurried out gaspingly without looking at Sam. Theo's mouth moved grimly.

In the end he had to seduce him, Sam thought.

Caesar Vinci said coldly, 'What are you waiting for?'

Theo knew. The man had feelings. 'The dead one at the Alcazar,' he said. Poor Willie. Already he was anonymous. 'He has been taken care of. Very decently,' he told Sam. He had an instant's worry. 'Does he have kin?'

'Nobody.'

Inexplicable. 'Everybody has somebody. No friends?'

'I was his friend,' Sam said.

'Yes,' Theo said begrudgingly. Almost with sympathy. I will never understand what makes people like that work. See for yourself. Not a dollar profit in it for him after so much risk, and shoes he must be ashamed to wear. There are some things one never learned in the fastness of the boardroom. What was the man waiting for *now*?

'What happened to the others?' Sam asked.

Of course. 'This Vic Diamond.' Theo turned away. He was thinking of the serenity of his yacht in the Aegean. He could be aboard in six hours. 'We let him go. Why should we do anything about him? Lew Cask will do it for us. He will hunt him down no matter how long it takes. The Mafia have contacts everywhere. He will efface himself somewhere like Hong Kong, but they will pick him up. Then he will die. They will try and make it painful for him.'

'And the girl?'

Theo Parnassus glanced fastidiously at Gregor. Let him reply. 'She is below,' Gregor said. Sam's eyes widened. 'I have given her a charming suite.' Again Sam blinked. 'She is very excited. She thinks she has made a conquest. I am something better than Vic Diamond it seems.' He lifted his leather case off the carpet, hefting it absently as if to check that it was full. It was. 'She is coming with me to Beirut. The night life is gay. She will love it. I shall show her Damascus and Baghdad. It should be a marvellous trip.' He made it sound enticing; a colourful travelogue brought to life. 'Then across to Abu Musa which is one of the Trucial States on the Persian Gulf. You have heard of it?' Sam stared at him blankly. 'Not many people have. There is nothing there but sand and camels and oil. A lot of oil. Medieval, of course.' Gregor shrugged indulgently. 'Everything revolves about the sanctity of the harem. They still do a thriving trade in Negroes with Dar es Salaam.' Did he share in the trade?

'The Emir is my brother-in-law. He has a delicate taste for fair-skinned girls. I think he will like Joey.' Gregor's large brown eyes glowed. Sam suddenly realized what made this apparently soft Levantine a most ruthless man. 'She is really very dangerous. She should not be at large. She is too lustful. Too improvident. She wastes lives without counting the cost. She will vanish into his harem. The Emir will pamper her like a poodle, she will grow fat and happy. But she will never emerge.'

He frowned. He saw Sam's eyes glaze. His face seethed wetly; Gregor thought the man might actually hit him. He turned with a sigh and went out.

He left the hotel, walking swiftly, head bent, whispering maliciously to himself. Then his spirits picked up; he was aware of the sun. It was going to be a bright day. Already the snow was thawing; it was dripping in gobbets from the trees. Far out in the Tuileries the kids were throwing snowballs and yelling. That was the age to be. Playful. But not as playful as Joey. His face wrenched; he had a poignant remembrance of the slim smooth body turning in his arms, laughing huskily as she prepared so expertly to manage the sexual act. Laughing Girl. He hurried his steps. He had a long way to go; though not as far as Joey would go. And not so permanently. He found himself making unthinkingly for Sybilla's apartment.

She opened the door to him sternly. 'Oh, it's you, is it?' Where had he been these past two days? Then she stared into his face and cried out, 'What has happened to you, Sam? You look as if elephants have trampled on you.' Three of them had, back in a lush hotel. 'Chèri, come in.' She drew him into the living room and pushed him into a chair. There was a warm fire. She said passionately, 'What a mess you are. Let me take your shoes off,' bending like a well-trained wife to slip them off. 'You are a fool,' she grumbled. 'You don't know how to take care of yourself.' He looked fondly down at her glossy auburn hair that was a little less auburn at the roots. His socks were damp and she stripped them off. She gave him a towel to dry his feet.

'Now rest. You look half starved.' He could smell coffee and crusty bread. It made his taste buds run. 'It will not be a minute.' She hurried into the kitchen, then came flying back with a flurry of pleasure to kiss his cheek.

'It is nice to have breakfast together again. Bon Noël!'